AS THE STAR LORDS COMMAND

I glared at that gorgeous bird, arrogant and bright in his power. "Dray Prescot, onker of onkers. Do you understand what the Star Lords demand of you?"

I burst out, "By Vox, you brainless bird! Do they know themselves?"

"They know, onker, and they know you are the man to fulfill their desires and to obey their commands. Now, hearken! You will stop the Iron Riders. The Star Lords command. You will drive them back across the sea to whence they came."

I laughed scornfully. "Stop them? With what? How am I supposed to halt that mailed cavalry single-handed?"

The raptor let out a squawking cackle. "Emperor of onkers, do as you must and then, why you may do as you wish with Vallia. For a space."

I opened my mouth to ask what the cursed bird meant by a space, but he struck his wings and soared aloft. In an instant he was gone. . . .

"What did she know of me? What, indeed?"

GOLDEN SCORPIO

—•—

by
Alan
Burt
Akers

Illustrated by
Josh Kirby

DAW BOOKS, INC.
DONALD A. WOLLHEIM, PUBLISHER

1301 Avenue of the Americas
New York, N.Y.   10019

FIRST PRINTING, DECEMBER 1978

1 2 3 4 5 6 7 8 9

PRINTED IN U. S. A.

Table of Contents

List of Illustrations

Dray Prescot

Dray Prescot is an enigmatic figure. Reared in the inhumanly harsh conditions of Nelson's Navy, he has been transported many times through the agencies of the Star Lords, the Everoinye, and the Savanti nal Aphrasöe to the terrible yet beautiful world of Kregen under Antares, four hundred light years from Earth. In chronicling his brilliant adventures on that exotic world I have been forced to the conclusion that there is much he does not tell us as he records his story on cassettes. A fresh supply has reached me and will form the subject matter for the next cycle of Dray Prescot's story.

His appearance as described by one who has seen him is of a man above middle height, with brown hair and level brown eyes, brooding and dominating, with enormously broad shoulders and powerful, even brutal, physique. There is about him an abrasive honesty and an indomitable courage. He moves like a savage hunting cat, quiet and deadly. On the marvelous world of Kregen he has fought his way to become Vovedeer and Zorcander of his wild Clansmen of Segesthes, Lord of Strombor, Strom of Valka, King of Djanduin, Prince Majister of Vallia—and a member of the Order of Krozairs of Zy. To this plethora of titles he confesses with a wryness and an irony I am sure mask much deeper feelings at which we can only guess.

Prescot's happiness with Delia, the Princess Majestrix of Vallia, is threatened as the notorious Wizard of Loh, Phu-Si Yantong, seeks to overwhelm the empire. Many factions rise to seize the supreme power and with the death of the emperor, Delia's father, and the burning of Vondium, the capital, Prescot and Delia are forced to flee Vallia. *Golden Scorpio* tells how Prescot reacted and how he came to terms with himself, if not altogether satisfactorily in his own estimation.

The volumes chronicling his life are arranged to be read as individual books. A clearly-marked change has overtaken the character of Prescot as he relates his story, and, indeed, the story itself reveals this, illuminating him in ways of which he

7

himself is probably unaware. Future volumes can only be awaited with the fascination of the unexpected.

The next cycle of volumes in the Saga of Dray Prescot I have called the *Jikaida Cycle*, carrying the linking word Kregen in their titles. Life is a continuing process and the enigmatic figure Prescot presents of himself might lead us to imagine that he understands only the belief that the effort of life is soldiering on dauntlessly against Fate. There is more to him than that. I feel sure he is fully aware of the many other facets of human belief in understanding our natures and harmonizing them, in the theory of abnegation, in the idea of letting oneself slide into the infinite, of bending with the current to cope with existence, of acceptance. But on the vivid world of Kregen under Antares, in the streaming mingled lights of the Suns of Scorpio, Prescot has had and will continue to have more than his share of setbacks and hurtful adventures. I do not think it is Dray Prescot's nature to allow the destruction of himself or those he loves.

Alan Burt Akers

CHAPTER ONE

Dragons in the Fire

We flew from burning Vondium.

Sulphurous masses of smoke rolling from the doomed city cast dark palls between the streaming mingled radiances of the fading suns. The spreading fans of jade and crimson light cupped the city below. Vondium burned. Along the wide avenues rivers of fire, across the canal-bordered islands lakes of fire, upon the terraced hills volcanoes of fire—incandescent, lambent, roaring with unchecked power, spurting yellow and orange flames, shooting myriads of sparks like discharges from Hell's furnaces, the fire burned.

Our airboat shook in the windrush.

"This was not planned," said Delia, guiding the airboat out of the last swathing bands of smoke. The suns shafted light behind us and swiftly the emerald and ruby spears drained down across the sky, dwindling and shrinking as the pit of fire that was Vondium blazed up. She shivered. "Not planned—"

"The factions fight it out down there. They all struggle for the supreme power and," I said, looking up, my fist closing on the hilt of the sword, "here come those who would dispute our passage."

Two fliers spun out of the shadows ahead, the light glittering along their sides, glancing from their brazen embellishments. In the weirdly coruscating lights the two airboats looked dark and magical dragons, glinting with fire-jewels.

"Hamalese," said the Lord Farris. He moved forward from the shelter deck aft, and his face lay shrunken in shadow.

At his side Lykon Crimahan spoke in words still slurred by witnessed horror. "They have destroyed all of value in life—I will have my due of them."

"The queen?" said Delia, not glancing back, but guiding our airboat skillfully upwards so that the cramphs of Hamal might not have the advantage of us. The airboats flitted up into the night sky and the smoke dropped away and the clouds were tinged in orange and gold about us.

9

"The queen sleeps." Farris had already drawn his sword. In the encroaching darkness the bulky firmness of his body as he moved up struck me as mightily comforting. "She is exhausted."

We were all exhausted. But only a fierce continuing, a savage determination to go on, an unyielding struggle against all odds would get us through now and save our necks.

In this airboat I had taken from the Hamalese were ready racked a dozen crossbows. I took one up and spanned it and said to Farris: "Put up your sword. Delia will outfly these rasts."

"Yes," said Farris. "The Princess—I mean, the Empress—has consummate skill."

The three airboats whirled about the night sky, leaves tossed in the maelstrom of the fire and the high winds of the night, darting and swooping, climbing to secure the height advantage. Delia swung us up superbly. I leaned over the wooden coaming and let fly. The bolt skewered into the dark mass of the Hamalian airboat below. In the wind bluster I could not hear a shriek of anguish, I did not know if I had hit; but I respanned the bow and let fly again as we circled in.

Farris and Crimahan joined in. They were unused to crossbows; but every bolt that hit the Hamalians would count.

And then in the way of these wild skirling affrays as fliers spin and grapple at night one of the Hamalians flew awkwardly across and fell athwart our bows. Delia made a last frantic effort to avoid the onrushing mass. The two airboats came together with a great crushing of wood and ripping of canvas. But the craft I had selected was stoutly built, as one would expect from the damned Hamalese who made the things and denied us Vallians the right to make our own, and she was stouter than the other. Amid a shrieking splintering of wood the foeman's airboat tumbled full into our own.

Men spilled out to stagger and stumble across our deck.

Over our heads through a rent in the clouds the fat blue shine of the first star of the evening suddenly caught me up with a swift and entirely unexpected sense of the beauty of the night. That first star that Kregans call Soothe was not as large or as fat now, as the conjunctions of orbits opened out, for Soothe is a planet of Antares as is Kregen, but that blue lambent luminosity reminded me of the fabled Goddesses of Love of Kregen. And as no Goddess of Love of two worlds has ever been or can ever be as precious as my Delia, my

10

Delia of Delphond, my Delia of the Blue Mountains, I hurled the crossbow down and leaped yelling into action.

Delia was ready for the Hamalese from the wreck of their airboat. Together, we hit them. Like two perfectly-machined parts, we meshed, she taking her man with her rapier, I chunking the Krozair longsword around into his comrade's ribs. Armor crumpled.

"Hanitch! Hanitch!" The Hamalese kept up their battle yells, fierce, predatory and yet highly disciplined fighting men.

"Vallia!" yelled Farris and hurled himself forward along the deck, his sword a glinting blur. "Vallia and Vomansoir!"

These warriors of Hamal did not carry shields, although their Air Service personnel habitually did so, and I guessed the shock of the collision had not so much left them with no time to seize up that article of combat as the demands of scrambling from the wreck of a flier about to plunge over into nothingness had made them concentrate wonderfully on having two hands free. Now, had they been Djangs, or Pachaks. . . .

The little fight raged for a space. I squared off my man and thrust the next one through. Crimahan was bashing away and yelling all manner of frenzied insults and taunts, half off his head with grief for what had befallen Vallia and him.

With every blow he struck, Lykon Crimahan, Kov of Forli, took out a payment for his lost lands on the hides of his enemies.

"Hamal! Hanitch!" screeched the Hamalese, and fought and struggled and died. I feel the very fury of our vengeful attack threw them off balance. They had flown up from their empire to sack and burn and overthrow the Empire of Vallia, acting under the veiled orders of the Wizard of Loh Phu-Si-Yantong whose maniacal ambitions knew few bounds, and if they were surprised at our vengeful resistance then they were fools. In that moment I felt the enormous weight pressing in on me that my own plans called for Vallia and Hamal to join hands in amity. To accomplish that with the blood-debt that now soaked the two countries seemed almost impossible.

So we fought.

Toward the end of the fight when but four Hamalese soldiers remained alive, the rest either slumped in death on the deck or pitched with a despairing shriek overboard, Queen Lushfymi tottered out of the aft cabin. She held a poniard. She looked distraught, her dark hair dishevelled, her violet eyes wide and drugged.

11

She would have rushed upon the last soldiers; but I got her right arm in my left fist. I held her very very carefully.

The poniard she brandished with drugged abandon had two dark channels cut into the narrow blade, and in those runnels clung a virulent poison. . . .

"Let me go. I will slay and slay—"

She spoke in a slurred, drugged fashion, her words heavy. Her face showed demoniac devilishness and exhausted despair, struggling to gain the ascendancy.

"They slew the emperor, they murdered my beloved—let me repay the debt."

That she had to be held back was quite obvious, although she was a queen—the Queen of Lome in Pandahem—and therefore might be expected to know how to handle weapons. But the Hamalese soldiers of the air were no amateurs. Their swords flickered in these dying moments of the struggle as they sought to take us and so win all—and, in truth, even now we could lose. I shook Queen Lush.

"Hold still. Do you want to throw your life away after the emperor's?"

That, of course, was a stupid thing to say.

I recognized that. I gave her a push back into the cabin, before she could screech out some cataclysmic determination to end it all and die to join the emperor, and slammed the door.

I swung back to the fight, raging.

Delia had taken her man out with that neat precision of effort girls are taught in the military establishments of the Sisters of the Rose. Crimahan missed his stroke and had to duck and dodge back, his left-hand dagger fending off a thraxter blow. Farris was in the act of withdrawing his rapier from the throat of his man. So that left the fourth, the one I should have been attending to if Queen Lush had not staggered out brandishing her poisoned poniard.

"By Vox!" I bellowed as I leaped. "I should have let the silly woman at these rasts with her poisoned dagger."

Then the Krozair brand flamed left, twitched right, sliced and was still, sheened in blood.

Farris looked at me and Crimahan staggered back, shaking with the violence of these last few moments. Delia tut-tutted and caught at a dead Hamalese by his belt.

"They're bleeding all over the deck. What a mess. Give me a hand to push them over."

We did so, with a will. If you imagine this to be strange behavior, insane, then you are not correct. Death is a part of

12

life. Delia fully understood that. But, even so, even so, no girl should have to go through the things Delia had been through, events and horrors that would have destroyed a being of lesser fiber. But Delia was right. We had a way to fly and we already had enough blood to clear up as it was.

Highly practical, highly professional, highly commonsense is Delia of Vallia—just as she is highly romantic. Her father, the Emperor of Vallia, had been slain this night. No—Delia could not act completely normally, not for a space yet.

I made up my mind. You who have listened to my story as the tapes spin through the heads will know how wrought up I must have been to nerve myself, actually to pluck up the courage, to open the talk I had promised Delia for long and long.

Tentatively I spoke to her in one of the aft cabins as Farris took the steering, speed and height levers and Crimahan having indicated he wished to be dropped on his own estates, tried to sleep. Queen Lush slumbered, her demoniac energy temporarily exhausted.

So, Delia and I sat on a ponsho fleece spread on a bench and talked as the airboat slid through the nighted air of Kregen.

"A world with only one sun and only one moon! But you can't expect anyone to take such a silly idea seriously."

"Yes, I know it sounds a silly notion. But I'm asking you to examine the idea. After all, it's not impossible, is it?"

"Impossible—one sun and one moon—we-ell—I suppose not."

"Look, Delia, my heart. Try to imagine a world very much like Kregen—well, something like—but instead of Zim and Genodras shining down in glory there is only one sun, a little yellow sun."

"But Opaz! The Invisible Twins visibly vouchsafed us in the fires of Zim and Genodras, the Eternal Spirit of Opaz— how could that be if the world did not have two suns?"

"That's a poser, all right. But say that the Eternal Spirit is manifest in some other form—that is possible."

"You would run into charges of heresy at many of the religious colleges for that, Dray. People have been burned alive for casting doubts like this. And talking of only one sun in the sky is blasphemy—"

"To some people. But the Todalpheme could discuss this as a proposition. The wise men, the Sans of the world—the Wizards of Loh."

"Oh, yes, as a theory. But it runs dangerously close to blas-

13

phemy against Opaz, and that is something no honest person can possibly tolerate."

I wanted to burst out into a roar of laughter, I wanted to shout aloud in frustrated fury, and I wanted to cringe away and have no more stupid talk of planets orbiting solitary stars. But I owed Delia an explanation, and so I ploughed doggedly on. This was one eventuality I hadn't bargained for, that religion would rear its beautiful head to deny the possibility that I came from such a crippled world.

"Instead of the seven moons of Kregen there is just the one—"

"Oh, Dray, Dray—if I didn't know you I'd think you were determined to blaspheme. So—there is only one explanation. You are making fun of me."

"No." I was about to go on by saying I was in deadly serious earnest; but I paused. Tsleetha-tsleethi, as Kregens say, softly, softly. "No, I would not do that. But what I have said merits thought. . . ."

This business about a world possessing just a single sun and a single moon was only the beginning. What would Delia say when I tried to explain to her the concept of a world that had no diffs, no splendid array of peoples, no enormous variety of morphology, no halflings; but only had a single sort of human being, apims, like ourselves? How could she accept such an absurdity?

For a space we were silent as the airboat sped on through the level air and Vallia passed away below. Poor Vallia. That was where our thoughts lay. Poor, proud Vallia, an island empire torn and savaged by implacable foes, by power-hungry maniacs, by coldly ambitious men and women—and we flew in all haste from a shattered city and a burning palace which provided a funeral pyre of somber magnificence for the body of Delia's father the emperor. Yet it was precisely at this point that I chose to begin this my late and lame explanation. I tried to talk to Delia of Earth, of that strange planet distant four hundred light years from Kregen, and hoped these transparent means might provide the anodyne she needed. Mysteries partially revealed, I thought, might exercise her mind. But I miscalculated the power of Opaz, the pure religion that, I felt sure at the time, was one certain way to raise Kregen from its barbarity and savagery. Perhaps I was being selfish. All I know is that I was savaged by grief for Delia, whatever may have been my ambivalent attitude to her father, and I was desperate to ease her suffering.

Up front the Lord Farris, Kov of Vomansoir, piloted the

14

flier and left Delia and me to talk in privacy. He had witnessed the death of the emperor, for I had not been there, and had struggled with blood-stained sword to prevent that deed. Now he, like us, was a hunted fugitive.

Lykon Crimahan, Kov of Forli, had also been there at the emperor's death. He had never liked me, being bitterly opposed to my schemes to create a strong Air Service to withstand the attack from Hamal we knew must one day come across the sea. Well, that day had come and gone. Even if the whole power of Hamal had not been thrown into the battle, as I judged, the maniacal Wizard of Loh, Phu-Si-Yantong, who controlled through his puppets all of Pandahem and plenty of other spots besides, had gained enough strength to do the work. And, as well as the Hamalese marching against Vondium, there had been traitors from Vallia herself. Layco Jhansi, Udo, the various factions, they were fighting and gnawing at the bones of empire, seeking to snatch the richest portions for themselves.

The Hamalese army that Phu-Si-Yantong had somehow got out of the Empress Thyllis had possessed no aerial cavalry of any strength that I had seen. Maybe the flyers were away in another part of Vallia engaged in the campaigns that Yantong must surely carry out to bring us much of the island empire under his heel as he hungered for.

If there were no aerial cavalry mounted on fluttrells or mirvols flying over the corpse of Vondium, there would certainly be plenty of red meat there for the warvols, those vulture-like carrion-eaters. The thoughts and images rose into my mind, most unprettily, most pungent.

All over Vallia as the days passed there would be slaughter. Vallians are accounted a rich people, and most of their wealth comes from trading. They are great seafarers. Inland they are farmers and stockmen and woodsmen. When Vallia needed an army to fight some war or other she would hire mercenaries, and the mercenaries would be secure in the knowledge that Vallia could transport them safely in her fleets of galleons. But as for indigenous fighting men, warriors, they were few and thin on the ground.

That enormous wealth existed within Vallia herself was undeniable. The forests, the mines, the broad cornlands, as the emperor had once told me, they are the sinews of wealth and the muscles of power.

At Lykon Crimahan's request we dropped him off near his provincial capital of MichelDen. MichelDen lies a hundred dwaburs northeast of Vallia's capital Vondium. The provincial capital of Forli stands on the River of White Reenbays, an eastern tributary of the Great River. The kovnate of Forli extends from the Great River to the eastern coast opposite the Thirda Passage between the islands of Arlton and Meltzer to the north and Veliadrin to the south. We had taken a dog's leg passage to Valka in order to let Crimahan off at MichelDen.

He stood with one hand on the coaming of the flier, looking up at us before he jumped down onto the grass. The stars glittered, She of the Veils cast down a sheening diffused golden light and the night was very still.

"I give you the Remberee, Dray Prescot, Emperor of Vallia. I—" And here Crimahan paused, and swallowed.

I own it, the sound of my name coupled with the emperor's landed with a strange sound in my ears, a leaden sound of doom. But Drig take me if I would let this fellow see all the hesitation and indecision tormenting me. I nodded; with a hard and curt gesture of my hand I hoped he would not mistake, I ground out in the old hateful way: "If I am the emperor, Kov Lykon, then your fealty I take and welcome. Now you will do what you can against these cramphs. I shall contact you." His face bore that pained expression of unwelcome comprehension. I finished, surly and domineering: "And mind you don't get yourself killed. May Opaz go with you. Remberee."

The others called their remberees as Crimahan dropped from the airboat and vanished into the uncertain shadows.

"Up," I said to Farris. "Valka."

The voller rose into the air as Farris hauled on the levers. "He may be going to his death, majister—"

"Very likely, Farris, very likely. But he wanted to go home and I forebore to prevent him. I know how he felt."

"As do we all. I do not need to be told what has overtaken my kovnate," went on Farris in his dogged way. "Vomansoir, like your estates, like Lykon's, must have been marked down for destruction. All those about the emperor and who gave him their loyalty will find only grief in their homes. Once the structure of empire creaks and bends, once the first blows succeed, the collapse is swift."

"There will be fighting and bloodshed all over the land," said Delia, and her lovely face shadowed with the horrors we had seen and the fresh horrors to come.

"Not always," I said in my intemperate, vicious way. "Sometimes an empire will hold out tenaciously. But, Farris, I hope you are right in your estimation when we return."

16

I said this, and all the time I was totally unsure if I had the right, the moral right, to return to Vallia. But I went on speaking in that old savage way.

"So," I said, only half-believing my own words. "Before we can do anything we must secure a base and see about men and resources—and that means Valka."

The voller rose against the stars and sped eastward.

"Only," I told Delia. "You will take Didi and Velia and Aunt Katri and fly to Strombor. The continent of Segesthes is far enough away from Vallia and these troubles. There they will be safe."

"But—"

I shook my head. Delia did not like the idea of leaving Vallia at this time, even for a short period and even for so important a mission; but she saw the sense of it and agreed to go.

Below us under the glinting moonlight the coast passed away. We struck out across the sea.

We flew across the Rojica Passage that separates Vallia from Veliadrin. We flew along the Thirda Passage, eastward, to the north of Veliadrin. We did not fly over the land. To the south we could see fires burning in the night.

Delia took my arm and I could guess her thoughts.

"Veliadrin is attacked, like all our lands. No doubt the Qua'voils have stirred their prickly selves again. But there are good men down there, as well as evil. Our duty lies elsewhere this night."

It was hard. No doubt of it. We could only guess at what deviltry was going on down there to the south. But little imagination was required to understand that all of Vallia was in turmoil, with old grudges being paid off and with rapaciousness leading men and women on to blood-soaked excesses.

From MichelDen to Valkanium is about two hundred dwaburs in a straight line, what the Havilfarese call as the fluttrell flies. But we circled around over the sea to the north and so took longer over the aerial journey. The Maiden with the Many Smiles joined She of the Veils and although the night was cloudy the two moons shed their fuzzy golden pink light upon the sea.

In the sheening water sparkle below in the light of the moons the dark shadowed mass of Valka rose before us out of the sea. Valka. Valka, the place I had made my home on Kregen. The place that, along with Strombor and the Great

17

Plains of Segesthes and Djanduin, meant more to me at that time than anywhere else. Valka. . . .

"Dray—"

I held her gently, for I knew what Delia intended to say, what pained her to say, how she had struggled and sought for the right words.

"Dray—Valka. All our lands have been attacked, we know that. Phu-Si-Yantong would not overlook Valka."

I spoke cheerily, and with a certain confidence, for Valka was not quite as other lands of Vallia, because the island had fought its battles and won. "I would not expect that villain to do so. One day he will be chopped. But Valka is not the same easy prey to mercenaries and aragorn and slavers as the rest of Vallia. We have regiments of strong fighting men—"

"But Phu-Si-Yantong is a Wizard of Loh. He will have employed sorcery—"

"Yes."

That was, indeed, an unpalatable thought. This damned Wizard of Loh sought to make himself the supreme lord of Paz. He didn't care what he did to achieve that insane ambition.

"If only Khe-Hi-Bjanching was with us—or had been in Valka." Delia's hand trembled against mine. I did not think she trembled in fear. "But he will have been sent to Loh as all our other friends were sent home from—"

"There are other forces of superhuman help," I said, cutting in briskly, over-riding Delia's words. I did not want Farris—or anyone who need not know, for that matter—being apprised of what had happened to our friends. They had all been incontinently hurled back to their homes from the Sacred Pool of Baptism. So far they had not found their way back. That was a contributory cause to the misfortunes that had overtaken us; but we would have been overwhelmed even if all my friends had surrounded us. That I knew with a somber chill.

The dawn would soon be with us, and I suggested that Delia try to sleep. It was not so stupid a suggestion, for she was exhausted and despite her feelings, despite the grief for her father, she did sleep. I could soldier on for a space yet.

I fancied, in thinking of Yantong, that the cramph no longer cared if I lived or died. I had to examine the notion with great care. He had given orders that I was not to be assassinated. I did not know if he had canceled those instructions. Yantong had contrived the death of an empire. His tools fought in Vondium and over the land against the armies of

18

other men, highly placed nobles and demagogues, who sought the throne for themselves. Of all those ambitious and greedy would-be-emperors, I fancied Phu-Si-Yantong would be the eventual victor.

And, among his instruments, numbered in the ranks of those who fought for him, was our own daughter Dayra. Unwittingly, perhaps, she served the Wizard of Loh, thinking in all honor that she fought for the rights of self-determination for the North Eastern section of Vallia and this damned fellow Zankov; but she had served Yantong well. Dayra. I would have to tell Delia about her, tell Delia about Ros the Claw, and of her entanglement with Zankov, that same cramph Zankov whose bloody brand had struck down the emperor, Dayra's grandfather.

This was a tangled web, and there was more, and I could not see a clear path to steer.

"Well," I said to myself, and if I had spoken aloud my voice would have cracked out harsh and ugly under the moons, "we will take Didi and Velia and Aunt Katri out of Valka if the place is closed up as tight as a swod's drum. We will see them safely to Strombor. And then—"

And then—what?

If I did what I had said I would do, speaking in the heat of the moment and out of anger and foolish pride, there would lie seasons of campaigning ahead. Vallia would run as red with blood as ever it had. How could I justify this? I had pushed these thoughts away before, but they recurred. What moral right had I, what morality was there in it, if I raised armies, fought the usurpers, destroyed their armies, restored the throne of Vallia to its rightful heirs? Did my honor demand that? Can honor ever justify the deaths of thousands of honest people?

Perhaps, as I had wistfully half-suggested to myself, perhaps I would just stay quietly in Strombor, that beautiful enclave of the city of Zenicce, and live life the way life is intended to be lived and enjoyed.

We had taken all night over this flight. The flier was reasonably fast, having covered three hundred dwaburs, about fifteen hundred miles, and it would be full daylight before we reached Valkanium and the Bay and the high fortress of Esser Rarioch.

Below us Valka fled past. Farris had gone back to sleep and as I cogitated with such melancholy with my tormented thoughts and watched the suns rise off to our larboard, I felt

19

the soft warm hand creep into mine and felt again all the magic of my Delia enfold me.

"Dawn," said Delia.

"Aye. And the Suns are rising on a sorry land this day."

"But it is a new day, my heart. A new beginning. A new chance. In Valka—" She expected me to interrupt; but I did not. "In Valka we must find help. We must."

"If we do not, if we do, it makes no difference. You and the children are for Strombor."

The Suns of Scorpio, Zim and Genodras, rose into the clear air. The day would be fine, with perhaps a little rain after the Hour of Mid. Delia sighed.

"I have been thinking of your blasphemous suggestions of a world with one little yellow sun and one silvery moon. It is possible, I grant you. But where is the sense in it? Why do you raise a philosophical point? Is there anything more?"

"Oh, aye," I said, turning so she could nestle into my free arm. "A lot more." I spoke slowly and carefully, trying to make what I said sound sensible, which, to a Kregen, it did not, could not.

"Only apims?" She stared up at me blankly. I leaned down and kissed her. For a space nothing else mattered. Then—

"Only apims. People like us. No diffs, none at all."

"Now I know you make fun. Such a world would be— would be flat, would be—dull!"

"Well—no," I said, defending this our Earth which is so marvelous a world in its own right. "Not flat or dull. Just that Kregen is so much—so much—more," I finished lamely.

She drew a deep breath.

"Very well, husband. Since you choose to mock all the religion and the learning of the wise men—suppose, just suppose a world could exist like that. Then what?"

It was my turn to swallow.

Below us Valka began to show all those myriad colors of her forests and lakes, the mountains of the Heart Heights, the wide open spaces, the serene areas of ordered cultivation, the thread of rivers and the glint of waterfalls. The air breathed sweet and clean, that glorious air of Kregen. This was my own island of unsurpassed beauty, wild and rugged, tranquil and fertile, rich with the goodness of the earth. I drew another deep breath and the fragrant dawn air of Kregen dizzied my senses. For this I would give much, give very much. . . .

Delia looked up at me, her brown hair catching the radiance of the suns so that those outrageous chestnut tints glinted. The richness of her lips, the clarity of her brown eyes, the perfect purity of her face and form—I swallowed again and opened my mouth.

"From such a world, distant a long long way, my heart, I—"

She broke away from me and her chin firmed and the danger signals flashed from those brown eyes that changed from melting tenderness to hard authority.

"Flyers! Hamalese! They see us!"

I swivelled about, checking my words, stared out.

Flyers lifted toward us, their wide wings spread against the light, the flyers on their backs shaking their weapons.

"Not Hamalese," I said after that first flashing glance. "Flutsmen."

The mercenaries of the skies wheeled their flying mounts up toward us like a gale-driven whirlwind of leaves.

Ahead of us the Bay opened out, and the City of Valkanium spread in beauty up the slopes where vegetation bowered in verdant beauty my home. The massive pile of Esser Rarioch reared above the city and the Bay. The light picked out every detail.

Our own flags of Valka still flew from the battlements of Esser Rarioch. But ugly smears of smoke rose from the city. There were sunken galleons in the Bay. Flames spat spitefully from warehouses and from the villas along the shore and overhanging the water. A confused mass hurled up and forward against the fortress and the wink and glitter of weapons splintered shards of light into the morning.

"Esser Rarioch is attacked," I said, and the bitterness choked me with bile.

"But it still holds out." Delia leaped for a crossbow. "We must break through these flutsmen and reach the fortress."

Feathered wings flickered about us. Feathers streamed back in those clotted clumps from their helmets that give to flutsmen their devilish, reiving, headlong appearance. True mercenaries, Flutsmen of Kregen, hiring out to the highest bidder and ready to betray him for a price. They share nothing of the high honor of nikobi that give Pachaks their unmatched reputation as paktuns. Flutsmen often band together and simply reive on their own account. Now, with Vallia torn by strife, these aerial devils struck out for themselves.

I slammed the control levers over to full and bellowed for Farris. The voller lanced up into the air, spraying flutsmen away. Delia, braced against the coaming, loosed and bent at once to respan the bow.

21

Some remnants of honor still cling to some flutsmen. I had no way of knowing of what calibre were these aerial foes; but I knew with everything I held precious that I would never allow Delia to fall into their hands.

Farris lumbered out and belted up the deck to the controls. Flutsmen were urging their flying steeds on. For a space we outclimbed them. I shoved my head over the side and looked down. The dark mass of men attacking Esser Rarioch had broken through the first portals of the long stairway and were forcing their way up. The pavises borne before them bristled with arrows. Esser Rarioch was due to fall soon. And the flutsmen bored in toward us, screeching, their weapons glittering.

"Down, Farris!" I bellowed. "Straight down—straight for Esser Rarioch!"

The Lord Farris flung me a single questioning glance. He saw my face, that ugly, demoniac, headstrong old face of mine with the look of the devil, and he thumped the levers over.

Straight through the whirling cloud of flutsmen we plummeted, down and down, hurtling toward the fight raging on the long stairway leading up to Esser Rarioch.

CHAPTER TWO

The Folly of Empire

The brave red and white flags of Valka still flew over the battlements, the treshes bright and defiant in the morning light. Down we plummeted. Flutsmen screeched and drove in and were buffetted away and left, trailing far above us. The wind scorched about our ears.

No flyers attacked Esser Rarioch. I smiled. I, Dray Prescot, smiled at the grim and bloodcurdling thoughts—for my Archers of Valka must have remembered and put to good use the techniques they had been taught of repelling aerial cavalry.

So we roared down toward the fight and I peered about intently. Birds and flying animals used as steeds had been virtually unknown in Vallia until the confrontation with Hamal had forced the unwelcome information upon the Vallians.

Down south in the magnificent continent of Havilfar there were many and many a variety of flyer, and of them all, I fancied—aye! and still do!—that the fabulous flutduin of my ferocious four-armed Djangs is the finest. A corps of flutduin mounted flyers had been formed in Valka, trained by Djangs brought to my island for the purpose. Where were they now?

Why was not this assaulting mass of infantry being harassed from the air?

These thoughts had to be banished as with the wind blustering past we dropped headlong into the attack.

Queen Lush staggered out, almost falling down the steeply canted deck.

"Take up a crossbow, queen, and let us see how you shoot!"

"I'll shoot, ma faril, I'll shoot—"

So we had three crossbows to loose and Delia and I spanned a half dozen more as we rocketed down.

White and colored blobs showed as the faces of the men in the ranks below looked up. Their wide pavises were studded with arrows. Varter-hurled bolts splintered off the rocky sides of the stairway, and chunks of stone ricocheted away. I judged that there were few Valkans left in Esser Rarioch to carry on the defense.

Time, time. . . . There is never enough time. . . .

Up the stairway the infantry struggled in the shelter of their large shields, and down we plunged at them. At intervals in the long flight of steps there are generously proportioned landings, places where a fellow might pause and catch his breath as he climbs to Esser Rarioch. The head of the assaulting column had reached one such landing and now it halted. Bows bent against us and arrows flew. The voller was of good Hamalian construction, built soundly of stout wood, mostly sturm, with lenken bracers. The arrows either failed to penetrate or missed and fell away.

The Lord Farris was a fine flier. He would needs be, seeing he was a Chuktar in the Vallian Air Service. Now he eased the voller out of her headlong downward plunge, aiming to bring us up over the heads of the foremost foemen.

Queen Lush leaned over the coaming and let fly. She loosed far too early and where her bolt went Opaz knew.

"Save your bolts, queen!" I bellowed. She glared madly at me, and seized up another of the crossbows.

Farris was swinging us up now in a sweetly contrived curve that would put us in a good shooting position. Queen Lush's second bolt disappeared into the dark mass below.

Delia began to shoot.

We discharged our crossbows and I saw one of the pavises sway and tilt as men fell, their hands lax in death slipping from the cross-struts. But our combined shooting would not make the decisive difference the desperate situation required.

Now Farris was a fine flier, as I have said. I bellowed at him as I frantically wound a windlass.

"Down, Farris! Drop full on them!"

He glared at me, and all the reluctance of an Air Serviceman to hazard his craft showed in his seamed, wind-lined face. The crow's-feet at the corners of his eyes deepened.

With a curse that apostrophized Makki-Grodno's foul and diseased anatomy I hurled myself at the controls. I thunked the lever down, hard. The voller dropped like a leaden plummet.

"Majister!" yelled Farris, aghast.

The airboat smashed down onto the head of the column, onto the pavises, onto the infantry. If there were squashing sounds they were lost in the uproar. The voller lurched. She stuck her stern down, over the rear of the steps leading onto the lower flight. I juggled the controls, lifting her and letting her fall. We ground down as a pestle grinds in a mortar.

Presently, with only a few arrows flicking about us, I lifted. The voller rose smartly enough and I turned her in the air. We looked over the side.

The column was in full retreat, broken into flying fragments. Men ran and scrambled down the stairs. Many fell to roll in brightly swathed bundles of uniforms and armor down the long stairway. I did not smile. But, for the moment at least, we had gained a respite.

"The chance," breathed Farris. "It was a gamble—"

"And the gamble succeeded," said Queen Lush. She had just spanned a bow, struggling with the cords, and now she took careful aim at a wretch running down the steps and sent the bolt full into his back. He leaped into the air, convulsed, and then collapsed, to fall and tumble headlong down onto the pressing backs of his comrades. In a wild tangle of arms and legs and weapons they all slithered down to the next landing.

"Now," I said. "We will find out what is going on here, by Krun!"

"It won't be good news, that is no gamble," said Farris.

"But," said Delia, her chin lifted, her face bright. "Esser Rarioch still stands. The flags still fly."

As we flew up to the high landing platform I fancied that

24

my fortress palace might still stand; but not for long. Anyone of the villians who wanted the downfall of the Empire of Vallia as a prerequisite to assuming the crown himself—or herself—would not allow any strong place of the Prince Majister's to stand. My plans for starting the counter-revolution from Valka must be re-thought. But, then, I'd half-known that all along.

The folk who met us as we alighted from the voller bore the marks of hard fighting. Yellow bandages bore ugly stains. But the men greeted me with a roar of welcome, the women smiling at Delia. Esser Rarioch is a place dear to me, as you know, a place where no slaves were kept. Everyone in the fortress capable of bearing arms did so. We were engulfed in a human tide of talk and explanations of what had happened here and enquiries of what was taking place elsewhere and a determined defiance of anything those rasts outside could do to us.

Chuktars hold high ranks in any army, the name in its original barbaric connotations meaning commander of ten thousand. Nowadays, a Chuktar commands a grouping of regiments or units each under a Jiktar. The Chuktar who met me as I went up onto the battlements gripped my hand in his own brown fist and beamed. I agreed with his decision not to meet me at the landing platform. He was occupied where he was and he pointed out what deviltry was afoot out there as we talked.

The flutsmen had been employed to bring the fortress to a rapid submission, and they had been seen off with volleys of accurately loosed arrows. Chuktar Nath Fergen ti Vandayha pointed at the gathering masses far below filling the Kyro of the Tridents, and he had no need to say they prepared themselves for the next attack.

As we talked I knew Delia would be seeing about Aunt Katri and the children, that Queen Lush would be exciting sidelong glances from the folk of Esser Rarioch, that our own preparations were being made. The Lord Farris joined us on the high battlements, and the pappattu was made between him and Chuktar Nath Fergen.

Jiktar Exand, the commander of the fortress guard, had been wounded early on, and I would go down and see him and give him words of comfort. Nath Fergen had chanced to be in Valkanium when the attack developed. As he said, with a round oath: "Tom took most of the army off to Veliadrin, for those Opaz-forsaken cramphs of Qua'voil burst out and burned three towns and started to march north. I came here to pick up the Fourth Archers and was just in time to get myself into the castle."

He sounded most wroth. The Fourth Archers, a fine regiment, had been scattered in billets around the town and only a half pastang had made it up the long stairs. Among that number was Naghan ti Ovoinach, now an ord-Hikdar. Panshi, my Chief Chamberlain, came up and superintended the supply of tea and parclear and fruits. Long before Esser Rarioch could be starved out the attackers would have broken their way in, for there were very many of them, and barely a hundred and fifty souls left in the fortress. As for the Valkan army, that was away in the island of Veliadrin, to the west, fighting those porcupine-like devils of Qua'voil who would rejoice to see the destruction of everything apim within their reach.

So, as I listened to the news tumbling out, there was precious little to cheer me. I remained firm in my decision to send Delia and the children to Strombor. All those incapable of fighting must be crammed into the voller. But, I thought with what I hoped was shrewd cunning and not footling incapacity, suppose the voller was used to take everyone out of the fortress by turn? They could be taken into the Heart Heights. We could resist from there as we had in the old days. Yes, I said to myself, and swung about to tell Chuktar Fergen what I proposed.

"But strom! To abandon Esser Rarioch!"

"Aye, Chuktar Nath. Aye! I would abandon this place that I love so dearly to those devils. What is the importance of stone and sculpture against flesh and blood? I would not lose a single man or woman of Valka to save Esser Rarioch." I thought of the emperor, grimly holding onto his fine palace, and getting the place burned down around his ears and himself slain for the sake of it. "The important strategy now is to save our people."

"Yes, my strom—and then we will rise and kick them out—all these invaders, every last one." His full-fleshed face showed the thick blood-pulse beneath the skin, his beaked Vallian nose outthrust. "As we did in the old days, when we chased the aragorn out of Valka! Hai, Jikai! We will write new stanzas to *The Fetching of Drak na Valka!*"

"Hai, Jikai!" shouted the others clustered on the high battlements. "Hai, Jikai!"

The moment was emotional, no doubt of it, and I responded, thinking that, perhaps, if we did what we said then it

26

might well be a jikai we did. And then those people of mine had to go on, and bellow it out, as they loved to do.

"Hai Jikai!" they shouted, and the swords whipped up, glittering in the lights of the Suns of Scorpio. "Hai, Jikai! Dray Prescot! Strom of Valka!"

It was all proud and stupid and a folly. Pride, pride—well, I have no truck with pride, having fallen flat so very many dreadful times. But, I own, if we all fought as well as we shouted, we should be home and dry.

On that sour mental note I looked out and saw that our shouting had attracted the attention of some of those miserable cramphs below. They were running about, mere black ants so far below in the kyro, preparing to ascend the stairs again and, I trusted, many of them to ascend not to any of their heavens but to the quickest way to the Ice Floes of Sicce.

Joining our group on the high battlements, Delia looked down. Her face drew down in a frown that always has the power to seize my heart up in a constricting grip.

"Is this to be Vondium, all over again?" she said.

I forced my craggy old face to smile for her.

"No. We will evacuate. Everyone will be taken to safety in the Heart Heights. From there, as we did in the old days, we will resist the invaders."

At once she fired up. For only the most fleeting of fallible moments I thought she would protest. But she saw at once that by abandoning Esser Rarioch, for all that we held the place so dear, we would shed an encumbrance and gain freedom of action. To be mewed up in a fortress with a hundred and fifty souls against an army is no way to fight a war. Memories of the Siege of Zandikar ghosted in, and scarlet memories of other sieges; but I looked away to the distant purple haze of those ferocious central mountains of Valka, and took heart.

We held that attack, shooting sheaves of arrows and bolts upon the attackers, rolling masses of stone down the steps, bounding, crunching into the shield, scattering them in a splintering wash of wicker and blood.

In a pause of the action, Jiktar Exand clambered up onto the ramparts, a yellow bandage over his neck and shoulder already glistening with fresh blood. The enormous arch of his ribcage swelled as I greeted him.

I said: "What in the name of the black lotus flowers of Hodan-Set are you doing up here, Exand? Look at that wound!"

Exand's square face bristled under his helmet and he bashed his red and white banded sleeve across his breastplate. I tensed up for his bellow.

"Strom! I cannot skulk in bed when there is fighting to be done! Strom! We fight to the death!"

He was just the same, massive, bulky, creaking in his armor, bulbous, filled with the fanatical devotion of all my fighting men of Valka.

"Well, Exand, my friend. It is indeed good to see you. Now stand you clear of that varter and get a fresh dressing on that wound. You hear?"

"Quidang!" His bellow vibrated against our eardrums. "I hear, my strom!"

The Lord Farris bustled up and took Exand's arm, leading him off, talking. I saw Exand halt as though shafted. He swung about. His quivering alertness took everyone's attention and the shrieking of the infantry below struggling to climb those murderous stairs faded. Exand's face turned that purple that the best Wenhartdrin wines hold within their bodies.

"Majister!" Exand fairly roared out, purple, immense, consumed with overwhelming joy. "Hai, Emperor of Vallia!"

My first thought was that Farris had to go and open his mouth. He was loyal to the emperor—to the emperor that was—and to Delia. I knew a loyal man, and I valued Farris far too much to fault him in so petty a thing as this.

After that, when we had thrown the attack back and could take a breath, the buzz went around the fortress. The emperor was dead: long live the emperor.

I have mentioned how my folk of Valka continue to call me their strom, somehow or other conveniently overlooking the rather comical thought that I was the Prince Majister of Vallia. Well, now they knew I was the Emperor of Vallia. Although, at that moment, I was the Emperor of Nothing. But they continued to call me strom, with occasionally a lapse into more formal majisters for the sake of propriety.

This somewhat farcical interjection of emperors and majisters into the grim business of staying alive within the besieged fortress served to force upon me the thought that I was more like the fabled Pakkad, the outcast, the pariah, than any emperor. I had not wanted to be emperor, had not sought the throne and crown of Vallia. And, the plain fact was, I did not have them. The corpse of Vallia was being fought over as lurfings fight over a corpse on the great plains.

28

The desire to dabble my fingers in that stew appeared more and more unattractive, more and more unworthy.

Thrusting these morose broodings aside I joined in the preparations. The voller would take out the people in relays and with them weapons and supplies. Up in the Heart Heights we would find refuge. As an accomplished flier, Farris offered to make the first journeys. For the moment the attackers had drawn off and so I decided to catch up on a little sleep. The first voller load was seen off and then I went into our private apartments and stretched out on the bed. Before I went to sleep two thoughts hovered lazily in my mind and the first of these was cheerful and reassuring.

Among these defenders of Esser Rarioch and all the other fearsome warriors of Valka who would continue the resistance there would be found no place for that robust figure of legend, Vikatu the Dodger, the archetypal Old Sweat of most of the armies of Paz. That mythical old soldier is loved and sworn by with enormous gusto by the swods in the ranks, a paragon of all the military vices, the old hand who looks after Number One and knows every trick in and out of every book and manual of soldiering ever written. The fighting men of Valka might cuss away in Vikatu's best style, but they were not soldiers in the strict regimental sense, not even the swods of the regiments we had formed, disciplined, controlled, trained. In the struggles that lay ahead I thought that not one fighting man of Valka would misunderstand the reality of Vikatu and dodge his duty.

So that, as far as it went, was all right. We would, as Kregans say, blatter them with a will.

But—by all the grey ones of Sicce—but the other thought coiling in my head made me twist and turn uncomfortably on the bed. I was still totally undecided. I had spoken out about returning, had half-promised to regain the throne and crown. But, even with all the strictures laid on me, the ideas of honor, the knowledge of evil that would cover the land unopposed in any meaningful way, even with all this and the high ideals of the Kroveres of Iztar, even then I was not fully committed to a course that would bring further bloodshed. What was Vallia to me? I cherished estates in other parts of the world. Delia's father the emperor was murdered and his empire sundered. Why should I seek to restore all that blaze of pomp and pageantry, resuscitate the power and the glory? Were those ends moral? Could the suffering be tolerated? How could all this maelstrom of future misery be justified?

So, as I slipped into sleep with a million torturing thoughts

29

troubling me, you will see I was in a most foul mood. Only that last thought before sleep of Delia held any power to sooth me.

CHAPTER THREE

───◆───

Delia Looses an Opinion at the Star Lords

The sleep lasted long enough to refresh. The voller made two more trips and the defenders of the fortress were very thin along the battlements indeed. We had to take thought to arrange the best way of the final evacuation.

"The folk are being cared for at friendly farms in the Heart Heights," said Farris. He looked windblown and tired. "But it is wild country up there—wild."

"Aye. Valka will never fall to invaders whilst the Heart Heights stand."

The remainder of the force was split into two. I moved along the sun-splashed battlements to talk privately with Delia. I knew I'd encounter opposition.

"I do not think, husband, that that is a very good plan at all. In fact, if you ask me, I'd say it was a plan suitable for Cottmer's Caverns."

Below us the incredibly beautiful vista of Valkanium and the Bay spread out, dappled in sunshine, the light drifting of rain after the Hour of Mid burnishing everything with a glistening patina of gold. The attackers far below were thinking of forming up for another onslaught. They had lost a great many men, and they could see no other way of getting at us in Esser Rarioch than of climbing up those blood-spattered stairs.

They did not know of the secret entrances and exits far below the rock.

I persisted stubbornly.

"You will fly out with the children and Aunt Katri. I want you with them."

"But Aunt Katri is perfectly capable—she may be getting old, now, true; but the nurses—"

30

"You. You will take the penultimate trip. We may have to cut and run for it on the last one."

"I know. And don't you think I would be at your side?"

A shadow fleeted between the ruby glory of Zim and the ramparts. I looked up. My fist tightened on my sword hilt.

Up there, planing in its arrogant wide-winged circles, flew the Gdoinye, the spy and messenger of the Star Lords. That gorgeous golden and scarlet raptor circled up there, his head on one side, one beady eye fixed upon us.

Delia said in a voice that almost but not quite trembled: "There is that bird again—"

"Aye . . . A Bird of Ill Omen. Delia—I have promised to tell you why I am sometimes dragged away from you when all I want is to stay with you. Not like now, when it is sensible for you to go with the children. But, the other times—"

"I remember them, I remember them all. They were horrible."

What was horrible to me in that moment, as well as the enforced absences I made at the orders of the Everoinye, the Star Lords, was that Delia could see the bird. I knew Drak my eldest son had seen it, and I had lied to him and said the bird was not there. But the Star Lords did not reveal their powers to many. I feared and hated the idea of my Delia being caught up in the schemes of superhuman unknown and unknowable beings who demanded so much from me without explanation.

"The bird is connected with your—disappearances."

"Yes. And the Scorpion."

"On the field of the Crimson Missals, when you said you did not want to go to Hyrklana—and I went there—and—"

I tried to make a laugh and failed. "I'd be sorry, now, if I hadn't gone to Hyrklana and fought in the Jikhorkdun of Huringa. Then we would not have Tilly and Oby and Naghan the Gnat and Balass the Hawk as friends."

"And where they are now, Opaz knows."

"We will fetch them back, if they wish to come."

"I think they will make their way back here, to Valka, for they are true Valkans now—"

"And what a sorry mess Valka and Vallia are in!"

The scarlet and golden bird circled, watching us. I shook my fist at it, and it continued on, indifferent.

"And when the shanks attacked that little village of Panashti, on the island of Lower Kairfowen, and you fell from the gate and we carried you to a hut. It was all a confusion. The walls and huts were burning. Those terrible Leem

Lovers were breaking in—the walls came down and the smoke blew—We fought. Oh, Dray! You should have seen Drak. He was like a young zhantil. You would have been proud."

Drak had grown up since then, become a man, a prince, a Krozair of Zy. His life had not been easy. Now Delia poured out all the wonder and the hidden-away hurt, the bewilderments she had felt over the years of our life together.

"I had gone to see you in the hut and—and you were not there! Only your armor and your weapons. I feared, then, remembering the other times, Jynaratha, over the Shrouded Sea—and then, even your weapons were gone. We fought as hard as we could and then Tom and Vangar came and we were saved. Drak was suddenly aware. Men looked to him. He and I, between us—and there was Turko and Naghan and Balass and all the others. There was such a lot of shouting and confusion. It was given out that you had gone to punish the shanks. Men believed. We were able to leave Panashti without any suspicion that you had died being voiced. Later, it was suggested—but you know—and, anyway, you have gone before to visit other lands, as all men know."

"Twenty-one years," I said, and I shivered.

The Star Lords had banished me to Earth for twenty-one long and miserable years because I had defied them.

Delia put her hand on my arm.

"And then you disappeared from the voller as we flew to Aphrasöe—that was mysterious and terrible—"

"The Scorpion," I said. "I will tell you why I sometimes have to go away, and why I have decided to resist in different ways that do not mean I go back to—go away for twenty-one years."

She looked at me and a wary look warned me.

"Back to—where?"

I did not reply.

"Back to the Great Plains of Segesthes? To your Clansmen?"

It would have been only a little difficult to lie. I shook my head.

"But where, my heart, where? Tell me—"

"If I do tell you you will believe, I think, for I love you enough to know that—but it will be hard."

She looked at me, and I knew my stupid remark had not only been unnecessary, it showed her how tangled up I was.

The wind blew the red and white flags of Valka out in a fluttering panoply. We would leave them flying when we

32

deserted this beautiful place. For a time they would convince those rasts below we still resisted them. The red and white of Valka. . . .

Among the treshes fluttering from the flagstaffs someone had hoisted my own old battle flag, the yellow cross on the scarlet field, that battle flag fighting men call Old Superb.

I wondered then if I could bear to leave that behind.

What I did know and with sharp agony, was that if I defied the Star Lords who had brought me to Kregen I would leave more than a flag behind me when I was ejected with contempt from this exotic and cruel world.

The bird volplaned away, turning in a gentle glide and the suns sheened a brilliance along his feathers. I wondered what Delia would do, what say, if the Gdoinye slanted back to us and spoke to me. The messenger of the Everoinye usually insulted me—well, we understood each other's tempers in that. But I did not want to risk what Delia might say if the bird did speak to us. I wanted to move us along. I wanted—what I wanted was just about anything than having to go through this.

The quick, intuitive empathy between Delia and myself has always given me a trembling feeling of possessing beauty beyond price. Always, I stress that we call each other 'My Delia' and 'My Dray' and the togetherness is complete, unshakeable, unremarked on save as I speak this record, and yet that possession is mutual, not a diseased obsession of property, one of the other. We are two people, two rounded persons, and yet together we are more than a single rounded one, more than merely one and one, more than two; and through all this rapturous spectrum of feeling the dark hollow secret I carried dragged at me, tearing at me, and I knew that Delia sensed that apartness and grieved.

So, with that empathy between us, I was not surprised when she began to speak in a low, serious voice, as we stood there in the radiance of the Suns of Scorpio. But her voice faltered, hesitated, her face was half-averted, and those brown eyes did not regard me with that same old brave look I knew and loved. All my primeval instincts flared into my thick old skull. Her mouth trembled as she spoke and yet she controlled herself, and I saw the way her hand fingered the brooch upon her breast and fell away and so crept up again. I felt the blood in my head.

"You have watched performances of *Sooten and Her Twelve Suitors*, I know." She would not look at me. "The story is old, as old as Kregen itself. An abandoned wife is prey. There are many men whose minds dwell on their opportunities, whose desires, whose hands—" She stopped speaking, unable to go on.

Sooten, as you know, is a legend of Kregen that parallels in emotional depth the brave Earthly story of Penelope, wife to Odysseus, mother of Telemachus. Like Penelope, Sooten kept her suitors at bay. I sensed that Delia was trying to feel her way to telling me things I had best learn at first hand, if at all, and my mind went back to what I had heard, posing as Jak Jakhan, in the Baths of the Nine called the Bower of the Scented Lotus in Vondium. There those oafs had nudged and winked and repeated tales of the notorious affairs of the Princess Majestrix of Vallia. The rubbish had passed from my mind as the cess pits are emptied and purified with that remarkable concoction made from the little blue fallimy flower. And, chained in a prison cell, I had heard other salacious stories.

In the many rich pantheons of Kregen there stands the archetypal figure of the seducer, suave, groomed, glib-tongued. He knows well how to comfort and feed the vanity of women and this Quergey the Murgey is charmingly versed in the ways of breaking down the defenses of wives who, for whatever reason, are estranged from their husbands. I should add that I give this contemptible figure a name that is not his own, his real name being much contumed over Kregen, and I choose to use this alias. Perhaps, one day, his own name and not his use name will be revealed. Odysseus was gone for twenty years. I had been gone many times, and once for twenty-one whole years. As I looked at Delia I understood that many men had essayed her, and I knew they had failed. Her own inner spirit and strengths would not fail her, and although she knew my opinion of the sin of pride, in this case her own pride would rise and she would draw her virtue from our love. Her strength would not fail no matter that I was absent, gone, removed. What we meant to each other remained steadfast despite my seeming rejection of her, leaving her distraught and abandoned and prey to the scum who batten on unhappy women.

One of Quergey the Murgey's favorite techniques is to practice the sympathy routine, offering help and a firm shoulder on which to lean and cry, and so lead on, subtly, delicately, to the fulfilment of his desires. He feeds the anguished ego with words the woman craves to hear. Delia would see through all that. But she felt she must try to make the oafish, foolish, thoughtless Dray Prescot understand the load she bore. And, understanding, my anguish for her agony almost destroyed me—almost, for my Delia of the Blue Mountains was with me now and no matter what happened we would be together in ways of love far beyond the comprehension of mere mortal flesh and blood.

That belief is not rooted in religion or mysticism of a mundane kind—and that is not a contradiction in terms—is not understood by the seducers of the world. The meretricious creeds that condone the acts of Quergey the Murgey offer cheap substitutes for reality, like the evil creed of Lem the Silver Leem, and claim their reality is of life when it is of death.

The scarlet and golden bird circled, watching us.

My wife must understand that my absences were forced on me and not of my own free will. The idea that she would fail to grasp my ludicrous story of a world with one sun and one moon and only apims for people appeared to do her a most injurious injustice. Was she not Delia? Of course she would understand, and understanding gain strength to repel with the contempt they deserved all those moist-mouthed, hypocritical well-wishers, the suitors infected by the poison of Quergey the Murgey. She looked up at me and her chin lifted. She looked marvelous.

"Yes, my heart. There are stories. I beg you—do not unsheath your Krozair longsword against those little people. They do not merit that worth of attention."

"You are with me, Delia." I spoke most soberly. "That is all I want."

"And all the rest," she whispered, and leaned toward me and the Gdoinye flew down and hawked out a coarse barking cry. She glanced up, and said: "These absences—you will tell me. But there are puzzles, sorely troubling, in the times. Time seems unreal." She spoke in a reflective way now, the storm over, searching for knowledge, remembering our partings.

The messenger and spy of the Star Lords hovered over us.

Delia eyed the Gdoinye with a speculative eye. "You made yourself Strom of Valka when—"

"I was made, my love," I corrected, mildly.

"Yes. You were Fetched to be Drak na Valka. And that happened—it *must* have happened—when you and I, and Seg and Thelda were marching through the hostile territories. I have thought about this. I have thought that I spent but one day apart after we met, whilst you were off in Segesthes and your Clansmen, or at least, so it seems. A person cannot be in two places at once, can they?" Here she moved a little way away, pensive, troubled and struggling with her thoughts. "Also, you are King of Djanduin and when did that happen?" She looked at me, and caught that luscious lower lip between her teeth. "And will you say you were Fetched to be King of Djanduin?"

"No." I spoke with humility and with anger. "No. I own I set out to make myself King of Djanduin. But I changed along the way. It was a long and wearisome wait through the seasons."

"So," she said, and sparked up. "So the sorcerer is very powerful. I do not think even a Wizard of Loh could match what I suspect."

"That is true—if you suspect truth. That, I do not know."

The Gdoinye angled closer, ruffling his feathers, slanting down toward us.

"And does this great bird come to take you away from me again?"

At my troubled look Delia gave me no time to answer. She whipped up the crossbow to hand, one we had taken from the voller. It was ready spanned. She triggered the nut, the bow clanked, the bolt sped.

I gaped.

I felt the chill. What would happen now?

Delia, my Delia of Delphond, had loosed at the Gdoinye!

What thunder would roll from the heavens? What lightnings spit down and split the castle walls? What hailstones might lash us to a bloody froth? I let out a yell and rushed for Delia, swept her up into my arms, pressing her head against my chest. I glared up madly. The bird circled and the bolt whickered up and in my heightened state I followed the cast with raking eyes. Delia had shot true. The bolt would hit. . . .

So fast it all happened, so fast, pelting fleeter than a zorca over the plains. A voice hammered against the brightness of the day.

"Fool! Onker! Have you learned no lessons, Dray Prescot?"

And a stunning flash of blue fire illuminated the sky, washed over the stone walls, burst in thunder about my ears. The bolt burst asunder, limned by blue fire, smashed and broken, falling away, twisting, dropping.

Even then, I knew no other eyes but those of Delia and my own would have seen that coruscating display of power.

For a heartbeat, for a single heartbeat, I thought the blue smash of fire destroyed the crossbow bolt alone. And then I knew differently, knew better—I, Dray Prescot, Lord of Strombor and Krozair of Zy, knew I had another lesson to learn.

Blueness coiled around us.

"Dray!"

The radiance twined grasping tentacles around us—between us. I felt the old hateful sensations of falling. Delia was no longer clasped in my arms. I glared up, my whole body and mind wracked with hatred. Up there, blazing against the sky, drowning out the refulgence of Zim and Genodras, the enormous bloated form of the ghostly Scorpion glowered down on me.

Gropingly, frantically, I reached for Delia. The stones of the ramparts beneath my booted feet scraped harshly. Coldness fell over me like the chill cloak of the grey ones. Delia—she was gone, torn away from me—no! I was being torn away from her as I had so often been dragged away before.

Hateful memories of those other times when I had been wrenched away from Kregen by this ghostly blue representation of a Scorpion battered at me. I tried to shout, and nothing came save a wheeze. The blueness deepened.

And that blueness wavered; the Scorpion trembled as though formed of smoke wafted from a campfire, and being blown this way and that by the evening breeze from the high mountains.

The Scorpion dissolved.

A flush of crimson light spread across the firmament from starboard, and I switched instinctively to search the larboard side for that welcome glow of yellow gold.

But the yellow fascinating gold of Zena Iztar did not appear to cheer me and give me comfort and help.

A vivid acid green jaggled into the sky, hard-edged, sharp, cutting across the blue.

Voices as though confined in an echoing cavern shielded miles deep in rock ghosted across, hollow voices, muffled and echoing, yet clear, distinct, so that I heard. And, hearing, I braced myself, prepared to meet the new challenge and attempt with all the will-power in me to resist. Perhaps—I had been told—perhaps a mental force alone would suffice. I did not know. All I knew was that I must resist and summon myself, the inner me that was plain and simple Dray Prescot, to stand against these superhuman forces.

"He is mine. I run him, for you are weak and old. . . ."

The acid voice dripped with power.

"Not so, Ahrinye! Not so. For we are the Everoinye—"

The answering voice boomed, muffled, half-choked, yet deep with the reverberations of habitual authority.

"You may be Everoinye, but you have forfeited your rights. I am a Star Lord, also. I—" And then the acrid voice screeched into an incoherency that jumbled the passionate words together like the screech of metal against the grinder's wheel. The bitter green light fluctuated wildly.

This quarrel among the Star Lords affected me and yet I felt a frail confidence that the Everoinye did not know I could hear them. Their own passionate natures were well hidden, repressed, controlled by the flame of their purpose, that I believed. They were superhuman and therefore would not think as a man would think. They wrangled and I listened, and all the time I watched for the yellow golden flush of light that would herald the arrival of Zena Iztar.

What they said contorted thought; I could not then comprehend all and it would not be proper to attribute what little I later learned to the Dray Prescot who was the me who listened in such awed and yet defiant fascination.

The Star Lord called Ahrinye, he of the jagged acid green light and sharp acid voice, showered his youthful contempt upon the elders of the Star Lords. As I braced myself up, ready, hating them all, raging, I yet had time to reflect that the Star Lords in this but followed the same time-consuming course as fragile humanity—except that, I knew, the Everoinye were by thousands of years older than the oldest man who ever lived, on Earth or on Kregen.

They wrangled over me. Ahrinye wanted to use me with a greater force than hitherto and, I realized, a greater harshness, a lack of even the rudimentary concerns for my skin the Star Lords had shown. Mind you, I did not think they cared for me one jot after I had done their dirty work for them. And then the name spurted from the maze of shrouded talk and I snapped into even more alert listening.

"Phu-Si-Yantong?" said Ahrinye. "Your lordling suffers from him and I would send a summary Gdoinye to settle that."

"You think you may stand against us, and you know so little. The lordling Prescot has been given a measure of protection against the Wizard—for their puny powers quail even at the thought of the Savanti. And the Shere'affo Iztar meddles—"

I winced. The viridian green light exploded into whorls of jagged lightning. Enormous thunders crashed about my head.

38

The blue light pulsed and, tiny, creeping, but there, real and penetrating, a golden yellow glow grew low on the horizon.

And I understood. At the mention of the name of Zena Iztar these puissant and superhuman beings took notice, took cognisance—I could not believe they feared. But they became wary—yes, wary would be the name for the emotions I sensed coiling there in the sky colors coruscating above my head.

The crimson beat a steady pulse of glowing ruby light through all the other clash of color.

All the time I stood upon the battlements of Esser Rarioch, in my capital city of Valkanium, in my island stromnate of Valka—and yet I might as well have been on Earth, or Esser Rarioch have been flung to the farthest depths of space.

And although I say I understood, I understood that I had grasped at a tiny fragment of what was going on. Amid all this frightening display of supernal power I gleed at the thought that Zena Iztar did, indeed, possess some vestiges of influence. However, she may wish to influence the course of events, Zena Iztar, I felt with a dim sense of prying perhaps beyond the evidence, must perforce direct the current, seek to steer events rather than to originate them. The yellow glow faded.

I tried to scream out for Zena Iztar to remain, to succour me; but I was falling, falling, feeling the chill biting into me, and I heard, faint and far-away, like the echo of a lost child in the darkling woods: "Dray! Dray! Where are you?"

The cords in my throat stood out as I tried to bellow back. "Delia! Delia—" But no sound forced its way from my ashen lips.

Once again I was being hurtled head-over-heels into fresh adventure, being flung halfway across Kregen to succour someone whom the Star Lords wished to remain alive for the sake of their future plans.

Where before I had insanely contumed the Star Lords and sought to fly back at once to Delia, and been banished to Earth for my pains, this time I would do what the Everoinye commanded, do it fast and quick and ruthlessly. Then I would return to Valka. Better, return to Strombor, for I knew Farris would make sure that Delia was taken with the children to refuge in my enclave of Strombor in Zenicce.

The blueness roared in my head like a rashoon of the Eye of the World.

The Scorpion writhing in blue fire sharded with the crimson glints of Antares had me in its grip. Wherever on Kregen

39

I was thumped down to get on with the commands of the Star Lords would not be too far for me to claw my way back.

As always I was thumped down stark naked. A ferocious screaming and bellowing lacerated the hot air. Joe Muggins, Dray Prescot, yanked from all he wanted on Kregen and sent to sort out a problem for the Star Lords. Well, this time I'd do it so damned fast even the Everoinye wouldn't have time to blink.

There was no hesitation in my mind over what I was supposed to do.

I had been hurled down into a small wooden cabin which had been ripped and wrecked and thrown into confusion, with odd bits of clothing and kitchen utensils scattered everywhere. A man lay sprawled on the floor, his right hand trapped under his body. He was dead, his head cloven in. I leaped to my feet, feeling a dragging weight pulling at my limbs, launched myself at the man who was trying to strangle the half-naked woman. She clutched a baby to her and screamed and screamed.

As I say, there was no doubt in my mind what I was supposed to do.

The people were all apims, like me, and the fellow whose neck I took into my fists, twisting a trifle, for I wanted to ask him some questions, wore a hide loincloth and a quantity of beadwork. His head was shaved somewhat after the fashion of a Gon or a Chulik. He tried to slash me with his little steel-headed axe and I ground down harder so that he slumped.

I threw him down and heard the betraying shush of a shoe across the floor. The cabin was lit by a cheap glass oil lamp. The light beamed out mellowly. It was a wonder the lamp had not been upset in the struggle before I arrived.

The turn I made and the immediate sideways step were all done without thought, heritage of the Disciplines of the Krozairs of Zy. The fellow who was in the act of leaping at me, his axe upraised, was dressed as his companion. A tangle of ridiculous feathers tufted about the haft of the axe. It was only a small axe; but I knew that kind of weapon and I knew the fellow wielding it would be exceedingly ferocious and swift, no matter what part of Kregen I might be in.

The axe-head sliced down, glittering. I slid the blow and stepped in and he tried to seize me with his free hand. His face looked a flat-nosed shriek of absolute resolve. He was a

40

savage, no doubt of it, in his fighting techniques. But so was I. I gave him no time to grapple or to bring the axe back.

A knee into his vitals, a chopping blow to his neck, and a slashing smash of my forearm as he went down, finishing with a kick to whatever came handiest as he rolled. He flopped. I gave them both a reassuring tap with the little axe-head, not to slay them but to keep them in cold storage for a space.

The woman was still shrieking. She glared at me with wide-eyed horror and she could not speak. The baby was yelling.

I stepped across to a pile of clothes all tangled up and then my head snapped up. My hand fastened on a pair of trousers made from some hard blue material. But, outside, shouts lifted, the sound of men yelling, muffled words and the trample of feet. Hastily pulling on the trousers, which had to be doubled up around my waist and yanked tight with the belt, I snatched up the axe and started for the door.

Men were yelling out there. I heard a sudden shriek which, if I knew anything, was the sound of a friend of these two sleeping beauties in the act of charging. The first one in the door wouldn't be put to sleep—he'd be flattened.

The door burst open. A man towered on the threshold, the lamp glinting from his sweat-soaked coppery skin. His axe looked identical to the one I grasped, save that I'd taken time to rip away the stilly tangling feathers. He saw me and he gave a single incoherent shriek and charged.

His lank black hair was bound by a fillet and he wore a few feathers there. I sidestepped, hit him over the head, smashed him down and so whirled as another appeared. This one tried to be clever, whipping a broad-bladed knife in with his left hand as he struck with the axe. But I'd fought for many and many a year with a sword and a left-hand dagger, the Jiktar and the Hikdar. I foined briefly, desperately anxious to get these idiots off my back and hightail it back to Valka or Strombor. I pitched him down to lie with his comrades, although, as I had bleakly surmised, he did not sleep. I'd had to slash half his face off before he'd consent to lie down.

The screaming from the woman and the baby went on and on and there was no time to shout at them as a fifth man leaped into the doorway. He took a single look at the scene within, the shrieking woman and the baby, his four comrades sprawled and bloody on the floor, and me, a right tearaway with an axe fronting him, and he half turned.

41

He stood in the doorway, the light gleaming from his powerful body.

I was perfectly prepared to let him go. I had no idea where I was, but I had no wish to slaughter more than was inescapable if I was to do what I had been commanded to do. If he attacked the woman and the child, he would probably die. If he ran away I might run a greater risk; but that was an equation that honor demanded.

I shook the axe at him, to help him make up his mind.

From outside the approaching beat of hooves heralded the arrival of a hard-riding group of men. The staccato hammer held much of the rhythm of a zorcatroop; certainly they were not totrixes with their awkward six-legged gait or nikvoves with their battering array of eight hooves. The man in the doorway threw me a look of so powerful a hatred I was minded to charge forward and settle his hash there and then. In the linen and beadwork band about his dark hair he wore more feathers than the others. He moved smoothly, like a chavonth, the lamplight running in gleaming shadow-filled highlights across his muscles.

A succession of strange noises broke from outside—noises I did not at once identify. The first impression was of some maniac hammering a dull but noisy drum, or repeatedly slamming a heavy door. The coughing bangs erupted with the violence of a summer storm, bursting thunder about our ears.

Ready to leap forward and make sure the woman and child were safeguarded from this fifth fellow who had tried to kill them, I stopped stock still.

The man jerked. He stiffened. He dropped his axe. He half-turned, shaking with some invisible force. He staggered and then, limply, collapsed.

From his back a gush of blood dropped down.

I stared.

I looked down on him.

And I trembled.

The banging sounds continued. But I knew what they were.

With a roar of rage and agony I hurled forward, reached the door, looked out.

The shack stood near the end of an untidy row of similar shacks, and a raised boardwalk connected them above the road. Other men clad in loincloths and wielding axes and knives, some with bow and arrows, ran this way and that, and many fell. Up the center of the street rode a party of men, wearing clothes I recognized.

42

And, over all, the silvery flood of light from a single moon lit the scene in hard metallic pewter brilliance.

Again and again the Winchesters and the Colts and the Remingtons flamed.

I felt sick.

Somehow I was back in the cabin, looking at the woman who stared in horror at me, her sobs shaking her, her cheeks wet. She cradled the baby to her. Slowly, I picked up a shirt, a red and white checked shirt whereat I felt a fresh pang, and put it on. Boots stood nearby. The woman's husband would not require boots for his last journey to Boot Hill.

"You are safe now," I said, and my voice made her flinch back.

I turned to the door and men crowded in. They were apims, like me—well, they would be, wouldn't they? There were no Fristles and Rapas and Chuliks and all the other wonderful assemblage of diffs within four hundred light years.

"You all right, pardner?" The man who spoke wore levis, a hickory shirt, a tin badge and a wideawake. He held his Army Remington easily one-handed, and the muzzle centered on my midriff. I own he was wise to show caution. Despite my pants and boots and shirt, I must have looked far more like the Red Indians he had been shooting at than any of the White-eyes with him.

"I'm all right. This lady needs help—"

One of the others turned the bodies over with his toe.

"These two ain't dead, Hank."

The leader, the one with the silver star, said: "See to Mrs. Story, Jess." He eyed me meanly. "Reckon I don't know you, mister."

Carefully, I placed the axe down. The men stared into the room, seeing the lax forms of the Indians, the mess, the sobbing woman—and seeing me, scowling, black-browed, looking more mean and savage than any painted Indian busted loose they'd ever run across.

"I'm Dray Prescot," I said, and although I tried to make my harsh voice easy, I knew my words spat out like the slugs from their guns. "This lady appeared in need of help."

"You did fer them injuns?" The men looked perplexed. The woman, Mrs. Story, was assisted to her feet. The men talked about 'gitting her to the doc' and so I felt she was now safe. If the Star Lords had commanded me to rescue her and her baby, then I had done that. But there was no easy way now of my returning to Valka or Strombor. I was once more

43

marooned on Earth, stranded and desolate on the planet of my birth.

My appearance was easily enough explained—I'd been raked out of bed by the fighting and had run to Mrs. Story's assistance. But the posse eyed me askance for a space, until the easy open-handed way of the West, and question and counter-question, plus the convincing results of my handi-work plain to be seen sprawled on the floor, assured them of my bona fides. I managed to keep track of the situation and not betray an almost impossible to explain away ignorance of local conditions. The Indians had broken out, as they were wont to do, for down here the main fighting had been fin-ished up a few years back.

Down around South Fork things erupted only now and then, and the main action had transferred north, where great disasters had shaken the nation. The local people were still jumpy. All the talk was of the frightful events of the 25th June last. The newspapers carried a leaked confidential report severely critical of Custer and his handling of the tactical sit-uation at the Little Big Horn. I remembered the braves who had tried to do for me and was forced to wonder if not only the tactical but the strategical handling was amiss. They were men, like me, even if their skin was a coppery color. They were not Fristles or Rapas or Chuliks, and they also are men, if not like me.

Around that time a considerable amount of English money was being invested in the West. Having to face the cata-strophic fact that the Star Lords had not pitched me into an-other part of Kregen but had despatched me back to Earth, the world of my birth, I was still in no frame of mind to settle down. I had the opportunity of going partners more than once in a fine ranch; but I turned them all down. I took a swing through the Staked Plains and checked out Charles Goodnight's JA Ranch, a spread he ran with John Adair's money. They were just beginning their fabulous build up. Then I drifted west through El Paso and had me a rip-roar-ing time in Tombstone.

This was a couple of years before Wyatt Earp showed up with his kinfolk and Doc Holliday. Rather to my surprise I discovered that men would shoot whole magazines of Win-chester ammunition away, or the full six shots from their Colts, and still not hit anything. I could draw reasonably fast; but did not make a habit of it. As to accuracy, given a gun I knew, I could hit what I aimed at. So I stayed out of trouble and drifted north. The 2nd August had witnessed the shooting of Hickok, in Carl Mann's Saloon in Deadwood. Already, men wouldn't play a hand of cards consisting of aces and eights.

So I drifted around the frontier, not doing much of anything. As I have said before, it is not my purpose to tell you of my life here on this Earth. Certainly I got myself into a few scrapes and tight corners during this period, and found out enough to know that a great deal of guff was written then about the West, guff that has been continued to the present day.

My bankers in the City of London sent funds promptly as requested, and I had more or less reached the conclusion of going east, at least across the Mississippi and south, and then of repeating my previous swing around the country ending up in New York. From there England tempted me.

The continuing improvement in repeating firearms interested me greatly. The Spencer I had known in Civil War days was now quite outclassed, although remaining a fine weapon, by the new Winchesters. The model '73 with its stronger receiver than the model '66 proved a reliable weapon, although lacking the range and penetration of military firearms. As for the revolvers, a plethora of different patterns and styles vied for attention. I studied everything I could, and this time I had very much in mind that the wise men of Kregen might be brought to a consideration of a repeating varter. The gros varters of Vallia, the best of their kind in my opinion, might work wonders on the Leem Lovers if some kind of repeating mechanism could be provided.

Of one thing I felt reasonably although not one hundred percent certain. It would destroy a great and intangible asset if gunpowder were to be introduced to Kregen.

By the time I'd reached Saint Louis the thought of spending time in England appealed overwhelmingly to me—until I ran across Amos Brown who had a hankering to go to California. Well, he talked me into it. We outfitted ourselves in great style, and Amos, who'd been a mule-skinner up around Laramie and ways west for a number of years, expressed himself as plumb pleased at our rigs. He was a short, spare, wispy-haired little guy with a mean shot-gun trigger finger. Well, we set off full of high spirits to cross Missouri just as fast as we could and then across Kansas. The place was already being domesticated, and Amos couldn't stand the smell of ironing and scrubbing and stoop-sweeping.

Dodge City was just about played out, too—or so it was given out. We got into only one good fight, and from then on

45

to Santa Fe the rest of the folks with us more or less kept us on our best behavior. But I never got to Santa Fe—leastways not on that swing.

The blue radiance descended on me as I rode drag to the remuda—for we had a few wealthy folk with us—and the dust biting into my throat and the shushing of the hooves for a split-second prevented the reality of what was happening from penetrating.

Then I understood and I let fly with a holler and a whoop and felt the pony slipping away from between my knees. I gave a convulsive snatch at the Sharps scabbarded under the saddle—it was a model '77 chambered for the three and a quarter inch, 45-120-550 load, not too hefty, with a beautiful full octagonal barrel of 34 inches, a real Creedmoor beauty with tang sight—and felt that vaporize under my fingers. No good going for the Winchester on its California saddle horn loop or the Improved Army Remington .44 at my waist—that revolver cost me eighteen dollars, plus a premium to get it—or, indeed, the Bowie knife. The Star Lords were calling me and all the gunpowder in the whole of the West wouldn't stop them.

Whirling up, seeing the radiance enfolding me and watching with a choked fascination the enormous shape of the Scorpion glowing against the sky, I had time for what was a remarkably lurid reflection on the reactions of Amos and the rest of the bunch to my disappearance. When my pony trotted in with everything in place and without me—they'd spend a heck of a time rooting around trying to find me or my body.

Maybe, I said, maybe one day I'll mosey back along the trail and find out what happened.

And then all reflection ended as I felt the ground come up and thump me, felt once again the blessed warmth of Zim and Genodras pour heat into every fiber, drew deep breaths of that glorious tangy air—and knew I was once again back on Kregen, where I belonged.

CHAPTER FOUR

Jak the Drang Encounters The Iron Riders

To be perfectly honest as I leaped up I felt my nakedness, felt it terribly. My hand went to my waist. My little arsenal had become a part of my daily round, the Sharps to hit 'em as far off as I could, the Winchester to cut 'em down as they charged, the Remington to finish those that wouldn't go down and the Bowie to take out the last, obstinate idiot who insisted on closing to close quarters.

All this was a long way away from the Sea Service pistol of my youth, the cutlass or boarding pike, and a very long way away from the rapier or thraxter, the spear or the longsword I needed on Kregen—and needed right now, by Zair!

I was on Kregen, right enough, there was no mistaking that. All the agony I had experienced as I'd realized just where the Star Lords had flung me last vanished altogether in that moment.

The mingled opaline radiance of the Suns of Scorpio streamed refulgently about me; but there was no time for anything other than getting on with the work to my hand, presented to me in the old familiar auhoritative way—I had to fight and do what I had to do, or be banished once again. Or, given the circumstances, to die messily.

It was, I thought then, all one to the Everoinye.

Judging by the frightened looks they cast over their shoulders, the merciless plying of whip and spur, the mob of men lambasting up the draw toward me were fleeing—were running away as fast as they could make their mounts gallop. These were a mix of various saddle animals of Kregen—hirvels, totrixes, preysanys, urvivels—with only two or three zorcas mixed up in the stampede. Dust flew up in a long ochre smear.

I ducked in back of a rock out of the way of the fugitives, guessing my task lay at the interface of pursued and pursuers.

Usually I was projected onto Kregen stark naked and headlong into action. Not always—usually. This time the Star Lords had seen fit to give me a little preparatory time. Of course, they did not deign to provide me with a helmet or spear, sword or shield, and we had struck our reactions to that idea. They would guess I would regard them with less estimation—although, truth to tell, I fancy that as I grew older I might come to regret that hot and impassioned surge of pride of my youth. I had not aged a day since the dip in the Sacred Pool of Baptism; but although my body remained young I know my brain had, slowly and painfully, accreted a trifle of wisdom in the intervening years.

Drawn by six piebald nikvoves the coach lumbered into view. Its felloes shrieked as it skated over the rocks. It kicked up one helluva dust and I could see nothing down the back-trail.

Most of the fugitives were apims, but there was a fair sprinkling of diffs, and a Rapa sat up on the box and flogged the nikvoves on. This coach, these six laboring animals, the dust, the racket—well, it caught at my throat, so like and yet so fantastically unlike the scenes I had just left. Had those different alien riding animals and the draught animals all been horses, had there been no diffs—this would still be Kregen. The smell, the feel, the empathy of the world was uniquely Kregen under Antares.

I saw what must be done. Had those crazed fugitives taken a mur to observe for themselves they must have seen it, too. I was just a lone, naked man. But if I did not do what had to be done I knew what would happen. So I got on with it.

The rocks at the lip of the draw scattered away in a detritus to either side. Starting a likely-looking boulder moving started two or three others. Pebbles rattled. Dust smoked. The rocks tumbled down. I cut it fine, and a couple of fist-sized pebbles bounced into the polished varnish of the coach. But the main mass of sliding rock rumbled down, spreading, filling the bed of the draw. So much dust hung about that it was impossible to see beyond and so I still did not know who or what pursued these men and scared them half to death.

Who or whatever—they or it were not going to ride over that still-quivering wall of rock.

The coach slewed and skidded. A wheel flew off, spinning gracefully, the spokes and hub never designed for this kind of hard hacking cross-country work. In a screech the coach bedded down canting onto its for'ard larboard axle. Slowly, I walked down toward the coach, watching the Rapa, who

48

wore a gaudy uniform, watching the painted and varnished door swing open.

No one down there took any notice of me. The distance was too great to make out features. A woman jumped energetically down from the coach and shook her fist at the Rapa. At once he began unhitching the nikvoves. Two other women and a man got out of the coach. They all stood arguing, waving their arms, looking back at the still-smoking mass of rock barring off the pursuit. I stopped walking down, fascinated by this display of human emotion and character behavior.

Presently, the whole group mounted up on the freed nikvoves and took off, hitting their mounts with the flats of their swords, galloping hell-for-leather. I stood and watched them go. I had carried out the commands of the Star Lords. I had no further interest in those people I had saved. I did not recognize any insigne, colors—the whole assemblage had been liberally covered in dust—or, more importantly, the country I was in. The coach looked to be of the kind I had seen in Zenicce, Vallia or Pandahem. I needed to know where I was to set my course for Strombor.

The Rapa coachman had freed only five nikvoves. So there was one left for me. I felt pleased. I walked down to the coach.

There are very few voves in Vallia, for that magnificent russet-coated, eight-legged king of saddle-animals is a native of the Great Plains of Segesthes. Yet Vallians and other people call his smaller cousin a nikvove, which always amuses me. This piebald specimen looked alertly at me as I walked up to him and stroked his neck, speaking soothingly. He and I would get on capitally.

The coach had been stripped of its interior fittings; but in the box at the rear was to be found a mass of clothing, and from its style of buff and shirts with colored sleeves I judged I was in Vallia. I felt dizzy. The Star Lords might have dumped me down anywhere on Kregen—apart from being put down somewhere near Strombor—or, even, Djanduin—Vallia was the next best place for me in my ugly old mood.

I found a piece of russet cloth, for there was no scarlet, and twisted it around my waist and pulled the free end up between my legs and tucked it in. A broad belt—not, unfortunately, of lesten-hide—held the breechclout in place. The only weapons I could find were two small daggers, half kicked under the seat. They were of reasonable manufacture, with far too much gew-gaw imitation jewelry; but they'd serve.

49

Despite all the cunning expertise of unarmed combat taught in the Disciplines of the Krozairs and of the Khamorros, Kregen is no place to wander around unarmed. Mind you, Turko the Shield would scoff with enormous gusto at these two ridiculous daggers, by Krun!

A number of the white shirts bore banded sleeves of gold and black. There were others in different color combinations; but the gold and black predominated. Thoughtfully I went back to the door and slammed it shut and brushed off the dust coating the varnished panel. The painted and gilded representation of a butterfly upon the gold and black blazon confirmed the view that I was in Aduimbrev. At least, the butterfly on gold and black was the insignia of Aduimbrev. If I was in the kovnate I knew where I was. Poor old Kov Vektor who had aspired with the emperor's blessings to the hand of Delia was long since dead, having got himself foolishly killed in the Battle at the Dragon's Bones. The memory of that famous old conflict heartened me.

A collateral line of the family had inherited, with the very necessary emperor's confirmation of their claim, and the present kov incumbent was Marto Renberg, whom I knew only to nod to politely. The Aduimbrevs had reckoned on being emperor's men; I had no way of knowing how their allegiances had fallen in the recent struggles for power.

I was pretty well near the dead center of Vallia. Across the Great River to the south lay Ogier. Across a tributary of the Great River to the west lay Eganbrev. And, eastward, the Trylonate of Gelkwa barred my path. Trylon Udo had led the uprising of the whole North East, or so I believed, and the mischief they had caused me with their damned revived corpse and the damage they had done to Vondium would long be remembered in the land. It had been that cramph Zankov from the North East who had slain the emperor. I thought of Dayra, Ros the Claw, and a great deal of my good mood vanished.

It was necessary for me to travel east. The best plan would be to swing across to Thengelsax and in that city discover what had transpired during my absence. From there I'd have to find faster transport and take myself off to Zamra, or Valka, and from thence fly east across the sea to Zenicce and Strombor. Yes. I decided, then, spitting dust, that that was what I would have to do.

Well, as they say, man reaps for Zair to sickle.

To the north spread the emperor's province of Thermin, and in its chief city of Therminsax I might find what I needed. But the obsession was on me to take the shortest route. East, then. . . .

The rout of fugitives had headed south down the draw. I fashioned a saddle cloth from the clothes and cinched it tight with ropes. I took what clothing I thought necessary and then, being a canny old paktun, a soldier of fortune, I broke a long length of hefty timbering from the coach. That would serve as a lance, and a shorter length as a wooden sword. Once or twice before a length of lumber had served me as a weapon, and on Kregen a man needs weapons as he needs food and water.

The piebald nikvove rumbled off with that special smooth elongated rhythm of the eight-footed. I cocked an eye back at the freshly created wall of rock. Nalgre ti Liancesmot, the long-dead playwright whose work is known over many areas of Kregen, is often quoted. "Better to know the smile of the friend who stabs you in the back than the scowl of the enemy who assails you in front," which comes from his cycle "The Vicissitudes of Panadian the Ibreiver" and contains a thought with which I do not always agree, allowing it to have a cogent point. It struck me I ought to find out just what that crazed mob had been fleeing from.

There was every chance now, that, their dirty work done, for them, the Star Lords would let me alone. I was coming to the conclusion, not as clear-cut as I may have made it appear, that there was strife among the Everoinye. If this Ahrinye really wanted to run me, as he so elegantly phrased it, with so much more force, I might find myself being run pretty sharpish in the future, and without recourse to any of the fragile obstructions I had erected to resist the Everoinye.

So, feeling pretty mulish and bloody-minded, I guided the nikvove up out of the draw. The land spread away in an opening panorama, superb under the suns, lightening from the dusty ochre near me to a fresher green along the horizon. And, in the middle distance, sparkling in the mingled radiance, the waters of a canal ran dead straight, northwest, southeast. I fancied this might well be a direct link through to Thengelsax. Certainly, the Ogier Cut ran east-west some way south of my present position. So, I turned the nikvove to follow the canal.

When I reached the towpath I frowned. So this was one of the results of the chaos destroying Vallia. For the cut was in vile condition, half-choked with weeds, the banks fallen away here and there, the water, although sparkling as the light of the suns glinted from it, sullen and barely moving.

51

A thin strip of vegetation grew along both banks, trees and bushes breaking the flatness of the land. From the shadows of a missal tree I looked back and saw the dun-colored dust clouds rising. I stared closely. A body of riders broke into view, rising up like a succession of trap-door devils. They appeared in no hurry. They trotted on. Probably the rock-fall had caught a few of them and time had been spent assisting the injured. For whatever reason, only now were they resuming their pursuit. Or, and what was far more probably the correct explanation, the fugitives had been in such terror they were fleeing from these riders when the pursuit was a long way off. Only now had the pursuit caught up with them.

At this unpalatable thought I frowned.

But the people of Aduimbrev ought to be clear away by now. Should I follow them and make sure? They were headed south. Damn those blasted Star Lords! So, undecided, I stood there and heard the splash of water at my back.

Without thought, without looking back, I rolled off the nikvove, hit on a shoulder, rolled under a bush and came up, quivering, ready to defend myself against—against a slender slip of a girl who climbed out onto the bank, half-naked, dripping, shining—and laughing at me with a rosy face beaming rapturous amusement at my antics.

"You don't have to be afraid of me, ven. I won't hurt you—" she started to say. Then she stopped and all the amused enjoyment fled from her face. She saw the dust cloud, she saw the riders, and she seemed to shrivel there in the streaming light of the suns. "Radvakkas." She spoke the word with so much of fear and loathing it was instantly clear these riders were a real and terrible threat. "The Iron Riders."

Standing up I put a hand on the piebald's neck, soothing, and looked again at the men out there trotting along with the dust spuming and the light striking sparks from their armor and weapons.

"The Iron Riders?"

"Yes—and keep you still and silent until they are gone. I pray to Vaosh they do not see us."

"We can swim across the canal—they are not of the canal-folk—"

I chanced my arm there; but I was right. She nodded, swiftly, her brown hair gleaming, her water-drenched tunic plastered to her. Her face was small and elfin, and her eyes were very frightened.

"That is true. But their benhoffs would swim the cut with the radvakkas safely clear of the water."

So we kept silent and watched and I digested what this girl had said. For I knew about benhoffs. The benhoff is a shaggy, powerful, six-legged riding animal from North Segesthes. The barbarians up there use them as my clansmen use the vove. And from short and ferocious wars the various tribes and confederations of the North Segesthan Barbarians had long learned never to tangle with a Clansman. They kept themselves well to the north of Segesthes and the continent is large enough for barbarian and clansman to live separately. Although, mind you, it is a truism to say that any honest Clansman is far more savage and bloodthirsty than any barbarian. . . .

But, here, in Vallia—benhoffs? To the best of my knowledge the benhoff was as little known or used as the vove in Vallia. I swallowed down what I was about to say, and instead, said: "You know these Iron Riders?"

"Aye, may Gurush of the Bottomless Marsh take them and suck them down and never spit out their diseased bones!"

"I am a stranger here, just riding through—tell me of these radvakkas."

She lifted one brown eyebrow at this; but let it pass.

She told me her name was Feri of the Therduim Cut. This canal connected Therminsax and Thengelsax. Before I could urge her to tell me of The Iron Riders, other canalfolk appeared. They had no narrow boat; they walked along the towpath, and I prepared for unpleasantness even though I was well aware of the hospitality of the canalfolk. In the event Llahals were exchanged and the pappattu made in a proper civilized way. We all waited quietly until the radvakkas had ridden out of sight.

Then a load was lifted from these people, and they began to smile and chatter again. Very briefly, I learned that trade had been thoroughly disrupted by the troubles, and these people had lost their two boats and, perforce were compelled to walk carrying what belongings they could, until they could reach one of the towns along the cut where they had friends. The Iron Riders had come sweeping in from the northeast and terrorized the whole countryside. They roamed in bands, ravaging and looting and burning, and no one was safe.

Despite the smiles and the warm comradeliness the impression I gained was that these canalfolk were mightily scared not only of The Iron Riders but of life in general. Vallia was no longer the empire it once had been. The country was split into warring factions. Vengeful townsfolk had sunk the two narrow boats. The town had been sacked by the rad-vakkas three nights previously; and the townspeople had vented their spite. No—I did not at all care for the truths I was finding out about Vallia.

This Feri had spirit. She had been out ahead scouting and had taken to the water to come up on me unseen. I suppose I'd satisfied her I was not an Iron Rider. But the rest of them were anxious to push on and after I had learned a little more of conditions—much of which I will relate when the telling is needful—I told them I must push on also.

"But the radvakkas went that way, ven." And: "But you are a lone rider, Ven Jak." And: "Come with us, ven." And so on, for I had given them the name of Jak the Drang, conceiving Dray Prescot would be a name with much gravity attaching to it.

"I thank you, vens and venas. But mayhap we will meet again in more happy times."

Amid the calling of remberees, I mounted up and turned the piebald's head. I waved to them, and guided the nikvove angling away from the Therduim Cut.

Deliberately, for I fancied I had not fully completed the task the Star Lords had set to my hands, I set off southwards, following in the tracks of The Iron Riders.

CHAPTER FIVE

——◆◆——

Of a Rout After Breakfast

Night would soon bring the brilliance of the Moons of Kregen to brighten the sky and I could feel the first tendrils of tiredness. After all, I had begun the day astride a pony riding drag to a remuda heading for Santa Fe, and was now riding a nikvove in pursuit of a bunch of rogues more ferocious than anything the West had witnessed—and had, into the bargain, been pitchforked four hundred light years through space. Not, I hasten to add, that I was then aware of the real distance involved. But I could soldier on for a spell yet and decided to take a swing around the band of radvakkas ahead and catch up with the fugitives.

The level ground began to roll into a series of long tawny-grass-covered dunes as I went on, and presently stands of trees showed throwing long twinned shadows. I kept The Iron Riders under observation and was somewhat surprised to see them pitch camp for the night and settle down. Anxious to press on I skirted their camp and rode on into the darkness as She of the Veils rose luminously over my left shoulder.

If I was on the right track then the fugitives had galloped fast and without let-up. Just before midnight the lights of a town showed ahead. I had only a hazy idea of the detailed geography around here; it seemed likely if I was right that the smot ahead was Cansinsax. In a long chain surrounding the North East the forts had been built in the old days against the reivers. The Therduim Cut was a later construction, running mostly along the borders between Aduimbrev to the south and Sakwara to the north. The saxes were not always built directly on the frontier, and, sometimes, the borders had been shifted by imperial decree.

I bedded down outside the town and saw to the nikvove and caught a little sleep, being up well before Zim and Genodras broke over the horizon. My urgency was being channelled into doing what I believed right. If I was wrong, well, I would be the sufferer—for I was still firmly convinced that Delia was safe in Strombor. She had to be.

For breakfast I had a few deep lungfuls of fresh Kregen air. The nikvove chomped the grass and appeared content.

Had I chosen to ride north and cross the border out of Aduimbrev I would have come into the emperor's province of Thermin. The odd thing was, I was in no way reconciled to the idea that I was supposed to be the emperor. Emperor of Vallia. By Vox! How empty could a title get?

Had I done so, I sourly wondered if, even there, I'd have found anyone willing to give me breakfast.

As the twin Suns of Scorpio rose and threw the land into that shimmering opaline radiance I saw a sight that astounded me. I put a hand to the piebald's neck, soothing him. I remained very still in the little stand of timber, peering out under the leaves.

Across the grassy ground a great host approached Cansinsax. Clearly I could see the long extended lines of cavalrymen. They rode benhoffs, shaggy and gray. Their weapons glittered. They wore mail. There were, I judged, something in excess of three thousand of them. So a junction had been made and the forces gathered in and now The Iron Riders rode against Cansinsax.

The evident terror these riders of iron struck into all they encountered was a most potent weapon; but not, I judged, their only or even their chiefest weapon. Just how they would manage the siege of the town I admit intrigued me. But then—well, they say the gods sharpen both edges of a blade—the gates of the town opened. Trumpets pealed brazen notes into the morning air. I watched, spell-bound.

Out from the gates of Cansinsax, a town of Vallia, marched with a swing and a swank the iron legions of Hamal.

Hamal. I saw them. The serried ranks of swods all marching in time, their rectangular shields all in alignment, their banners blazing a rich tapestry of color, the plumes in their helmets whiffling in the dawn breeze. Swods from Hamal. Real soldiers, men trained to fight under the strict laws of Hamal. I marveled. Regiment by regiment they marched out. Squadrons of cavalry surged out and extended into wings on the flanks. A little dust plumed; but the grass here was altogether richer and lusher than the sere tawny-grass along the Therduim Cut.

My vantage position gave me a perfect view.

Following the regulars of Hamal crowded a swarm of mercenaries. Among their ranks were many diffs. Also, as I was quick to observe, there were masichieri there, also, which was surprising, seeing the masichieri are mercenaries but soldiers of fortune of an altogether different stamp from the paktuns, who more often than not fight with honor and earn their hire.

Two regiments of totrixmen spurred out ahead, and trumpets rang and they hauled back. It was clear this army was anxious to get to grips with the radvakkas. Running an old soldier's eye over the serried array I estimated the Hamalians as putting into the field four or five thousand infantry—ten regiments—and a thousand or so cavalry. The mixed bunch of mercenaries probably added up to another couple of thousand.

Numbers favored the Hamalians. What, I wondered, of the native Vallians of Aduimbrev? Mind you, as I have already explained, Vallia was a powerful trading empire, whose wealth came from her seapower, the superb Galleons of Vallia. If the empire needed soldiers, she would hire them.

The Hamalian army halted. The regiments of foot braced their shields. The regiments of crossbowmen spanned their crossbows. Soon the bolts would fly. I watched, scarcely breathing and, I admit, not a little puzzled as to where my cheering should be directed.

The Iron Riders were clearly a grave menace; but, then, Hamal was the deadly foe of Vallia, temporarily in the ascendant. So, I merely watched and studied, and if my right hand twitched and the fingers curled around the length of lumber—well, they were only simple, stupid reactions of an old fighting man.

Three thousand Iron Riders against around eight thousand Hamalese and paktuns—it seemed to me my services would no longer be required.

The Hamalese cavalry wings overlapped the radvakkas. The totrixmen again almost boiled over into a charge. There was a regiment of zorcamen there, also, whereat I at once thought of Rees and Chido. But the general in command held them in the rear in reserve.

The Iron Riders shook out into three battles or divisions, a thousand cavalrymen each.

I saw no signal given. The distant trumpet notes pealed. The front ranks of benhoffs began to move, lumpy gray beasts surging forward like the gray tide beating against rocks. But the center division rode forward faster and faster. The crossbowmen loosed, pastang by pastang, and the bolts fell like rain, and still the benhoffs came on. A few, only a few, tumbled down to thrash on the trampled ground as their comrades thundered on.

The central division galloped rapidly through the beaten zone and crashed into the Hamalese infantry. The whole front two ranks caved in instantly. Infantrymen were sent bodily flying. The great six-legged beasts rampaged on. Swords rose and fell. Shields were splintered. And now the totrix wings of Hamalese cavalry closed in—and the left and right wedges of radvakkas spurned them. In an instant amid a ghastly racket the whole line was engaged. For only an instant—for the Hamalese army sagged back and back. Totrixes were bounding riderless from the field. The infantry were being cut to pieces. On and on surged that enormous battering wedge of Iron Riders.

The field became a sea of boiling action—I did not see the end of the zorca regiment. It merely ceased to exist. The Hamalese were running. Iron Riders were breaking away from the main divisions now, were hunting and slaying.

Time was being cut so fine I almost did not make it.

My services were, after all, still required.

Piebald roared ahead, his eight hooves battering the grass. A party of Rapas offered to halt me at the gate; but already fugitives were streaming in and the situation was plain. If it was a case of sauve qui peut than the saruvest would be the peutest, that was for sure. I had no trouble entering Cansinsax.

The trouble lay in finding where away was the party I had already once rescued. Just which one in that party was the particular one the Star Lords wished preserved I did not know, which simply meant I had to save the lot.

The town was in the most frightful uproar. Men and women were running every which way—men and women wearing the buff of Vallians. Slaves were being beaten along staggering under loads of household equipment. Everyone was raging toward the western gate in a crazy flood. Just how they expected to get away when the benhoffs of the radvakkas would overhaul them in no time at all did not appear to have occurred to them. The scenes of chaos rang and thumped on and I forced my way through.

A bad time this, when a town falls, a bad time.

In this instance, I think with some degree of certainty, the Star Lords took a direct hand. I remember I shook my fist at the indifferent sky, and hurled a few lusty Makki-Grodno cusses upward—conduct that aroused not one whit of interest from the crazed mobs about me—and so saw a piebald nikvove bolt from the broken-down gateway of a villa. The mobs pushed past and I came up with the nikvove and got a hand into his harness. I hauled back and lay my own steed into him and some of the crowd staggering away managed to turn him. Together, we went racketing back into the villa. Slaves were looting the place, which was a very proper thing to do, considering.

The woman who stood in the doorway of the house yelling furiously, purple of face, wearing riding clothes, slashing about with a thraxter, might have been one of the three women who had descended from the coach. The air was filled with noise, people screaming, the crash of furniture being hurled through windows, the thump of many feet. The smells were interesting, too. I barged across. She looked up.

She saw my face. Her own face, which was filled with that aristocratic fury, venom-filled, that overtakes the high and mighty when they see slaves breaking out or people not obeying them instantly, abruptly hung slack. I vaulted off Piebald.

"Here, lady, a mount for you. Where are the others?"

She was saved a reply as a man rushed at me with his rapier held ready to stick me. I slid the blow, took the rapier away, hit him over the head with it—gently, mind—and caught him as he fell. Even then I felt the old familiar sensa-

58

tions as my fist gripped around the rapier hilt. Two other women, dressed for riding, appeared, screaming. I bellowed them all down.

"Silence, you famblys! The four of you—you will have to share the two nikvoves. Get mounted and get out. The Iron Riders will be here in a mur or two! Ride!"

They were yelling and screaming; but they retained sense enough to mount up. The man held his head, glaring at me with sadistic hostility; but I saw his eyes, and they slid away and would not meet mine.

A preysany stood at the steps ready-loaded. I snapped him across the rump and started him after the nikvoves. We headed out through the gate. Truth to tell, riding through the panic-smitten mobs was not easy and I, afoot, would have been quicker than the riders. But, once they were outside the walls, the story would be different. I knew benhoffs and I knew nikvoves. The half-vove is not a true vove, but he can still outrun a shambling, shaggy, gray-haired benhoff any day of the month.

Now the remnants of the Hamalese army were crowding into the town. The confusion was splendid and awful. I sweated along. The woman who rode like a man and held the man upright as he swayed and cursed weakly, glowered down on me as I led them along the crowded street.

"You, rast. Why do you save us?"

"Just be thankful I do, lady. And no Lahal between us."

She colored again at this, fully aware of the sarcasm.

"Be very careful how you address me. I am the Kovneva of Aduimbrev, Marta Renberg, and your head lies most shakily upon your shoulders."

"Then Llahal, Kovneva. I did not know Marto Renberg; but I once met old Vektor—"

She tried to hit me with her thraxter, and I laughed and ducked away and hauled the nikvove on. Oh, yes, I laughed. It was certainly no time for crying.

She was not very old, I judged, although that is always a tricky business on Kregen where a person changes but little and slowly over two hundred or so years. She had the brown Vallian hair and eyes, a trim figure, a high color, and she was most decidedly a very important person in her own eyes.

Some quality I at first thought indefinable about her—perhaps the way her nostrils curved, the curl of her lower lip, the tensioning lines around her eyes, something—offended me. I felt I would try to like her and fail. We pushed on along the street with the fugitive mobs and I found that, once again, I did not much care for the task the Everoinye had set to my hands.

When a victorious army follows up a victory of this kind and the defeated do not have the nous to run into their town and shut the gates, much may be learned of the character and temperament of the victors by the way they go about consolidating. As we debouched from the western gate in a yelling struggling mass of people and animals, I hauled myself up by the nikvove's mane and took a searching look around.

There was no sign of Iron Riders sweeping in around the city. Then they would be simply bolting in through the eastern gate, charging down the remnants of the Hamalese's soldiery and the paktuns, just driving on through the gate into the city. They had not aimed to cut off the fugitives. Not slavers, then . . . ?

Many carts harnessed to the refreshing variety of draught animals of Kregen lumbered away across the plain heading for the forest a dwabur or so off. Mounted people set spurs to their mounts and pelted headlong for safety. Those afoot, wailing and crying, ran and hobbled in a great untidy mass. It was one diabolical scene, I can tell you.

The Kovneva of Aduimbrev leaned down toward me. Her flushed face looked dangerous.

"Take your hand from the rope, tikshim.* There is the forest. We can manage perfectly well now."

She was quite serious. The situation was perfectly plain in her eyes. I had appeared and had helped her to escape from Cansinsax. And this, very properly, was the duty owed to her as the kovneva by everyone of her people. I did not let go of the rope.

"Now, tikshim! We must gallop to the forest before the radvakkas overtake us—"

"Cramph!" bellowed the man, thickly. I had his rapier and so he whipped out his left-hand dagger and tried to slash at me or at the rope. I did not care for the first idea.

I said: "You may ride for the forest, and you will. But if you get yourself killed I shall be most wroth." She could not, of course, understand just why I would be annoyed. "Do not ride with the main bulk of the fugitives—"

* Tikshim. The form of address used by the higher to the lower orders. The higher consider it neutral. As it probably equates with "my man" or even "my good man" the lower orders are almost invariably provoked by its use although quite unable to articulate their reaction or to explain it. Prescot has used the word rarely; but here it fits perfectly.   A.B.A.

60

"Do you presume to give me orders?" She half-turned and swung the thraxter at me. This time the blade was not turned. She cut at me.

I slid the blow and jumped back, letting go the rope. I held myself under control—but only just. How they conduct themselves, the high and mighty of the land!

"Ride, kovneva. Ride. I shall find you in the forest. Just be very sure you are still alive when I do—and not a bloody corpse."

With that I gave Piebald a slap across the rump and started him off at a run. The other nikvove with the two handmaidens lumbered after. Pretty soon the two angled away from the main mass and lit out for the trees. Nikvoves can run. I let out a gusty breath. This hoity-toity Marta Renberg should be safe now and the Star Lords satisfied. But, all the same, I'd wander across to the forest and make sure.

Amid that swirling mass of terrified folk I had to think about getting myself away; but, I admit, a few nasty thoughts about these mysterious purposes of the Star Lords crossed my mind. I had been given evidence that the people the Everoinye wished preserved did, indeed, affect the destiny of the world. The mad genius king Genod of the Eye of the World proved that. What the Star Lords wanted of Marta Renberg, Kovneva of Aduimbrev, I could not know. But I wished them the evil of it, for I found myself in a black humor with the foolish woman.

Of course, I could not even be sure it was she the Star Lords had their eye on. It might have been the man—she'd called him Larghos and no doubt he served some function or other in her establishment—or one of the handmaidens, pretty, washed out girls whose terror rendered them mute. The preysany, loaded down, I did not doubt, with choice and expensive items, followed the nikvoves. I turned about and looked at the doomed town.

Already smoke drifted over the red roofs, dun, swirling, skull-like in outline, mushroom-headed, vile. Soon the flames would break out and seek to dim the glory of the suns. It was all a ghastly mess, butchery and rapine and pillage—and here, in Vallia, Vallia that had been so puissant an empire.

The cultivated fields swallowed up many of the fugitives who vanished from view in the crops. On the other side the plain was suitable only for those with fast riding animals. Reflectively, I weighed the chances, walking smartly away from the town. The rabble thinned about me, and mostly those who were delayed by excess of baggage, infirmity of limb or care for children, labored on about me now. I gave a hand to people who needed it—hauling a cart out of a rut here, carrying a child for a space there; much though I would have liked to remain and help I could not chain myself down to just one party. In the event, we were all within the first rows of crops before the leading elements of radvakkas debouched from the western gate of Cansinsax and spurred after us.

The appearance of The Iron Riders drove the fugitives into a fresh panic. Shrieking they stumbled on through the crackling fronds. One or two sturdy fellows and I sought to make them move as swiftly as might be along the tracks left for the cultivators. We yelled and waved our arms.

"Go as far as you can before you hide!" bellowed a fellow who sweated away, a leather cap awry over one ear, his apron marked with the burns of his smithy's trade. He carried a blacksmith's hammer. He looked as though he might be useful. His family trudged along, helping a woman smitten with chivrel. I hoped they would make it. So, because I am something of an idiot, I found myself at the tail end of the rout. I could not force myself to run on ahead, as I might easily have done. Somehow—and I cursed myself for it, believe me—I could not run off and leave these people.

The crops swayed about us. Here, where the grass was weeded away, puffs of dust rose. It was hot and sticky work. We pushed on. I kept swiveling about to look down the narrow track between the crops.

Inevitably, out of the mobs hurrying through the cultivated fields some would be found by the radvakkas, and, equally inevitably, along the row down which I moved after those ahead an Iron Rider should trot into view. He moved his benhoff with that lumpy power that so deceives. Big ugly brutes, benhoffs, with an immense roll of fat around their chests to store nourishment against the rigors of their northern habitat, with spreading withers, and with loins and croup a trifle too mean for my taste. The Iron Rider saw me and his head went up.

He wore the usual shaggy pelt of furs—no doubt liberally infested—but because the weather was hotter than the thin mizzle to which he was accustomed the furs were thrown back exposing his armor, a simple leather shirt riveted with iron plates, and iron strips riveted down his trousers. His helmet was bulky and square in outline, with a fantastic conglomeration of feathers and benhofftail plumes. He carried a broadsword scabbarded to his saddle, and a spear; but as was the wont of the Segesthan, he bore no shield. He looked ugly and purposeful, a packed arsenal of power.

From the front rim of the helmet hung down a series of metal plates, jointed and sprung together, with eye-slots, which together formed what was in effect a mask. The sides joined the cheek pieces of the helmet. This Iron Rider had no beaver to his helmet, although the fashion was known.

Oh, yes, I knew these radvakkas well enough. My Clansmen did not often confront them, for, as I have said, the radvakkas had learned the unwisdom of tangling with a Clansman. But, from time to time, they drifted south onto the Great Plains, and if they created a disturbance they had to be dealt with. That meant they had to be dealt with, for if they were good for one thing at all that was creating disturbances. I suppose one should not call them barbarians; but we did, and the appellation fitted well enough.

Dark and ominous, clad in iron, the radvakka urged his mount into a trot and then a gallop. His spear came down. He would spit me as I stood.

My Clansmen learn to stand the charge, to stand alertly, poised, empty hands half-raised, watching the glittering spear point as it hurtles forward. At the last minute they hurl themselves sideways. One hand will rake out and snatch at the spear shaft. It is not an easy trick, it is extremely dangerous; and more than one youngster had his side or thigh cut open or his chest caved in. But with their ferocious abandonment they persist in the sport—for to a clansman this is sport, akin to Rakkle-jik-lora.

So I stood as a Clansman stands, and, withal, as a Krozair would stand awaiting the onslaught of an Overlord of Magdag.

The spear point dipped in at the last moment in the thunder of the hooves. I swayed, not jumping, brushed the spear aside, swung my length of lumber crackingly against the fellow's ribs.

The timber broke across.

How many ribs broke I did not know. The radvakka's yell burst out from him, and he swayed. I threw the rest of the wood at his head, heard it clang on that iron helmet, and then with a leaping spring was up on those narrow hindquarters of his benhoff. One arm went around his neck, and jerked back most cruelly. The other hand pushed his helmet, forward and sideways.

He slumped.

After that I was able to slow the benhoff down and cast

the radvakka into the dirt. I jumped down beside him. His armor he could keep. His weapons and his mount I would take.

So, mounted up on a shaggy grey six-legged beast, with a broadsword, a shortsword, a spear, and the rapier belonging to the kovneva's man Larghos, I trotted along after the fugitives toward the forest.

I admit—to my shame, I suppose—I felt in a much more cheerful frame of mind.

CHAPTER SIX

◆◆◆

Of the Scorpion and the Ring of Destiny

"And you believe this ring will solve all your problems, kovneva?"

"I am sure it will! I have been assured, personally assured, that the ring will restore all."

We led our mounts along the forest trails. I had ridden in, not without a few quaint comments on the benhoff, and found the kovneva and her party. Larghos had taken his rapier back, and his face was a study. In the dead radvakka's pouch I had found food, crude fare, rough bread and hunks of odoriferous cheese, and had wolfed it all down. Now we walked circumspectly through the forest to Thiurdsmot, a sizable town, larger than Cansinsax.

There we would find other regiments of the Hamalian army—and the kovneva's comments on the conduct of the Hamalese curdled the air. She reviled them bitterly. She had been promised support and aid by the Hamalese and they had sent an army which had been frittered away. I listened. I knew what I knew about the charge of mailed cavalry against sword and shield men, even with crossbow support. One of the handmaidens had told Marta Renberg that she had recognized me as the man who had saved them in the draw. The girl had long eyesight. I passed the incident over; but the kovneva's attitude changed subtly. I was still "my good man" to her; but she used my name now and then, condescendingly, and it was clear she was mightily puzzled why I, a common oaf, should be so tender of the welfare of her skin, when I was not even of Aduimbrev.

"A paktun?" she said. "Well, you earn your hire."

"May I enquire who told you of the powers of the ring?"

"You may not!"

"I am not, my lady, in your employment. You do not pay my hire."

"Are you threatening me, Jak the Drang? Be very careful—I have powerful friends who have dark and sorcerous powers."

"The necromancers of the North East can scarcely be your friends, since Aduimbrev has for many seasons been a buffer against them, against the Hawkwas. All along the area where now the Therduim Cut runs was a March—a bloody battlefield for season after season."

"Once—but not now."

"But they raid—"

"They used to raid, before the empire collapsed."

"So, kovneva, you are all friends with the Hawkwas now?" I chanced my arm. "And Trylon Udo of Gelkwa? Perhaps he—"

"He is vanished, no one knows where. The High Kov of Sakwara has now come forward into the open as the true leader of the Hawkwas."

I pricked up my ears. This was vital news.

And then, even as I opened my foolish mouth to speak, a thought hit me. A horrific thought. If this silly kovneva was mixed up with the Hawkwas, who had the support of the devil Phu-Si-Yantong, perhaps it was he to whom she referred when she spoke of great sorcerous powers?

After a space, as though changing the subject, although you will readily perceive I but planned ahead, I said: "And your people, your retainers, your guards? They have not all deserted you, my lady?"

Her face bunched tightly at this, spitting fury and venom. "Those that fled from me are as good as dead. There are others loyal to their kovneva in Aduimbrev! I shall raise a host—paktuns, masichieri, the rasts of Hamal. Together we shall return and sweep the radvakkas away into the sea."

"Caution, Marta," said Larghos, from where he walked on her other side.

I did not fail to notice his mode of address.

"Caution, good Larghos? When the Hamalese promised so much for *my* aid, and fail to give me *theirs?*"

65

Quickly, I said: "And your aid assisted them greatly, I think."

Still shaken by her passion, she burst out: "Assist them? Did I not drive into Thermin and sweep them away, and cross into Eganbrev and drive that insolent numim, Fyrnad Rosselin, from his palace and into hiding, destroying his puny forces? Did I not faithfully adhere to the treaty in every part? Did I not materially contribute to the great victory and the destruction of the emperor? Did I or did I not? And now these cramphs of Hamalese fail me, fail me utterly and leave me to flee through the dismal forest with—with—"

And here she paused in her outburst, and cast me a sidelong look, and clamped her mouth shut. She breathed heavily. The color flushed her face. She was silly, foolish, vindictive; but she was also a kovneva and this she had almost forgotten.

I said nothing but tramped on. I had learned much. So this headstrong woman—girl, really—had sided with the Hawkwas, with the Hamalese, and attacked her neighbors. It was a simple and effective method of taking out of play those people who would have rallied to the emperor. The Third Party had employed the stratagem before, and it would, I guessed, be used again.

And, if this hoity-toity Kovneva of Aduimbrev had sided and assisted the Hamalese, she had in that helped Phu-Si-Yantong.

I still did not know the full commitment of the Empress Thyllis of Hamal to this invasion of Vallia. She would glee in it, of course, hating everything Vallian. But it was Yantong who pulled the strings here and his the puppets that fought and struggled and died on Vallian soil.

The aisles of the forest passed by. We saw only a few other fugitives. The green dimness about us savored far more of Genodras than of Zim. The day wore on and we walked and rode alternately. The nikvoves were not too happy about this nearness of the benhoff, for the two animals dislike each other's scent; but by judicious management we kept them calmed down.

Marta Renberg maintained much silence after her outburst. She had nothing to fear from me, she would think, of course; but no doubt her own words scored into her mind, making her scratch over the sores of wounded pride, the feeling of being used. It would not have helped to have told her that ten regiments of the Hamalian Army, and a thousand cavalry, were no mean force. The absence of fliers and aerial cavalry

66

puzzled me; but I understood later that the Hamalian aerial forces were very thin in Vallia and the local contingents were all centered on Thiurdsmot. As to fliers in private hands, I soon found out that all the airboats Vallia possessed had been confiscated by the victorious parties. The Hamalese took most; but the Hawkwas took many and many more remained in the hands of Layco Jhansi, who was continuing to fight on, despite crippling losses. All these things I learned, one way and another, and stored them all away and pondered.

Despite her personal anger and humiliation, Marta Renberg remained fully convinced that the new emperor, Seakon, would continue in power and subdue the forces still in arms against him.

Seakon?

"A fine young man," said Larghos, across Marta Renberg. "He has already defeated Layco Jhansi in open battle. But I do not think the Hawkwas and the Hamalese can remain in alliance for very much longer."

From the way he spoke I saw at once that he thoroughly disliked the new emperor.

"What do you understand of these things, Larghos? You are supposed to be a fighting man—you have served as a paktun, have you not? Somewhere in Pandahem? Let me deal with politics." The kovneva's petulant words served to illuminate the depths of her personal frustrations and cares.

I cocked an eye at Larghos. A paktun he might be; he did not look like one. There was not a scar on his body as far as I could see. But he was a spare, limber fellow, with a straight back and a cut about his jaw that showed there was more to him than Marta either allowed or recognized.

He managed a light laugh.

"Oh, I am not a politician. I know that well enough." He glanced across at me, a thing easy enough to do seeing that the kovneva reached up only to our shoulders. "But a paktun—no. No, I was never honored with the pakmort as were you, Jak the Drang." He looked away. "Although I do not see you wearing the silver mortil-head at the moment."

"When I turfed that pile of stones down after your coach I had less than I have now."

The two handmaidens giggled at this.

I had offered no explanations. They would not get any, however much they might ask.

"This ring," I said, harking back to a subject that intrigued me more by its infantilism than anything else.

"The Ring of Destiny, once owned by La-Si-Quenying, a

67

mighty Wizard of Loh of the distant past. Quenying's Ring. Once I have that in my hand no one will stop me."

I did not smile.

"I know the Wizards of Loh hold great and mysterious powers," I said. That was true enough, by Krun! "I have heard of a great Wizard of Loh in these latter days. A most powerful man—"

"Can you call them men?" said Larghos. His face had lost a trifle of its color as he spoke.

We moved forward into a small clearing where two fallen trees had intertwined their branches high above, leaning one against another, and a third lay along the ground, rotting quietly away. Beetles and ants and woodlice were busy about their own businesses. Here we rested for a space and they told me about the Ring of Destiny, Quenying's Ring.

It seemed clear enough to me. Phu-Si-Yantong it was whose murky schemes coiled about this possessed woman. She believed that if she could take possession of this so-called magical ring she would miraculously find all her problems solved. She could at a stroke dispose of the perils of the rad-vakkas, gain everything she coveted. As she spoke I saw more. From the way Larghos glowered, and then smoothed out his face, I saw the way this pretty little scenario was scripted. For the kovneva fancied her luck as empress. She would wed this Seakon, who was without a bride, and become Empress of Vallia. The ring would do this for her, as a mere part of its miraculous properties. And, to cap it all, I was absolutely sure it must be Phu-Si-Yantong who had sold her this stinking kettle of fish.

But she believed passionately.

She had been on the way to the fortress town of Nikwald in the kovnate of Sakwara when the radvakkas had attacked.

Nikwald was in Sakwara, Hawkwa territory. Now it was over-run by the radvakkas. The Iron Riders would not take kindly to the notion of a Vallian kovneva driving up to their encampments in search of a magical ring.

I rubbed my nose.

The thought that occurred to me, to be instantly dispelled, also occurred to Marta Renberg.

She turned from where she sat on a fallen branch and surveyed me, her head on one side. A shafting of the mingled light cast her face for a moment into a softer mold, with all the petulant lines smoothed away. She looked radiant, in that moment, almost beautiful. She was well aware of the im-

68

pression she created. Larghos shifted and cleared his throat; he did not spit.

"Jak the Drang?"

I sat silent.

"You are a paktun, a renowned soldier of fortune. You could fetch me the ring."

"Perhaps."

"There would be a great reward in it."

"Would not the ring itself—?"

"No!" She flared up, agitated. "No—for Phu—for I have been most solemnly informed that only I have the power to raise the magic within the ring. Only me! I have been told and it is true."

Poor silly stupid girl!

She went on, and now she spoke in a breathless, winsome way she supposed must flatter me, overbear me, favor me with all the forbidden paradises known to Kregen. "Why have you been so good to me, Jak? You saved me from The Iron Riders. Then you saved me again from Cansinsax. You ride with us and are a good companion. Why do you do all these things?" She leaned down from her branch to where I sat with my back shoved against the wood. "Perhaps I can guess, Jak the Drang. Perhaps I know the secret of your heart."

I couldn't laugh; but the statement, the situation, demanded a great gut-bursting bellow of crude and raucous laughter.

What did she know of me? What, indeed!

"The ring is in Hawkwa country, and The Iron Riders—"

"You do not fear them. Do you not carry their weapons, ride their mount?"

About to bellow out some uncouth comment, I was struck dumb.

Among all the scuttering beetles and ants and tumbling woodlice under the rotting wood a bright orange-brown form waddled out. On eight hairy legs he poised, his arrogant tail upflung. I stared, feeling the bile rising. Larghos sat with his booted foot less than six inches from the scorpion, and did not move, did not see. He was not a scorpion. He was The Scorpion.

The forest fell silent. The leaves no longer chirred in the breeze. The very suns' beams lay quiescent, with motes of dust trapped and motionless.

The arrogant stinging tail lifted and dropped. The Scorpion surveyed me very deliberately. So I knew.

69

After a space of time very sinister to me, The Scorpion ambled to the flaking-barked log and disappeared. The breeze blew, the leaves whispered and the dust motes danced within the radiance of Zim and Genodras.

And not a word had the damned Scorpion spoken!

"Very well, kovneva. I will go to Nikwald and bring back the Ring of Destiny."

CHAPTER SEVEN

In the Camp of The Iron Riders

Lumpy carried me jogging across Aduimbrev and over the Therduim Cut and so into Sakwara. I'd called this shaggy old gray benhoff Lumpy, out of a mixture of disreputable feelings; but, truth to tell, he wasn't all that bad. It is difficult to feel at odds with a faithful saddle-animal for very long.

Seeing the kovneva and her party safely into Thiurdsmot, I had refused the offer of a flying mount from the Hamalian aerial cavalry squadron. They acted under the orders of Marta Renberg. People in Vallia were becoming more and more used to flying cavalry, great birds of the air being used as saddle flyers; but I refused the offer of a fluttrell since I considered that would attract more attention than a benhoff, attention I wished to avoid. I had insisted on going alone. Larghos had offered to accompany me, which made me look at him afresh; but I managed to convince him his duty lay with the kovneva. Truth to tell, he might have attempted to prevent my return with the ring, seeing that if Marta did as she intended then it would be a quick exit for Larghos.

A different route from the one I had followed previously swung me a trifle to the north. The same gradual trending of the land from forest to grassland to the sere plains progressed. On a bright morning I broke camp and set off and just before the Hour of Mid observed a dark mass approaching over the plain. Lumpy and I took ourselves as quickly as might be into a hollow. I watched.

These people were Vallians. They wore Vallian buff and their colors were a mixture of many of the provinces of the North East. But they were no advancing army bent on conquest. Carts were piled high with homely possessions. Women strode along with children clinging to their skirts. The men rode guard on the flanks. They were Hawkwas, well and true; but they were refugees, seeking to escape from the wrath of The Iron Riders. They passed away traveling west. I mounted up again and set off eastwards.

If ever I could say about the island empire, as I often say about other places, my Vallia—then my Vallia was in sorry shape. And I was pattering off on a footling errand for a silly ambitious woman who wanted to be empress, searching for a confounded ring said to be possessed of magical properties. Almost, I drew rein and turned back. But The Scorpion had left me in no doubt. I had to get that damned ring. It was a quest of the most farcical kind; but however ludicrous that side of the quest might be, the reality on the other side was dark and horrifically serious.

Despite all the appearances to the contrary, this was no splendid game of quest in the high tradition I played. I fought and gambled for stakes far greater than those of a simple quest.

I have no desire to go into the full details of all that went on during that search for the Ring of Destiny. Marta had given me all the information she had on its whereabouts, and this proved highly accurate. Phu-Si-Yantong would not fail on that. I guessed he used this ploy to distract the poor woman, seeing that his iron legions of Hamal had failed. He, like any other man, had to work through the tools available. In Yantong's case the tools were more often than not other men and women. But the Hamalese had been humiliated in the field. No doubt Yantong in his insane ambitions would assemble other forces; for the moment he kept this woman working for him by means of a transparently dishonest folk tale.

The defeat suffered by the Hamalian Army outside the walls of Cansinsax was not the first time they had been bested by The Iron Riders; but they would not face the humiliating fact that all their expertise, their professionalism, their famous Laws, could not withstand the mailed cavalry charge delivered by the radvakkas astride benhoffs. The talk in Thiurdsmot had been of a fresh battle with flyers and vollers to give aerial support and with batteries of varters to supplement the crossbows. The job could be done, of course; I did not know if I wanted to be there at the time to witness the horror and the splendor of it.

The shrill battle cries of the Hamalese as they clashed with

71

their enemies—the vicious, shrilling, demanding: "Hanitch!" "Hanitch!"—had rung with a desperation, almost an hysteria, over that stricken field outside the walls of Cansinsax.

Nikwald bore the marks of its altered status. Many of the brick buildings and wooden outhouses were mere shells and charred skeletons. But a central section remained around a kyro with pretensions to architectural respectability, and here the radvakkas stabled their benhoffs, set up their cooking arrangements and their armory and generally conducted themselves in the way of bombastic barbarians two worlds over.

Originally there had been four temples in Nikwald, the chiefest being dedicated to Junka, a manifestation of godhood well-thought of in the North East. The second, which should rightfully have been the first in view of the real importance of Opaz for all the genuine self-negation that is a small part of that belief, was dedicated to the Invisible Twins. Both had been partially destroyed. Benhoffs and calsanys were tethered within the shattered walls.

Shuffling along leading Lumpy, an old shaggy pelt flung over my shoulders, I passed well enough for a radvakka slave caring for his master's steed. Other slaves went about their businesses, and all wore that hangdog defeated look of the oppressed when in private, and all put on that inane cheerful look of happy subservience when their masters bellowed at them.

All I saw convinced me that the radvakkas had sailed from Segesthes and landed in Vallia in strength. The fate of the eastern islands concerned me profoundly—what had befallen Veliadrin, Zamra and Valka? Had my people managed to hold out against this new threat? The moment the Star Lords were satisfied, I knew where I was going—before, even, I thought, Strombor.

The temple of brick and wood erected to the greater glory of Mellor'An, a local god of agriculture, husbandry and fertility in general, was of altogether lesser proportions and only a part had burned. Men moved about purposefully and I saw they had set up a forge in the outer court where benhoff shoes were repaired and where the iron fittings of gear and equipment might be made good. The armories did not share the same fires and anvils as this blacksmithing work. I meandered along past the outer wall.

In a crumbled corner of brick I took a swift look around. No one watched me. The town hummed with activity. Working with a deceptive smoothness I probed a nail loose in

Lumpy's middle offside hoof. I already had a broken chain, and cursed it. I walked Lumpy lumpily back to the smithy.

Inside, the radvakkas in charge bellowed slaves about their work. "Here, slave, hurry!" rumbled one at me as I approached. Then he spat out that vicious, cutting order: *"Grak!"*

So, being sensible in these things, I grakked and handed the broken chain across. Radvakkas, like many barbarians, set no store by money; when it fell into their hands they melted it down for the precious metals to be used in ornamentation. Communal work was done on a communal basis. The radvakka blacksmiths grasped whips instead of hammers, and beat their skilled slaves into the work. The broken chain would be mended as a mere part of maintaining the military equipment of the whole band. Then I led Lumpy around to have his shoe fixed.

For the moment freed of observation I wandered away from the busy activity of the fires, as though seeking a corner where I might eat my bread and cheese and, if I was fortunate, munch on an onion. A hierarchy existed among slaves. Those attending personally to radvakka masters were a cut above the poor devils tending the fires or bashing iron. A group sat on sacks in a corner, and they called out to me to join them in their game of knuckle bones, as they waited for repairs to be completed.

"I have had the luck of Ernelltar the Bedevilled lately, doms," I called across. "Give me leave to sit awhile and eat. Mayhap later I will chance a round or two."

They made crude remarks at this, all of them pleased for the moment to be on a duty that gave them a trifle of spare time so rare and precious in their lives. I moved on into the shadows past where the altar to Mellor'An had once lifted and now lay in shards of broken brick and pottery and charred wood.

Without a shred of modesty I can claim that no ordinary Vallian would have escaped detection for a moment. But I was a Clansman—a Clansman of Felschraung and Longuelm and now of Viktrik. If Hap Loder had not been out collecting obi from other clans, also. I knew the ways of the radvakkas passing well. Talk of Ernelltar the Bedevilled raised uncouth and sarcastic comments, for all knew that runs of bad luck were attributed to him in North Segesthes.

The space at the rear of the altar was badly broken down. In a cavity within the pediment below the altar, Marta had said. I kicked charred timbers aside and swiped at the clouds of dust and ashes. The rumble of voices and the clang of the smithies' hammers resounded comfortingly from the exterior. I poked around. There was a crevice, a slot in the baked bricks. I reached down. A box? Something hard-edged. I got my fingers around it and then took a quick look back. I was still alone.

With a grunt and a heave the box came out. Sturmwood, scuffed, with a brass lock and hinges, it looked nothing special. It went under the shaggy pelt as a warvol devours flesh.

Then I yawned and wandered back to the knuckle-bone players.

For the look of the thing I played a few hands, and lost one of the daggers, and felt too amused even to curse.

The slaves laboring at the fires, at the bellows, hammering the iron, would slide liquid envious glances in our direction. Hardly slaves at all, these fellows who so liked to lord it over the less fortunate, cowed before their masters. In a sense they were more like the militarily employed helots of the Spartans. With good and faithful service and the signal proof of courage they might even be given a kind of manumission and join the hard-riding ranks of the radvakkas. The process was continuous, Iron Riders in the making.

Not all the slaves were apim. There was a marked brutality in the treatment the radvakkas meted out to the diffs. They would in their rough uncouth ways stand far more from an apim slave than a diff. I saw a Rapa knocked headlong into a fire. A little Och whose job was to bring water for quenching was tripped and his bucket upended over his head and rammed down around his ears. The Iron Riders were intolerant of diffs, that was known.

Many diffs bore the savage marks of barbaric punishments.

"Here, slave!" bellowed a radvakka, and he cracked his whip. "Your work is done. Now schtump. Grak!"

I detest that hateful word grak. As the radvakka yelled so the slaves all jumped, quite automatically, when the vicious cutting word of command bit into the stifling smoke-filled air.

As humbly as might be contrived I took Lumpy and the chain and went out. The air smelled sweet after the singing stink of the smithy.

All this time I had been alert, strung-up, making myself appear relaxed, expecting detection at any moment. Now, as I led Lumpy out along the street, with Nikwald filled with the clamor of The Iron Riders about me, I thought I had done it. I was set. Clear away. I had only to mount up and ride.

That would have been a disastrous mistake.

Since when would a slave, even a master's slave, a helot, dare to ride his master's steed back from the smithy in the barbaric encampments of The Iron Riders?

"By Getranchi's Iron Fist!" bellowed a radvakka as he kicked heartily at a Khibil carrying a sack of flour. "Grak, you useless worm. Or I'll cut your hide to pieces."

They were but a pair acting out the lunacy of their respective social positions, one swaggering, the other staggering. Perforce, I had to look the other way. One day, Opaz willing, we'd have sanity back in Vallia and do away with slavery for good and all. I led Lumpy on and ground down the instinct to whip out the broadsword and lay the flat against the arrogant Iron Rider's skull.

A hullabaloo broke out ahead, with people shouting and running, so I guided Lumpy into the shadows of a tumbledown shack at the side of a ruined house. Men were pointing up. So up I looked, shielding my eyes against the declining rays of the suns. Up there, high, three vollers fleeted across the sky, traveling southwest and going fast. They were mere petal-shaped outlines; but they were Hamalian and they were scouting radvakka Nikwald. Judging from the comments of The Iron Riders, they thirsted for the chance to drive a spear into the marvelous flying craft up there, and were stumped as to how to do it.

An odd sound as of a piece of wood striking the palm of the hand, although heavier, meatier, floated from the ruined building. I ignored it. In this concealment seemed a good time for me to discard the sturmwood, brass-bound box, which was too awkward for easy carriage. I took the ring out. The Ring of Destiny. It looked an ordinary enough ring, with two emeralds, a ronil and an indeterminate whitish stone, not a diamond, all fastened with gold claws. I stuck it down safely into my breechclout.

The slapping noise continued and I pushed further back and looked through where once a window had been and where now a gap stretched from ground to sky. the tamped earth space within was clearly illuminated by the angled rays of the suns. I saw.

The foul bile of disgust rose into my throat.

A circle of radvakkas stood with whips, with pieces of wood, with iron bars. They surrounded a stake. Tethered by his tail to the stake a man stood and was struck and struck again. The game was to make him run round and round the stake, his tail fastened to an iron ring that enabled him to

75

circle, to duck, to dodge and weave. At the side a radvakka was totting up the bets on a wooden slipstick. The Iron Riders sweated over their work; but they did not call out or make any noise. So I guessed there were bets on the shrieks of pain of their victim, also, and they would not wish to miss these.

In a corner lay the corpses of a number of men—all diffs.

The fellow who was now being tortured for sport did not run. He stood there, his four arms bound at their four elbows into his back. His face—his face showed a dark and passionate hatred of these radvakkas, a tawny-haired face, with tawny moustaches and a golden beard, a savage, noble, suffering face. But he did not cry out. He stood there and I marveled at the way he moved himself, shifting on his feet with a litheness that reminded me of the way great unarmed combatmen fight in their disciplines—a fluid shifting grace of movements that avoided many of the blows. But many more struck home. His naked body, banded with muscle and yet slender and limber, bore the bloody marks, the weals and cuts, the bruises.

He was a marvel, this man. He was of the Kildoi, a race of diffs not very well known mainly inhabiting Balintol. The immensely powerful physique, the fluid shifting movements, the slide and rope of muscles, all added to the clear and intelligent anticipation of a blow, enabled him to last out in his suffering where lesser men would have been shrieking in shredded agony. But—there was about his anticipation of a blow more than mere intelligence. Much mumbo jumbo is spoken and written about the mystic means whereby a man may judge a blow although blindfolded, and there is great truth in this. Certainly I know what I know of many Disciplines. The Krozairs, chiefest of all, of course, and the Khamster syples of the Khamorros, the Velyan techniques of the Martial Monks of Djanduin, and many more. Much foolishness is written and believed about mysticism in combat; but the kernel of truth remains. In this fellow, this Kildoi, I saw a man who was a High Adept, a True and Proven Master.

This was no business of mine. So why did I stand there?

This was something of a different order from that radvakka who had so thoughtlessly kicked his Khibil slave up the rear. That was of the daily nature of a slave's life and a vileness I and Delia would try to end as soon as we might—a thankless and difficult task, Opaz knew. But this obscenity before me was something else again. Still and all, all the same, without doubt—it was nothing to do with me. So, you see, I prevaricated.

One of the radvakkas slashed his whip and the Kildoi slid the blow easily and instantly swayed the other way and avoided a lashing blow from an iron bar. He was very very good. In the event, before I turned away—for I hewed to my main task and would not imperil that even for so marvelous a fellow as this—one of The Iron Riders threw his wooden bludgeon to the ground in disgust.

"You see?" he bellowed. "By the Iron helm of Getranchi. Did I not say so?"

"Maybe you were right," said another. "But he affords sport."

"Sport? I have hit him once only. Once! You call that sport?"

"Maybe," put in a third. "You cannot hit straight."

I rather hoped they'd start a brawl at this; but they went on arguing. The Kildoi stood, poised, lithe, his bruises hard and shining upon him, the blood trickling down that plated chest. I felt for him. And, although this was no business of mine, I did not go away.

"Give him another few murs," said the aggrieved radvakka at last. "It was a waste of time exchanging him. He must be kept in chains all day—he's far too dangerous for a good slave. A waste of time."

"A few murs, then. I own, he is worse than a Kataki."

They started it up again, hitting and slashing, and despite all the wonderful alacrity of the Kildoi he took blows. The blood shone upon his tawny skin.

Of course this was no business of mine—a strange diff, a camp of enemies, in a part of Vallia hostile to the center—what possible business was it of mine, who had urgent business with a ring and a willful kovneva and the commands of the Star Lords? And those just for starters—with all the rest of my problems looming and gibbering at me?

Emperor of Vallia. That was just a laugh. But, just suppose I was the emperor. Then the concerns of all Vallia were mine, and the concerns of all the people in the empire. And, anyway, I'd taken a great liking to this tailed, four-armed marvel who stood, shining with blood, yet golden and still defiant. He was a man I fancied I could understand. No business of mine—this situation was the business and concern of all men.

So, not reluctantly, but joyfully, I hauled out the broadsword and stepped silently into the ruined building.

"I hauled out the broadsword and stepped silently into
the ruined building."

CHAPTER EIGHT

Korero

This was no time for chivalry. No time for the honored traditions of combat. This was going to be nip and tuck.

I hewed through the necks of the first two radvakkas, just above the iron corselet rims, back-handed a third across his face, chunked the reeking broadsword into the eye of a fourth. But there were ten of them, nine in the circle and the slipstick man taking the bets. The others roared at me, raving, ripping out their swords.

The first two fell smoothly enough, and I leaped across their collapsing bodies to get at the last three. The slipstick man tried to throw a knife. Well, he threw it, but the aim was deflected by my left arm. The broadsword went in and out, swung left-handed, and there was just the one left facing me.

He was mumbling something incoherent about a devil; but I smacked his blade away sharply and chunked him down into the tamped earth floor. The slipstick man was almost at the ruined window-opening, shrieking, getting away.

The broadsword lifted into the air, I caught it at the point of balance. I drew back, let fly. Point first the blade skimmed across that dolorous room, burst into the back of his neck, spouted on out. He stopped shrieking and staggered forward and sideways, collapsing in a quivering heap.

The dagger whipped out and a swift succession of four slicing cuts freed the Kildoi's arms. The rope around his handed tail chained to the ring slashed and fell away. I managed to force a smile for him.

"Llahal and Llahal, dom. Let us get out of here, sharpish."

"Llahal, dom. You are very—welcome—whatever kind of demon you may be."

I padded across to the window and retrieved the broadsword. I looked outside. Someone must have heard the racket and be coming to investigate. I swung back.

"Devil I may be. But we're both consigned to the Ice Floes

of Sicce if we don't use our noodles. Here—help me strip this fellow. He looks big enough."

Between us we got the riveted iron from the corpse and I shrugged it on. A helmet from the pile in the corner slammed on my head. The cunning metal plates flapped into place before my face. I slung the shaggy pelt over my shoulder and looked through the eye slits in the metal mask.

The Kildoi had snatched up a shaggy pelt and draped it about himself.

We stepped through the shattered window opening and I leaped up onto Lumpy.

"Take the reins. Lead us along—gently. Keep your head down."

He said nothing but did as I bid. Sitting astride the benhoff, led by a cowed slave, I rode sedately out into the street. A few radvakkas were riding up to find out what the racket was. One of them reined across and started to speak.

"A pestilential fellow," I said, making my gruff old voice harsher and more malignant still. "By the Iron Fist of Getranchi! He took a long time to die."

"Hai!" quoth this Iron Rider. "Did you win?"

"Aye. I won."

We rode on.

As quickly as possible I guided us away from the main street and away from the campfires. Nikwald was only so big and we would never avoid eventual discovery once the hunt was up. We had to get clean away, and the suns would not be gone for a bur yet. I kept listening for sounds that would indicate the massacre had been discovered; but as we approached the broken-down wall of the onetime fortress town nothing sounded apart from the familiar noises of warriors encamped.

We found the second benhoff at the lines under the wall. One radvakka who wanted to know why we took the beast fell down. I did not think he would get up again. The Kildoi mounted up, and I noticed that he fought the stiffness of his cuts and bruises with the phlegmatic calm of one inured to hardship and the injustices of life.

"We must wait until the suns are gone. She of the Veils will give us a bur before she rises. In that time—"

"Aye, dom. We ride."

"Just so. Until then, we keep out of sight."

That was not too difficult in a brawling barbarian camp, even when the racket broke out that told the discovery had been made. Parties of Iron Riders began galloping in all directions. Useless to try to disguise this Kildoi in the time available; I decided we had to try.

Dismounted, we stood in the shadow of the crumbled wall, ready to ride out. A radvakka had the misfortune to approach, without seeing us, to investigate the breach in the wall at this point. The suns were almost gone. Mingled jade and crimson light speared through the gap and threw opaline-bordered shadows across the detritus. I was about to reach out for The Iron Rider when the Kildoi said: "Mine, I think, dom."

"My pleasure."

His tail hand, so much like that of a Pachak, whipped out. It fastened on the throat of the radvakka, choking off his cry, hauled him from the saddle. He crashed to the ground with a savagery that told me much. There was no need to silence him after that. The Kildoi was halfway through trying to fit his artfully articulated shoulders into the riveted iron when the patrol rode up. We two froze. In the shadows, we ought to escape detection; but if one of our benhoffs reacted to the presence of the others. . . .

Our hands fondled the benhoffs, massaging the rolls of fat, giving the benhoffs pleasurable sensations, keeping them quiet.

The riders drew off. I let out a breath.

The suns were nearly gone, drowning in an opaline glory.

"Close," I said. I stared at the shadows that chingled with iron as they rode away.

"Close. I am Korero, dom. Your name?"

My mind was on those damned Iron Riders. I said: "I am Dray—" And then I caught myself, and said, swiftly: "I am Jak the Drang. Lahal, Korero."

"Lahal, Jak the Drang."

He passed no comment. But, even then, I fancied he had heard that confounded stupid word "Dray" and stored it away.

The dying radiance of the Suns of Scorpio stained across the sky of Kregen. In silence we mounted up. He was an old hand, this Korero, a fellow used to the kind of nefarious business we were about. He made no fuss about what had to be done but got on with it. An old campaigner, and yet he was young, I judged, although tall for a Kildoi, being a good four inches taller than me. He moved with a contained muscular alertness, a springiness, a limber strength. And his reflexes were quicksilver, I had witnessed that.

We rode away from Nikwald, very quietly, into the shadows before She of the Veils rose to shed her fuzzy pink and golden light across the land. I made sure the Ring of Destiny still snugged in my breechclout. We rode. If pursuit there was we saw nothing of it.

We spoke very little, aware how sound travelled at night over the plains. I taxed Korero on the absence of any appellation to his name, whereat he half-smiled, and said: "You are Jak the Drang. I have been Korero this and Korero that, from time to time. Mayhap, one day, I will tell you."

We rode companionably back the way I had come and in due time reached Thiurdsmot. Carrying the ring I found the kovneva.

CHAPTER NINE

◆•◆

Bird of Ill Omen

Thiurdsmot girded itself for the fray, everyone engaged in a grim preparation for the coming conflict, and Marta Renberg, Kovneva of Aduimbrev, was in raptures over the Ring of Destiny.

She turned it this way and that, holding it out at arm's length, admiring it as it glittered on her finger.

"Splendid!" she declared. "With this ring all my troubles are over."

Larghos looked at me, and away, and said nothing. We stood in the wide window embrasure of a tower given over to the kovneva's use. The trappings and furnishing were luxurious, as was to be expected. The handmaidens were flushed of cheek and brighter of eye. All in all, absolute confidence radiated about the walls and turrets of Thiurdsmot and nerved the ranks of the Hamalian army and their mercenary allies.

Standing respectfully before the kovneva I looked out through the window. Troops marched in their strict formations in the kyro far below. The colors of Hamal and Aduimbrev floated everywhere, mingled with the colors of the freelances and the paktuns with their own bands. A fluttrell formation winged past, the big birds keeping a beautiful precision of formation, the flyers on their backs leaning into the windrush.

Vollers sailed down to land at the vollerpark. These I eyed with a covetousness I trusted did not show on my savage old leem-face. One of those—one of those airboats I'd have this night and be away, or my name was not Dray Prescot. Zamra, Valka and Veliadrin, to scout, to discover, to do what might be done. And then—Strombor and Delia. Yes, my course was plain.

Marta was transported with pleasure. She had not actually said thank you or commended me on my action and this did not surprise me. As far as she was concerned my usefulness to her had finished and one did not expect civility from a great noble, male or female, in these circumstances. Had she wished to employ me again no doubt she would have remembered to toss me a crumb of some tawdry kind as a reward. Mind you, this forgetfulness of favors is not confined to the nobility or the gentry alone. The poor people, for all there are a great many of them, often share the same distressing character defect.

To carry out Phu-Si-Yantong's demands in this part of Vallia a Chuktar had been appointed in command. He was an ord-Chuktar, and therefore an important man in almost any army. He and Marta appeared to get along together and as she began to tell him just how the ring would discompose the mailed cavalry of The Iron Riders I was able to ease away out of their notices. This Chuktar Nath ham Holophar was a strom, the Strom of Warhurn, and I'd been ready to take action in case he recognized me. But that was highly unlikely, for the desperado Jak the Drang did not look much like Hamun ham Farthytu, the Amak of Paline Valley.

Their plan was one of the obvious ones, given the circumstances. Once the ring had exerted its power, controlled and directed by the kovneva, the army of Hamal would ride over what was left of the radvakkas. the aerial might they could bring to bear would finish them off. They saw no problems.

Scouts brought in details of the radvakka's movements. The battle was imminent, and I intended to be long gone before that.

The only note that ought to have indicated caution to the Hamalese sounded in the increased numbers of Iron Riders. Reports estimated at least three bands had joined, making nine thousand.

Chuktar ham Holophar had thirty regiments of infantry, foot and crossbows, and five thousand totrix and zorca cavalry, together with a strong varter force. With the aerial wings that ought to be enough to see off the Riders—so ham Holophar said, with some grimness—without the magical influence of the ring.

Myself, I owned with a matching grimness that I'd as lief see the paired opponents mutually exhausted, Hamalese and radvakkas alike, so that honest Vallians could claim back their own land.

Filled with her busy plans Marta Renberg saw me as I crossed to the door. Her face clouded and then brightened.

"You will fight in the battle, Jak the Drang?"

Standing with my hand on the door, aware of the guards posted at either side, I felt the need for a little gentle stirring. . . .

"Mayhap, kovneva. I remember a certain promise, made upon a fallen log in a clearing."

She flushed up, as she did so easily, and her lips tightened.

"I have warned you aforetime, eeshim. I do not forget old scores."

"But promises?"

"I do not wrangle in public with a rast like you. Guards! Seize the insolent cramph—"

I went through the doorway before the guards could react and slammed the heavy lenk shut. I was down the stairs of the tower and out into the inner ward, the outer ward, and the kyro swallowed me up in its busy activity long before anyone got a glimpse of my departure. Silly woman! Well, she had her Ring of Destiny. I almost felt sorry I would not be here to see how efficacious it was in action.

Just how serious this petulant kovneva was about having me taken up I was not sure; but it appeared a wise plan to keep myself out of sight until evening. The parallel between this action and the action of hiding in radvakka Nikwald occurred to me, you may be sure, and with an unpleasant reminder of the evil days fallen upon Vallia. a sprightly young Hamalian Air Service man went to sleep in a side alley, perfectly unharmed save for a headache when he awoke and a chilly feeling around his nether regions, because his smart uniform was missing. Wearing that uniform and almost busting the stitching, I sat myself down in a tavern, in a dark corner, to await my chance. Thus placing myself in the jaws of the beast, as it were, seemed the safest course.

These men were off duty, and in the nature of off-duty soldiers or airmen they drank and gambled and chased the girls and sang. They sang the songs of Hamal. Well, I'd sung them, in my time. I listened, not joining in, marking down a weasely little fellow with the insignia of a shiv-Deldar who was trying to sing and could only manage a croak or two because he was so far gone, half-falling off his bench, lolling foolishly near me.

They sang "Anete ham Terhenning," a stupidly tragic song about poor Anete who for the love of a stalwart crossbowman of the emperor's guard hurled herself from the Bridge of Sicce. I felt easier when they passed on to the good old favorite: "When the Fluttrell Flirts His Wing." The shiv-Deldar lurched and slopped his ale and I moved smoothly across and caught him, supported him up against the wall. He waggled his head at me, owlishly.

"Whereaway, dom? The old voller's in a real hurricane—"

"Rest easy," I said. "Have another drink."

So we sat and drank companionably and he talked. He was not at all sure he'd been as clever as he'd thought, volunteering for the Army against Vallia. I learned that the Hamalese regiments and aerial wings and cavalry were not regular units of the Hamalian army; they'd been given the chance of volunteering and, as the shiv-Deldar, who was called Naghan the Boxes, said, the Empress Thyllis wasn't paying them. Their regimental cash boxes were filled by prompt and regular payments from the person he called the Hyr Notor. The High Lord. I did not have to be told that was what Phu-Si-Yantong had adopted as a cover name for himself in dealing with Thyllis and her people and army.

Vallia was being cut up into different areas, dominated by the forces of different factions and nobles. His lot had been run out of the North East and they did not like it. Come the morrow, said Naghan the Boxes, and drank deeply, come the morrow and they'd chuck their firepots down on these nurdling Iron Riders and crisp 'em in their iron.

You may judge of my joy when, by casual enquiry, I discovered that the Deldar actually knew of Rees and Chido, and could assure me they yet lived and were hale and hearty. This pleased me greatly. Other things I learned, which you shall hear when they are germane to my narrative.

The Deldar blinked at my broadsword. "Naughty," he said. "Where's your thraxter? Your Hikdar will not allow non-squadron equipment." He belched. "He'll mazingle you as the Law allows." By mazingle he meant discipline. The uniform I had acquired was that of a simple aerial soldier, a voswod, so I forced a smile and nodded and offered another drink.

The conversation came around to the vollers of the

squadron and I learned what I needed to know. So I excused myself and the suns having set and my appetite for the moment satisfied by the ingestion of a superb vosk pie, I sauntered out into the moonlit darkness. Now, as you know, I have some skill in the art of stealing airboats. It is not a gift of which I am particularly proud; but I console myself with the reflection that I practice the art only to use a voller when the need is dire. It is not a skill used for mere self-gratification.

As I left the tavern with the lights shining from the windows the swods were singing "Black Is the River and Black Was Her Hair," another farcical tragical ditty. They'd roar and roister until the patrols hoicked them out, and they'd maybe have sore heads in the morning; but I knew they were Hamalian swods and they'd fight like demons when The Iron Riders charged.

I hummed a few bars of "The Bowmen of Loh," in a manner to redress the balance, and went up to the voller park. I took a voller. I hurt no one. The flier lifted into the moonshot dimness as one of the lesser moons of Kregen hurtled across the sky. The night air breathed sweet about me. I turned the airboat's head eastwards. I was on my way home.

Looking back, I realise the futility of anger. I should have known. That dratted Scorpion had not crawled out from under a rotting log and given me implicit instructions to let me get away so easily now.

The tempest boiled up in a maelstrom of whirling winds that buffeted the craft this way and that, that scythed me with a pelting blast of hail, that drove the voller swooping and skimming to the ground. I hauled at the controls; but the voller flattened out and skidded along the ground, less than two ulms from the town. The noise racketed about my head.

And then—and then the noise and the tempest vanished in a heartbeat, and the Gdoinye flew down, arrogant and bright in his power, and perched on the coaming.

I glared at that gorgeous bird whose plumage sheened with metallic luster in the moonlight as She of the Veils rose.

"Dray Prescot, onker of onkers."

My harsh old lips clamped shut. Confound the bird! The raptor would get no change out of me. . . .

"Do you not understand what the Everoinye demand of you?"

So, my resolution flung to the winds, I burst out: "By Vox, you brainless bird! Do they know themselves?"

"They know, onker, and they know you are the man to

fulfill their desires and to obey their commands." The Gdo-inye stuck his head on one side and regarded me balefully from one bright avaricious, beady, *knowing* eye. "A crossbow bolt was loosed at me—"

"I wish to Zair it had pierced your foul heart!"

"You do not. And you know you do not. Now, hearken! You will stop The Iron Riders. The Star Lords command. You will halt the radvakkas and drive them back over the sea to whence they came. This, Dray Prescot, king of onkers, you will do."

I laughed. "Stop them? With what? How am I supposed to halt that mailed cavalry?"

"You saved the Miglas and halted the Canops, I remember."

"Sarcasm, Gdoinye, ill becomes you. And to fight the Canops I brought my Freedom Fighters from Valka and merce-naries from Vallia. You know Vallia never has had a national army—"

"Do not prevaricate, onker! You know the answer. We do not ask you to perform a deed beyond your powers, puerile though they be."

"If they are so puerile, by Makki-Grodno's diseased tripes, then you should be able to do it all yourself!"

The Gdoinye let out a squawking cackle, of amusement, of scorn, I didn't know or care. I glared and shook my fist.

"I'm going back to Strombor—"

"Your empress is safe, Dray Prescot, safe in the Heart Heights of Valka surrounded by your Freedom Fighters. They take a heavy toll of those who invaded Valka."

"She is safe? Delia is safe?"

"Assuredly. Now, emperor of onkers, do as you must and drive back the radvakkas. And, then, why you may do as you wish with Vallia. For a space."

I opened my mouth to ask what the damned bird meant by a space; but he ruffled his feathers, struck his wings and soared aloft. In an instant he was a dot against the face of She of the Veils, and then he was gone.

So I, being in truth the onker of onkers the Gdoinye dubbed me, cursed and cursed again. I would have to do as the Star Lords commanded. And, of course, I'd mightily en-joy discomfiting the radvakkas. But I had to admit I would far rather tilt at The Iron Riders on my own account.

Back to Thiurdsmot I flew and replaced the voller. Scowl-ing ferociously, I took myself off. Only one thing pleased me, and that tempered by parting. Delia was safe. I hungered for

87

her and I knew she yearned for me. The quicker I saw The
Iron Riders to the Ice Floes of Sicce the quicker I'd see Delia
again.

CHAPTER TEN

━━◆━◆━━

"Give me your sword, jen, and you would see!"

I, Dray Prescot, Lord of Strombor and Krozair of Zy, hunkered down under a thorn-ivy bush with a crossbow bolt
through my thigh and could no longer curse. There was another bolt through my arm; but I was able to break off the
leather flights and draw the confounded thing through and
wrap a chunk of breechcloth around to check the bleeding.

All about me the yells and screams and moans of wounded
and dying men beat fearfully into the lowering sky. The Suns
of Scorpio were sinking over the field of carnage, and already
the scavengers were out, slinking like gray wolves from body
to body—if the body was not dead at first, it soon became
dead after.

"You will fight in the battle, will you not, Jak the Drang?"
that stupid Kovneva Marta had said, and so I had, and had
fought and this was the result. The Iron Riders had ridden.
They had ridden well. They had ridden clear over the ranked
regiments of Hamal and the mercenaries, ridden slap bang
through the cavalry, gone rampaging on to Thiurdsmot itself,
which was the prize they coveted. As for the famed aerial
cavalry and the squadron of vollers, they had made no impression, and were long gone. Only the Hamalian varters had
put any real impediment in the way of the radvakkas, and
that had been for a short space only, the artillery being swept
away in the rout.

And the ring? The damned Ring of Destiny?

Opaz knew what the woman had done. She believed fer-
vently in the magical properties of the ring. Well, they hadn't
worked. If she knew Phu-Si-Yantong as I was beginning to
know the devil, she should not have been surprised. Poor old
Chuktar ham Holophar—if he still lived he'd not lightly put

his trust in a silly woman's belief in a magical talisman again. . . .

The quarrel through my leg was a nuisance. It had to come out and the wound attended to. The crossbows the radvakkas had used had been shot off with a fine abandon, much jollity must have been evinced as the barbarians played with these toys of civilization. Their own bows were puny, mere flat arcs of wood and sinew, and the captured crossbows were, for all the mockery, rather wonderful to them. Anyway, some dratted barbarian idiot had sent a quarrel into me, and his mate had slapped a second to follow the first. Mind you, I must blame only myself. Being hit by a flying arrow or bolt in the midst of a hectic battle is a chance all fighting men must take.

Not wishing to dramatise my predicament unduly, I will only add that here I was, wounded, without transport, abandoned on a stricken field, surrounded by implacable foemen—and with the stricture laid on me to defeat and drive out of Vallia the very enemy who was now so triumphant.

Well. It was a task. It was a challenge. I fancied I would go into the task with a greater zest now.

First things first. . . .

The bolt drew out of my thigh with a deal of unpleasantness. The breechcloth had to be wrapped and pulled tightly. I peered out from under the thorn-ivy. She of the Veils was not yet up but in the last dying wash of light of the suns set the Twins rose in the east, eternally orbiting each other, lurid with a ruddy light. The wind blew soughingly. The yells and screams had mostly died away now and only occasionally a long groan broke that whispering silence.

I crawled out and stood up—very shakily.

The broadsword had snapped across in the melee and the shortsword had been carried off wedged in the breastbone of a radvakka whose iron corselet had been burst through. It had been hot work there, in the press.

Vague ideas of what I was going to do had already formed in my vosk-skull of a head; but I fancied I'd have to walk in on my own two feet—as I have done before, Zair knows. So, grumbling and cursing, I started off, hobbling along. That dip in the Pool of Baptism of the River Zelph in far Aphrasöe would most certainly speed my recuperation and leave me whole and unscarred; but the process of recovery was none the less highly fraught for all that.

Half-under a corpse of an infantryman I found a thraxter.

One of the gray scavengers approached and I showed him

the blade, lurid in that ruddy light, and snarled, and he withdrew.

One hell of a racket was breaking up out of Thiurdsmot as I skirted the town. The townspeople would have made good their escape—or I devoutly hoped they had—the moment they had realized the battle was lost. The rout would have been a Cansinsax on a greater and more ghastly scale. Now the barbarians whooped it up in best barbarian style. I flung a few ripe curses at them as I hobbled past in the dappled moons light.

The three water bottles I had picked up were soon emptied and I had to cast about for a stream. I was ragingly thirsty.

The light of a small fire twinkled ahead. Carefully I scouted the little camp. These were Vallians—all of them natives of Vallia, I judged, and not a Hamalese among them. They sat hunched around their fire by the stream and their conversation, low-voiced, made me realize just how low-sunk we Vallians had become.

When I made my presence known the first awkwardness when fists grasped knives was overcome in a quick pappattu. They saw my wounds and one of them, Wando the Squint, helped me bathe them and dress them again. There were about twenty men here, mostly tradesmen of Thiurdsmot of that sturdy class who although employing slaves yet did much of the manual work themselves, being masters at their trades. I gathered their womenfolk had gone back over the Great River a few months ago. And, with them, was the blacksmith with whom I had fled from Cansinsax. When I asked him what had happened, his face clouded over and he beat that thewed arm and iron fist onto his knee.

"The Opaz-forsaken radvakkas! They slew my family—all of them, they slew, and I could do nothing." His agony pierced me. "But I shall have them." He spoke quite rationally, this Cleitar the Smith. "I shall wreak my vengeance on them all."

Very carefully, for I had an inkling of what they purposed, I said: "You pitch your camp perilously close to the town."

"Aye," said the fellow who was clearly their elected leader. Tall, darker-complexioned than most Vallians, he lowered down on me, a deep scar furrowing down his left cheek from eye to lip. "Aye. We shall take any stragglers, and send them one by one to the Ice Floes of Sicce. They have conjured up great evil and a greater than they can imagine shall punish them."

"Amen to that," I said. "But—"

90

This Dorgo the Clis broke in: "We were told the iron men of Hamal were our new friends and allies. The kovneva told us. Well, we did her bidding. And Opaz punished us and sent The Iron Riders to destroy the men of iron. It is just. Now we shall avenge ourselves, as is just."

"Oh, aye," I said. "I'm all for slitting a few radvakka throats. But, as you see, I am in no case for running. And you will have to run—if you can."

They weren't too happy about this. They had a few weapons apart from their knives. One had a bow, a compound arm barely stronger than the bows of the radvakkas. Dorgo the Clis and another hulking fellow had swords, Vallian clanxers. Some of the others had spears, and Cleitar the Smith hefted his hammer. I tried to reason with them—uselessly.

"We may be honest tradesmen and no warriors. I think you are a paktun, Jak the Drang. Well, your paktun comrades ran and were cut down in the battle, as the Hamalese were. Now it is the turn of us to—"

"Listen, Dorgo! What do you know of fighting? I mean real fighting, as a warrior fights, in battle, with edged weapons? You have your town brawls with cudgels and a knife or two. But a real battle is a vastly different affair, by Vox!"

One of the men, a fellow who hefted a spear meanly, said: "My son was always reading the great stories, the legends, tales of the heroes. He ran away to be a mercenary, seeing, as he said, Vallia gave no place for a soldier in his native land. I have heard from him once. He is now a paktun, and fought in a place called Khorundur, wherever in the Light of the Invisible Twins that may be."

I did not tell him that Khorundur was a nation of the Dawn Lands of Havilfar. His son had traveled widely.

"And what is the meaning to your words, Magin?" demanded Dorgo the Clis.

"My son is not here to fight. But I shall. I shall stick my spear into the guts of a radvakka, at the least."

The real meaning behind Magin's words was there, plain as a pikestaff; but he had not yet teased out what he meant himself. He and his comrades, like the great mass of the people of Vallia, had not yet fully understood what they felt, had not yet come to a comprehension of what they must do. And what they must do had ramifications quite beyond the immediate knocking of a few Iron Riders over the head.

Trying to tell them to wait was like trying to melt the Ice

Floes of Sicce with a half-ob candle. In the end, when I had told them I intended to raise a proper army to fight The Iron Riders and they were properly incredulous—not to say suspiciously contemptuous of any such grandiose concept—I said: "I am for Therminsax. If you can, join me there."

Dorgo the Clis stroked a broken thumbnail down his scar.

"It is certain you can be of no help to us, Jak the Drang. So we wish you well. But I do not think we shall meet in Therminsax."

"I think perhaps you will," I said. "May the light of Opaz go with you." And so, regretfully, I hobbled off into the night.

That journey recurs now, not, perhaps, with the frightfulness of other journeys I have undertaken on Kregen but, certainly, with a certain frisson. I hobbled. Thoughts of the Hamalese intruded along with all manner of nonsenses as I labored on. Rees and Chido, thank Krun they were safe. Even then I recalled how the Hamalian Army had been suspect against a heavy cavalry charge. Rees being overset by a hersany charge in Pandahem; our own wild charge at Tomor Peak. . . . With an irony I did not relish I had to face the unpalatable fact that in this section of Vallia the only hope for Vallia at the moment was her enemy, Hamal. Nothing stood between the radvakkas and the soft heartlands of Vallia but the Hamalian Army. If I could find someone to listen to me—and I'd do it in the guise of the Amak Hamun nal Paline Valley—we'd strew caltrops, we'd dig ditches, we'd set ambushes, we'd smother The Iron Riders with bolts. It could be done; but at a price. Then I brightened up. That price, by Krun, would be paid by the Hamalese! Capital!

But, no—as I hobbled on through the night to the nearest canal, I knew that was a base thought. Good men would be sacrificed and die and I could take no pleasure from that.

Therminsax lay in a north, northwesterly direction and altogether too near the border of Sakwara for comfort. But all reports spoke of the city as holding out so far against the radvakkas. The treacherous attack by the Kovneva of Aduimbrev against her northern neighbor and the subsequent occupation by the Hawkwas and the forces of Hamal had gone through very rapidly. What conditions would be like now I had no idea. So I pushed on and curved around and at last found the Therduim Cut and a little group of canalfolk anxiously pushing on to Thermin. They had seen parties of Iron Riders crossing the cut; but so far had been unmolested.

All the North East must lie under the iron heel of the radvakkas. Layco Jhansi and the provinces he had taken with his own forces and the mercenaries he had hired would be the next on the list. What was going on up in the north, down in the southwest, in the southeast, was anybody's guess. Vondium, the capital and the surrounding provinces owed allegiance to this new emperor, Seakon, and if the radvakkas or Layco Jhansi did not deal with him, then I would. Vallia was a disturbed ants' nest these days, with every man's hand, it seemed, turned against every other man's.

We glided along the cut and as my wound healed so I helped haul. The canalfolk accepted me as one of themselves, as I was able to drink the canalwater, a true test. The kutven of this group was Rordam na Therduim, a brawny, cheerful fellow much cast down by the evil days and the disreputable state of the cut. Often we had to drop over the side of the lead narrow boat and with spades slice a way through the mud fallen in to make a passage. Once we halted in the shade of a group of missals as a long line of radvakkas passed, and with them wagons hauled by benhoffs, wagons no doubt containing much plunder.

"If only there was some way of getting back at them," said Rordam, wiping his forehead, frowning.

"There will be, kutven. We have to plan and organize."

"Plan what? Organize with what?"

"Once we get to Therminsax we'll be able to see better what to do."

But, I own, my own words sounded hollow even to me.

Of the towns and villages along the cut it were best not to speak. This canal, as I have said, ran for much of its course through border land, march country, and men had not in the old days built anything other than frontier forts. With the establishment of the empire by Delia's ancestors, the need for forts had gone; but the land was barely suitable for anything other than desultory grazing. The few towns were uniformly abandoned, looted and destroyed by The Iron Riders. We did meet other canalfolk and with them hauled on to Therminsax.

Approaching the city the land took on for a space a much wilder aspect, with rocky outcrops and precipitous descents alternating with broader open rides of grassland. The canal scythed through between cutting walls. Then, when Kutven Rordam said Therminsax lay half a day's haul away, the country opened out into the broader fields and pastures I remembered from my previous visits to the city. We hauled on lustily.

It fell to my lot to take the turn at striding out ahead along the towpath, well in front, to scout our safe passage, when we ran into the fight.

Standing immobile in the shade of the trees fringing the towpath I watched the scene on a grassy bank near a tumbledown village. Men fought and struggled there, and yet I saw they struck at one another with wooden cudgels, and fists, and feet, and bellowed and roared their mutual fury. There were two sides to the combat, and one side wore the blue and green of the high kovnate of Sakwara, and the other side wore the colors of Thermin, an emperor's province, colors of crimson and brown. I thought of The Iron Riders and felt my fury rising. This was a nonsense.

The city could only be an ulm or two beyond the next curve in the cut and when I barged out into the fight and grabbed a man wearing the crimson and brown and hoicked him out of it, he confirmed my suspicions of what was happening here. He saw my face and the thraxter, and he was very ready to talk.

"Yes, jen, yes. The devils of Hawkwas tried to cross and we must stop them—"

I shook my head.

"Who is in command of your men here?"

He squirmed around in my fist. The fight raged, with men staggering away holding their heads, and the dust lifting, and the uproar bellowing on. He pointed. "Yonder. Targon the Tapster." Targon, bellowing, struck wildly with his cudgel at a beefy individual who ducked and struck back.

I turned on the fellow I gripped and stuck my face into his. "Just you stand here, dom, peaceably, whilst I sort this out."

He nodded his head frantically, almost choking. I let him go and waded into the fight, got a grip on a Hawkwa. The question to him produced a string of swear words; but he sobered up quickly enough after I spoke to him, and he said: "There. With the black beard. Naghan ti Lodkwara—"

So, for the third time, I plunged into the fight. Men fell as I barged through. I hit Targon on the chin and dragged him along by my left arm, heaving struggling men away, pounding on, took Naghan ti Lodkwara by the neck. I hauled them both back out of the scrum and plunked them down against a ruined wall.

I glared at them as they stared up, quite unable to understand what had hit them.

"Now, you two hulus. Listen and listen well. You may be

94

of Therminsax and you may be a Hawkwa. I can guess why you are fighting. You stupid onkers! Haven't you heard of The Iron Riders?"

"These cramphs of Hawkwas stole six ponshos!"

"They wandered about, lost—we but gave them a home—"

"Aye! In your swag bellies!"

They'd have started up again; but I waggled the thraxter at them.

A couple of men spun out of the fight, saw me and their respective leaders, and came over to lend a hand. I was forced to stretch them upon the ground, where they slumbered. I glared at these two, this Targon the Tapster and this Naghan ti Lodkwara.

"Now, you two, you hulus. Call off your men. Stop this fight. Or, by Vox! I'll go in there and really thump a few heads."

Targon looked pretty sullen. "We are not used to fighting with swords—"

"So tell you men, sharpish. *Bratch!*"

In the event between us we managed to sort out the confusion. Men sat on the ground, panting, holding their heads. Others leaned on one another, gasping. They were a sorry looking bunch, and no mistake. I stood up and shouted at them. Shouting at people seems to be an occupational disease; but needs must when the devil drives—in this case, far more devils than the immediate deviltry of The Iron Riders.

"The Iron Riders are coming to sack your city—:"

"They are way down south," objected Targon sullenly.

"They drove us out," shouted Naghan viciously. "That is why we run and take your skinny ponshos."

"Our ponshos are fine and fat! We do not need nit-stinking Hawkwas to tell us about our ponshos."

"You will all be ponshos in the jaws of the leems," I bellowed at them. I went on in fine style, rhetoric, threats, not blandishments so much as promises of what lay in store for them when the radvakkas had been seen off and peace and prosperity once more enfolded Vallia. I watched their faces. "You are all Vallians. The North East is the northeast of Vallia. The Hamalese—"

At this a chorus of curses and blasphemies and threats of what they'd like to do to the Hamalese broke out. Kovneva Marta had wrought well with her mercenaries in Thermin, and these men were not likely to forget.

"Do the Hamalese hold Therminsax?"

"Aye, dom—" began Targon.

"I am Jak the Drang," I said, and, as though that was a kind of signal allied to what I had done and said, they at once started calling me jen, which is Vallian for lord. I let it pass. If I was to do what I had to do, then any additional slender threads of authority were useful, no matter how ludicrous or despicable in my eyes.

The Hamalian Army was represented in Therminsax chiefly by a regiment of foot and a regiment of crossbowmen. The balance of the forces was made up of paktuns and masichieri, and of men hired by Aduimbrev. That would have to be sorted out. Also, there was a mercenary force of flutsmen.

"If I know flutsmen," I told these men who were stanching their cuts and rubbing their bruises, "they will fly off the moment the going gets tough. After all, Therminsax means nothing to them, nor does Vallia and the North East. They are not Vallians. But, doms, you are."

"Maybe," spat out Naghan ti Lodkwara. "But we have no money to hire mercenaries to fight for us."

I let his words hang. I wanted these men to examine them. I repeated what he had said. Then, putting contempt into my voice, I said: "Gold—you pay gold for other men to fight for you. If you see your wife and child about to be killed and your house burned, you hold out a purse of gold and pray someone will come along and save your family, your home. Is that it?"

"No—no!" shouted some. They were growing warm. "It is not that at all," shouted others. They were all struggling with preconceived notions. Ordinary citizens just didn't go out and fight as common soldiers. Foul-mouthed mercenaries did that, and got paid to do it.

I pointed at Targon. "If you stood in your house and saw your wife and child about to be murdered—" I thought a subtle or not so subtle notion might enhance my argument here, and so I said: "Assuming any girl has been misguided enough to wed you—" which brought a few guffaws out. "And you had that cudgel you've been trying to brain these Hawkwas with—would you not strike down the assassin?"

"Well," flared out Targon, mightily angry. "Of course!"

"So when The Iron Riders get here—will you hit their iron with a wooden club?"

I was surprised to hear a few guffaws at this, and realized I was making headway.

"Give me your sword, jen, and you would see!"

I let out a sigh. About to speak, perhaps to come to the crux, I halted as a man yelled and pointed up.

"There are the flutsmen," he shouted. "What do they want? Have they seen The Iron Riders?"

The mercenaries of the skies, self-centered, wheeled on their wing-fluttering birds, circling the village. Then they descended steeply through the bright air. I saw the way they handled their weapons. I knew flutsmen of old.

"Take cover!" I bellowed, furious, seething. "They are true devils. They will slay us all for mere sport!"

CHAPTER ELEVEN

Sport for Flutsmen

"No, no, jen," quoth Targon, easy, assuming a superior attitude at my ignorance. "They have not troubled us so far—or, at least, no more than any rasts of mercenaries trouble honest men."

"They'll have you all as slaves—"

The other men of Therminsax made little attempt to conceal their amusement at my agitation. What a fuss I was making, and all over a patrol of flutsmen out scouting. It was clear enough that, detest the Hamalese and the treachery of Aduimbrev though they might, they had adapted and come to terms with the new order.

The flutsmen steepled down through the thin air, seven of them, the clotted clumps of feathers streaming back from their leather flying helmets, their long toonon-like weapons slanting down. They did not intend to shaft us with their crossbows, then. Sport—that was what they were after, sport. . . .

Then I remembered just why I was here. The narrowboats! I was supposed to be scouting for Kutven Rordam and the canalfolk.

Naghan ti Lodkwara pushed up from the wall. He stared up and scratched that black beard. "Flutsmen. They are very devils—"

"Get your Hawkwas into the houses, at least, Naghan. I must back to the cut—"

I started off running, waving my arms, haring along the

towpath. The narrowboats were just in view. There were two parties of people and both claimed my attention.

"Get inside and bolt the doors!" I bellowed. "Hurry! *Flutsmen!*"

The haulers eased up and the tows slacked. Kutven Rordam appeared shouting questions. I bellowed over the uproar.

"Bolt the doors. If you have weapons, use them."

Then I went pounding back up the towpath again past the concealing clumps of bushes toward that stretch of greensward.

On the edge of the village I skidded to a halt. The flutsmen had landed. Naghan must have shuffled his men into the houses, for the colors in badge and favor of the men huddled into an apprehensive and gesticulating ring were all crimson and brown. The flutsmen prodded them with their long polearms, cunningly adapted to aerial work, the narrow blade and curved axe on a shaft that might be anything from seven to fifteen feet in length, the infamous ukra cowed these men of Therminsax.

I had faced the toonons of the Ullars in Turismond and the ukras of flutsmen in Havilfar and I was in no mood to be cowed by these rasts before me now.

Two of the flutsmen carried volstuxes, the aerial throwing spear. They were not all apim, there being a Rapa and a Brokelsh in their number.

Reiving mercenaries of the skies, flutsmen, and they accept any man into their bands, apim, diff, it does not matter providing he swears allegiance to the flutsman band, and obeys their harsh protocol and discipline which, despite their savage ways, control their wild and barbaric way of life. I stepped out into the open and I did not draw my thraxter.

"By Barflut the Razor Feathered!" shouted the nearest flutsman, an apim, with a volstux poised. "Here is one who gapes like an onker! Rast! Get with the others, whilst we decide how you shall die. Bratch!"

"Barflut?" I said, not moving. "A cramph of cramphs, so I am told. A nulsh."

They went mad at this, their enjoyable conversation on just how these onkerish prisoners were to die so rudely interrupted. Some had wanted to tie ropes to the wrists and ankles of a man and then fly aloft with him attached to two fluttrells. How long, the game went, how long would he last before he was torn asunder. Now they heard the name of one of their sacred patron spirits defiled. They foamed with rage.

The apim cast his volstux. I stepped aside. The shaft flew

and no doubt stuck somewhere into the ground. I did not turn around to look.

The other one with a volstux, the Rapa, cast also, and again I moved.

Leaving three of their number to guard the prisoners, the other four rushed on me. Two ukras and two thraxters whipped toward me. I drew the thraxter. The swordsmen first, for I slid past the long polearms and crossed steel with the Rapa. He came at me in fine fettle with his sword; but, somehow, his thraxter was not where it should have been, and mine was through his throat above the feather-adorned corselet. Withdrawing, I grabbed an ukra in my left hand and swung its owner around into his comrade. The other swordsman died as he tried to degut me and then I could turn my attention to the last two. One had the sense to drop his ukra and go for his sword; but he was too late and too slow. The other one tried to run and I had to do as I dislike and chop him from the rear. But, then, even as he went down, he would understand that if a fighting man runs then his back becomes the target.

The remaining three shrilled their rage and raced for their fluttrells. They were going for their crossbows; they were not intending to fly away.

And then—and then an arm reached out from the mass of prisoners and fastened on the neck of a flutsman. Targon the Tapster lifted him and shook him and the ukra fell, to be immediately snatched up by another Therminsaxer. The two flutsmen reached their birds. The crossbows came out of their boots with twinkling speed and the next instant they were leveled at me. The two bolts sped.

Because flutsmen habitually shoot from flying birds their crossbow bolts are short and heavy. I had no Krozair longsword. So, not wishing to take any chances, I hurled myself forward and hit the ground. The bolts hissed past overhead. When I sprang to my feet again the two flutsmen were whipping out their thraxters, determined to finish me once and for all.

A chunk of rock flew and hit the Brokelsh in the stomach. He grunted. Quite apart from his armor, his Brokelsh guts were strong enough to withstand a blow twice as hard. With his companion he charged for me, ignoring the rabble who were now throwing rocks with abandon.

I bellowed, high and hard. "Targon the Tapster! Tell your men to capture the fluttrells—the flying birds—before they fly away! Hurry!"

Then the two flutsmen were on me and it was a fine old skip and dance before I thunked them both down. I swirled away to the fluttrells and let out a yell of disappointment. Six great saddle birds winged high into the air, disdainful of the half-scared, ineffectual attempts of the Therminsaxers to arrest them. Only one remained, and he fluttered his wide wings and kicked up an enormous stink, tugging at his clerketer which was held by half a dozen of the men, all hauling as though they dragged a narrow boat up a vertical cut. I laughed.

"By Vox! A single fluttrell, and you act as though you would chain a city down."

"We know nothing of these outlandish beasts!" And, and I swear, one of them, a little squiffy-eyed fellow with a broken nose, snapped out furiously: "If Opaz had meant us to fly he'd have given us wings when we're born."

In the end, more laughing than anything else, I got the fluttrell under control, and then an arrow winged in past my shoulder and buried its steel head in the fluttrell's breast.

Outraged, I swung about. What my face looked like I do not know. But the canalfolk, running up, abruptly fell back. A tall limber lad, a good hauler, lowered his bow. He looked perplexed. Kutven Rordam, wielding an axe, strode up.

"We saved you in time, Jak the Drang! By Vaosh, it was close."

So, I couldn't flare out at them for onkers, for idiots, for hulus—I needed the fluttrell, and now the poor bird was dead, and these canalfolk thought they had saved my life. I shook my head. I would tell them the truth, by Krun, yes! But not right now. . . .

But Targon the Tapster had no such inhibitions. Panting, dishevelled, with a raking claw scratch on his arm, he pushed up to Rordam. "You stupid calsany! We risk our lives to capture the bird—and you strut up and kill it! Onker!"

I pass over the next few murs in painful silence.

In the end they were sorted out, and their ruffled feathers soothed. I'd lost the fluttrell. But we had gained a small arsenal. And, more importantly, these people understood a little more of what was asked of them in the future, of what I would demand of them.

Three different cultures were represented here.

The canalfolk, fiercely independent, with a way of life peculiarly their own, reserved, withdrawn from the hurly burly of the political life of Vallia, doing their job and proud

"I got the fluttrell under control."

of that and their heritage and traditions, the canalfolk formed, as it were, the powerful skeleton of Vallia.

The Hawkwas, wilder than the general run of Vallian—if you excepted those howling Blue Mountain Boys of Delia's—driven from their lands just when they believed they had struck a blow for freedom, the Hawkwas harbored a savage sense of repression and injustice.

And the Therminsaxers, townsfolk, for many years accustomed to city ways and an ordered existence, habituated to a way of life centered around their city and its trade, their guilds and societies, the full living of the good life in a wealthy imperial province of Vallia, these citizens were bemused by the catastrophe that had befallen them.

When I had first come to Therminsax, flying in an ice voller, the place had been ranked as a market town. Now it was a city, the dignity conferred by the emperor in recognition of the place's growing size and importance and wealth.

"Gather up all the weapons. You—" and I singled out the man I had first dragged out of the fight, Yulo the Boots—"go and find the volstux that went into the bushes. You—" and I gestured to the Hawkwa I had first questioned, he who swore over-abundantly, Foke the Waso, for he was the fifth child— "go and retrieve the two bolts." They caught the urgency I felt, and all obeyed without question—at least, for the moment. This dominance, this habit of taking command and giving orders, is often hateful; but in the present circumstances a lead had to be given and I am, as you know, blessed or cursed with the yrium, that charismatic power that bedazzles men into total acceptance and loyal following—well, some men and some of the time, as you will have learned.

"Naghan ti Lodkwara," I said. "Targon the Tapster. Stand before me." In the busy bustle of men scouting around finding the fallen weapons and collecting the gear from the dead flutsmen the two leaders did as I bid. "Now," I said. "These ponshos."

They both started in a-yelling and I quieted them and glared at Naghan. He scraped a foot. "We are hungry. My people have marched many dwaburs without provender. Anyway, the ponshos were wandering—"

"That," pointed out Targo, breathing deeply, "is why we are out here looking for them."

"They are safe," said Naghan. He looked up, half-defiant, half-abashed. "In yonder broken-down house."

So we went to look. The ponshos were tied up with cloths around their heads. When we loosened the bindings the poor

102

beasts set up a great baaing and bleating. Targo beamed, pleased to see his ponshos still alive and not eaten.

"Your people?" I said to Naghan.

"Aye, jen. We heard what the radvakkas mischiefed in the south and we came north. Some would have asked the burghers of Therminsax for food and help; but others preferred to take what we could and press on."

By south he meant the southern borders of Hawkwa country. And by some who preferred to take what they wanted, he meant himself, I did not doubt.

"You lead them?"

"Aye, jen. They wait for the ponshos we would have brought a few ulms off—"

There was no doubt in my mind of the correct course. So, in the fullness of time and loaded down with the gear stripped from the flutsmen, we set off for the city. It was not far; and, indeed, Therminsax looked mightily refreshing with its red and white houses sheltered behind the long walls. Those walls were in poor shape now, and suburbs had sprung up outside.

"They will not welcome us, jen," said Naghan.

"Leave that to me," I said.

He and Targon, both, looked at me oddly.

Foke the Waso had been sent off to fetch in the rest of the Hawkwas. The Hawkwas I had run across, down in Gelkwa, had been a tough wild raffish lot. I did not doubt that those living in Sakwara were just as hard-bitten. Their reduced circumstances spoke volumes for the impetuous overaweing effect of The Iron Riders.

When Udo, Trylon of Gelkwa, subsidized by Phu-Si-Yantong with Hamalese money and arms, had set off to attack Vondium, the High Kov of Sakwara had sat still, biding his time. Now he was the acknowledged leader of the Hawkwas, in fact as well as by rank. So Naghan ti Lodkwara had not been involved in the earlier fighting. That, I admit, afforded me a little pleasure.

In Therminsax I anticipated making the first real opposition to the radvakkas, as I was commanded by the Star Lords. There might only be a handful of Hamalese there; but there were many mercenaries, paid by that damned Wizard of Loh. His wealth would be colossal, seeing he controlled all of Pandahem as well as much of Hamal and what other lands besides Opaz alone knew. So the reality of what had happened hit me shrewdly. I felt the shock. We had all seen the dust clouds to the south and west, and marked their progress as we came into the city, wondering what they portended.

Now I knew.

The Vallian citizens of Therminsax stood about their charming city, wringing their hands, wailing and crying. I did not see any guards of the Hamalian Army, nor did I see any sign of mercenaries. The reason was simple. The Hamalian Army and their mercenary allies had taken every saddle animal, every draught animal and every cart, and had gone. They had marched out, to the safety of the Great River some one hundred and fifty miles due southwest. And long before the citizens could think to abandon everything they could not carry and hurry after the deserting forces, young Wil the Farrow had ridden in on a preysany with the frightful news that the radvakkas had closed in from the south, and had cut off direct escape. Even as we assimilated this information and Naghan's Hawkwas hurried into the city, almost unnoticed, so more dust clouds rose ominously from east and north. The city was ringed. We were cut off.

Abandoned by all the professional fighting men, the citizens of Therminsax faced a future filled with horror, with sack and rapine and death. There seemed to them to be nothing else left to them in the whole wide world of Kregen.

Doomed, they shouted, screaming, distraught, crazed. Doomed.

CHAPTER TWELVE

We Shut the Gates

Useless to shout and attempt to calm the frenzied mobs who ran, shrieking and wailing, this way and that. Here and there men stood, alone, in groups, who did not scream but clenched their fists and scowled and knew not what to do. Pushing my way through and being buffeted about and trying not to retaliate unthinkingly, I led the Hawkwas to a central kyro I knew beside the Vomansoir Cut. This joined the Therduim Cut in a sizable basin, with wharves and slips, and here Rordam would bring his people to tie up. I headed for the palatial palace of the Justicar, the emperor's governor of the city.

Damn these Opaz-forsaken radvakkas! The Iron Riders had drifted westward across North Segesthes in comparatively recent seasons, although it seemed we Clansmen had been resisting them for ages. Where they had come from no one could be sure, for most of Eastern Segesthes was completely unknown to us, save for a few coastal free cities and the islands of the east. Once Hap Loder had said to me that I could weld all the clans of the Great Plains together into a single mighty fighting force, and I had chided him, my right-hand man, my good comrade, asking of him who the enemy would be we would fight. Well, in these latter days we knew who that foe was, and rued the knowledge.

The mobs thickened about the streets as I approached the kyro before the imperial Justicar's palace. I pushed through and worked my way toward the front. People were shrieking and tearing their hair, some had fallen onto their knees, their arms lifted imploringly to the façade of the palace. They shrieked to the imperial Justicar to save them, to find some way of salvation, to prevent their destruction at the cruel hands of The Iron Riders.

There were no guards. I guessed the small honor guard maintained here in normal times had been suppressed by the Hamalese. I was able to push through the throngs who surged into the inner courtyards and up the ornate stairways and into every room and chamber. The noise would have been upsetting to a man of stone. And, still, there were these knots of citizens who did not scream out, but clenched their fists emptily, and scowled, and did not know what to do.

Eventually I found the Justicar, standing with his back to a tall window where the crimson drapes shadowed the brilliance of the suns. He looked shrivelled. I knew him. He was Nazab Nalgre na Therminsax—an honor title adopted on his appointment. He stood there, created a Nazab by the emperor, trembling, holding his head, surrounded by a few loyal servants and slaves, quite unable to answer the imploring shouts and frantic pleas of the citizenry.

Without ceremony I ripped out the thraxter and angled it so that the light caught the blade and runnelled an ominous glitter into the faces of the citizens. I bellowed over their cries.

"Out! Outside! Stop this caterwauling. Let the Nazab have time to think and plan. Out—or I'll crop your ears."

Dazed, abruptly panic-stricken in an altogether more personal way, the people in the chamber hustled to the door, pushing, crying that a madman had arrived, yelling—oh, it was all a bedlam, and not very splendid, either.

I glared at the slaves.

"Out! *Schtump!*"

They scuttled.

I was left alone with the Justicar of Therminsax, Nazab Nalgre. He recognized me. He stopped shaking. His eyes grew round. He put a hand to his lips. I slammed the door and, swiftly, yanked it open and bellowed along the carpeted corridor.

"If anyone hangs about by this door I'll blatter him!"

Slamming the door again I swung back to Nazab Nalgre.

"Lahal, Nalgre. You know me. My name is Jak the Drang. Do you understand?"

"Yes—No, my prince—"

"Jak the Drang, onker!"

"Yes, yes, majister—Jak the Drang."

I lowered my voice. "Not prince, not majister. Jak. Now, Nazab Nalgre, we have work to do."

"Work? We are doomed. The soldiers have all gone. The Iron Riders approach—what work can we do but pray to Opaz?"

"I'll show you," I said, and hustled him to his desk. "Write at my dictation. A proclamation. Have your stylors copy it out, fair, and have it displayed all over the city. By Vox! We're Vallians. We do not run screeching like a pack of witless vosks when cramphs sniff around our city! Write!"

"Yes, majis—pri—Jak."

So I drew a breath and told him what to write. It was all good rousing stuff and I will not repeat it word for word. Briefly, I told the citizenry that the city would not fall, that we would outface these miserable radvakkas, that we'd see them all buried in their damned iron armor, and anyone who skulked would have his ears cropped, if not worse. Then I went on to give orders the import of which will become plain as I go on with my tale. Very quickly, the stylors were summoned and began to copy out the proclamation for distribution.

Then I ran Nazab Nalgre out onto the balcony fronting the kyro and by gesticulations we obtained a quietness in the mobs.

I shouted. I put forth that old fore-top hailing voice and reached out well into the square, and waited between sentences so that they might be repeated to those farther back.

Again I will not repeat all I said. It was perilously near boasting.

"People of Therminsax. Vallians. Hearken. Your Justicar, Nazab Nalgre, has given me the high honor and duty of resisting The Iron Riders, of saving Therminsax, and of burying every radvakka in a plot of soil. Those that are not burned to a crisp, that is. Think how a radvakka would broil in his armor! All the gates will be closed. Now. Those men who wish to shut the gates they know best—shut them. Those men who have iron bars to hand place them in the canals under the gateways so that no skulking radvakka may gain entrance there." I went on bawling, detailing work to be done, seeing groups of men running to obey. I scaled the work so that the most obvious tasks were performed first. Soon I was able to finish with a resounding burst of oratory, rousing stuff, and then go to meet the leaders of the city. The masters of the guilds, the heads of each ward, the magistrates, the Hikdars of the Watch, the chief of the fire service and, most important, the high priests of the various temples. Therminsax is well-served with temples, fine imposing buildings, and the priests held great if tenuous powers.

With this collection of frightened men in the main chamber of the palace I called for quiet and then told them, simply and forcefully, that Therminsax would not fall, that if they obeyed me they would be saved, what unpleasant things would happen to them if they did not obey, and finished off with a direct statement. "You are Vallians. Do not forget that. You have a pride in your city and your land. These rasts of Iron Riders are uncouth barbarians, illiterate. They have no idea how to lay siege to a city. All they know is charging in their mail, brainless. Obey me and you will be saved."

Then it was a matter of giving each group its orders.

All weapons must be gathered up for ordered distribution. If a man possessed a favorite sword—or spear, for they were spearmen of a sort—he might keep that, if he would use it. The weapon most used by the tumultuous townsmen was the stave with the cudgel held ready in the belt. The spears were used in vosk-hunting, and this was not done for a living but as a sport. The wild vosks were vicious beasts, as all men know, and quite unlike the domesticated vosks from which come such succulent rashers. I already had ideas on the old vosks, as you may imagine. Then I took myself off on a circuit of the city. The suburbs built outside the walls were a handicap, no doubt of that.

Barriers were erected across the ends of the streets, from house to house, where we could. In other places I gave orders for awkwardly placed houses to be pulled down. Now that the citizens had a task to do, had been given some hope, and had an intolerant devil to goad them, they saw fresh hope where all hope appeared dead. They worked. City folk are accustomed to working together, in disciplined order, their habits of mind are orderly. They work together, each relying on the next. That is for work. For play they are a wild tearaway bunch, of course, given the opportunity. Both these traits would be used by me in the defense of Therminsax.

The herds of vosks and flocks of ponshos were being driven into the city through the gates specially left ajar for the purpose. Cattle were brought in. The drovers had, perforce, to work afoot, for the only saddle animal in the entire city was young Wil the Farrow's preysany. At my direction stylors were making a count of food. Well and well—for now. If the siege was protracted—and I did not think it would be—then would come the time to search out hidden hoards.

The iron bars under the gates through which the canals flowed were fixed firmly, and I checked them all, ducking down into the water, conduct which brought knowing nods, and whispers that this Jak the Drang was a canalman, then. . . .

A small but cheerfully clear stream ran chuckling through the city, flowing on across the country to swell other streams and eventually to empty into a tributary of The Great River. Along both sides of this little stream, called the Letha Brook, grew tall stands of the letha tree, well mixed with a kind of beech. The letha tree gives a tough, elastic wood, very white, much used for the handles of agricultural implements. The leaves of the letha are light green, frondulous, very pleasant, and afford a pleasing contrast to the red and black buds and flowers. In the bed of the Letha Brook I made sure the iron bars were firmly fixed against the flow of water. The Iron Riders were perfectly capable of pulling off their iron armor and wading up the stream into the city.

These preparations, rushed though they were, filled in the time until the approach of the radvakkas signaled the time for me to go up onto the wall facing their serried ranks. They ringed the city in metal, sitting their benhoffs lumpily, watching us, and an embassy rode forward, under a great banner of benhoff tails, and trumpets blew for a parley.

Chivalric ways of warfare were not for the radvakkas, and

108

a parley to them meant nothing like what it would mean to a professional soldier of more civilized lands. So I did not go outside the gates to parley.

A fellow clad in iron with much gilding and a profusion of feathers and benhoff tail plumes spurred forward. He bellowed.

I heard him well enough.

I was pretty sure they were perplexed that an army had not ridden out to meet them and, in the familiar and highly satisfactory fashion they had established in this new land, be crushed to powder beneath their iron hooves. This fellow wanted us to open the gates pronto, to stand aside as the radvakkas rode in. He made no promises. His absolute confidence was, in truth, somewhat amusing. I guessed this band—an offshoot of the westward horde—had heard of the prowess of their fellows down south and burned to emulate them here. The city lay before them, open and defenseless, for they were well aware that an army had marched out— had run off. Their astonishment that we did not let them in abruptly ceased to amuse me. It affronted me. I leaned over the battlements and bellowed back.

Well—I cannot repeat what I said. It might burn out the machinery of this tape recorder. But I let fly with a choice selection of insults nicely calculated to upset these haughty and brainlessly arrogant barbarians.

I finished: "And any one of you can enter the city any time he likes, horizontally with his guts hanging out."

For a moment a dead silence hung over the assembled host.

Then a deep and passionate diapason of fury burst out from the crowded ranks. A cloud of arrows flew up. Every one fell short. The Iron Riders set spurs to their steeds, put their heads down, and charged. In a thundering roaring mass of iron they hurtled on.

Nazab Nalgre standing next to me took a few paces back across the ramparts. I stood watching the oncoming avalanche and I half-narrowed my eyes, studying them, thinking, scheming, imagining standing on the ground and facing that little lot. . . .

Of course, the radvakkas had to halt as they reached walls and buildings. Some tried to hack through the barricades we had erected across the ends of the outer streets; but the men I had stationed there reported that the defenses held against this passionate, headlong, ill-considered charge. . . . .

The riders began to mill, some fell back, others started to
109

gallop around the city seeking an entrance. All the time they were blowing trumpets and horns, yelling, kicking up the devil of a racket. Looking down on them I longed for a great Lohvian longbow and an inexhaustible supply of clothyard shafts.

Presently, the band drew off, waving their spears, shouting, reforming their ranks. They had no real organization apart from the war band clustered about a leader, and of discipline their ideas were that anything they did to an inferior was lawful, and if an inferior objected then they'd strapado him or do something equally unpleasant. Sheer brute force was their guiding principle. Everyone in the city was fully aware of the horrors that would ensue if the radvakkas took the place.

For the rest of the day they surged about, like aimless waves, rushing forward, recoiling, riding about, showing off, attempting to awe us. Steadily the citizens improved the barricades. The radvakkas were cavalry—heavy armored cavalry. They had many campfollowers and slaves, who walked or rode in the band's wagons. Of infantry they had none. The concept of a man attempting to conduct fighting standing on his own feet was to them not so much ludicrous as insane.

Mind you, in the last idea, my Clansmen shared much. They did fight on foot, for they had experience of the occasional necessity of that on the Great Plains. But any Clansman would regard saddleback fighting as the normal fashion.

When the suns began to decline the radvakkas hauled off and rode back to their camps, which ringed the city, and the fires blazed up. They were finished for the day. The morrow would bring fresh problems, and I would be up nearly all the night organizing.

At meetings with the various civic leaders their questions were all the same and my answers uniformly simple.

"How can we resist them?"

"They cannot break into the city."

"But they will starve us out."

"If we let them. We have food for six or seven months of the Maiden with the Many Smiles. In that time we shall organize. Do as I tell you. Obey me. Have courage. Have confidence."

"But, Jen Jak—"

"Buts are not wanted here, koters. You are citizens of a great city. You have the skills, the discipline, the power. I

110

shall channel that. Believe in me. And, always, remember you are Vallians."

"Vallia is destroyed, the empire fallen—even the emperor is dead."

"So I am told. So we fight for Vallia through the pride you have in your city of Therminsax. Are you not a city of an imperial province?"

"We obey the Justicar through habit, we think, and we tremble for the fearful evils—"

"Enough!"

In one fashion or another the meetings ended on the same note.

"Enough babbling like witless onkers, like wailing women. You are men. Vallians. From Therminsax we will destroy these Iron Riders who camp so uselessly outside our walls. And then we shall march and destroy the remainder. I have spoken. Do as I command—in the name of Vallia!"

CHAPTER THIRTEEN

◆◆◆

The Raid Against the Radvakkas

Clouds sped erratically across the faces of the Twins and the Maiden with the Many Smiles. The land breathed with the quietness of a country night. At our backs the bulk of the city rose against the sky, ill-defined, speckled here and there with lights. The civic leaders were carrying out strict instructions to make sure their people stood an alert watch along the walls and at the barricades. I stole silently across the sleeping land, heading for the nearest radvakka camp. With me came a choice band of desperadoes from Naghan ti Lodkwara's Hawkwas, and a few lively spirits from the city.

The days had been spinning past and I had already set in motion many of the measures needful for the safety of the city and the prosecution of the war against The Iron Riders.

Although it had seemed to me everything lay to my hand; the task was not easy. I had already fashioned a number of armies for specific purposes on Kregen—Fetching the young people of Valka out of the Heart Heights to defeat the slavers and aragorn; creating an army for the Miglas to defeat the Canops; forming the phalanx of my old vosk-skulls from the slaves and workers of the warrens in Magdag; and others I have not mentioned. But now when I thought the task would be relatively simple I was finding odd, stupid, little impediments.

Naghan whispered. "There is a camp, jen."

We approached cautiously upwind so as not to alarm the benhoffs, tethered out in long lines. We carried flint and steel and armfuls of combustible. We were a grim and deadly bunch and were not a party to be met with lightly on an overcast night.

Stealing on we passed the first rows of leather tents. We left them strictly alone. A sentry, riding his benhoff, for no self-respecting radvakka would walk when he could ride, was dealt with, silently. A leap onto those skinny hindquarters—hind-sixths—and a grip around his mouth, a heave and a thump. We pressed on. And all the time I was only half there in this raid to create mayhem, for my thoughts kept going to the preparations to be made.

The rapier and left-hand dagger were the arms of the gentlefolk of Vallia at that time, and the clanxer—the common clanxer, as it was called—was coming more and more into favor as the people witnessed the execution of the Hamalese thraxter, which the clanxer resembled. I had with Naghan the Gnat designed new styles of weapons in the armories of Valka, and the new sword we had developed from the thraxter, the clanxer and the shortsword, now equipped the regiments of Valka. Those regiments had been dispersed through the orders of the emperor and the wiles of Ashti Melekhi and Layco Jhansi. Well, much good it had done them. . . .

But Therminsax was not plentifully supplied with iron and steel. We must husband all we had. The women and girls were busily making arrows, and we were using flint heads, for flint is often sharper than steel and is never scorned by even the famed Bowmen of Loh. The bows themselves were compound, fashioned from horn and wood and sinew; but even then our numbers of men who could use a bow were limited. We were fortunate in having Larghos the Bow with us, for his family had been making bows for generations for the city and the districts around.

Now we approached the compound where the slaves were

quartered. The meanest of the slaves would be chained up for the night. Those more privileged, those whom I, probably erroneously, call helots, would sleep nearer their masters.

Cautiously, we stole into the compound and started our work.

Slaves—well, there were many slaves in Therminsax, and they were going to prove a problem.

Because of the ease with which The Iron Riders had ridden over and through the legions of Hamal, it was clear to all that a relatively thin line of sword and shield men would never stop a radvakka charge. We had no aerial cavalry and no fliers. We did have one preysany, though. . . . At that comical thought I came back to the present and heard Naghan whispering fiercely to the freed slaves. I did not think they would wait until we had fired the tents before they broke out; but we had to try.

Just as Foke the Waso struck a light and blew on the tinder the Maiden with the Many Smiles broke free of cloud wrack and cast her fuzzy pinkish light over the sleeping camp. We froze. The freed slaves, taking this sudden appearance of the Moon as a sign, broke out. Yelling and screaming and whirling their chains, they surged in a tide of vengeance against the leather tents. I cursed.

"Time to go, Naghan. Pull your men back. Chuck the fire pots and let us get out of here."

"Quidang, jen!" The firepots flew, setting the nearer tents afire. The dried leather burned clammily, belching smoke. But fire shot up satisfactorily from piled stores. We ran from tent to tent, hurling firepots, which contained combustibles and were surer for this work than simple firebrands. We reached the benhoff lines. The animals were restless, stamping their hooves, tossing their heads, letting rip with that raucous whinnying belching sound they have.

"Up with you, Hawkwas all!"

There was only fractional hesitation.

"If you can ride totrixes and hirvels in Sakwara, you can ride benhoffs in Thermin. Mount! Ride!"

There is a fellow in North Yorkshire in England who has trained bulls to be saddled and ridden and jumped. To a Kregen the idea of riding any sort of suitable animal is natural. The Hawkwas mounted up and, bareback, we belted out of the camp.

Uproar rose behind us. Flames leaping, slaves shrilling,

113

radvakkas roaring in rage and tumbling out, women screaming.

We left them to it and racketed back across the land toward the gate of the city where a guard waited to open for us.

I twisted around to look back. By Krun! Following the lead we gave a whole bunch of benhoffs charged out of their lines, pelting along in our wake. Their hooves thundered. We sped along. Clouds obscured the Moon for a space and then shifted across, intermittent shafts of pinkish light flooding down as the Twins rode free. In that hallucinatory light I saw a group of riders bearing in from the side, aiming to join us.

Naghan shrilled a warning, and then the newcomers were yelling: "Vallia! Vallia!"

Well, that is an old trick. I hefted my thraxter, ready to fend them off. My only object this night was to cause confusion to the radvakkas, as much damage as we could, but, mainly to let them know they fought warriors and their task ahead was going to be difficult and unpleasant.

The riders raced along on our flanks. There were totrixes, hirvels, a couple of nikvoves, and a few zorcas. Fleetly, the riding animals closed with us. I saw the fierce dark faces, the flash of eye and teeth, the glitter of weapons.

Now the radvakkas were swarming out of their camp, like a swarm of enraged bees, racketing over the plain after us. In a bunch, we raced ahead of them.

"Vallia!" yelled a man on a zorca, riding with that long-legged, loose style. "Let us into the city!"

As to that, I said to myself, we will see. . . . I didn't like the way he said Vallia, the way his tongue twisted around the word. I kept a wary eye on the newcomers as we fleeted toward the walls. Riding the benhoffs bareback my people jerked and swayed, gripping on, grasping their mounts convulsively. The zorcas moved ahead with their superb speed, and their riders eased them back, to pace the slower totrixes. To pace the slower anything, I should say, for, indeed, the four-legged, close-coupled zorca with his single central spiral horn is an animal of fire and spirit and enormous heart and gusto, superb, superb. . . . We crashed on and the radvakkas shrilled in pursuit.

By the time we neared the gate and saw the busy figures of Therminsaxers swinging the lenken portals wide I had more or less convinced myself that the riders who had so unexpectedly joined us were in truth Vallians. Riding as we were without saddles, we would have been easy meat for these men

114

settled firmly in their saddles, booted feet thrust deeply into stirrups.

In a mob we avalanched through the gate. Nodgen the Potter was in charge of the gate detail, and he had sense enough to allow the following benhoffs through as I yelled to him. The three Moons now chose to shine forth at last free of the clinging clouds. We saw the mass of Iron Riders pelting along, the pink light gleaming and sheening on their armor, their shaggy pelts flaring in the wind of their passage.

The last free benhoff lumbered through and Nodgen the Potter yelled to his men to slam the gates and set the bolts and bars. He was a potter, a master of his khand, his guild, and violently resentful of being called Nodgen the Pots. The gates slammed in the furious faces of The Iron Riders. Some of the citizens on the walls above called down taunts and insults, catcalls that infuriated the radvakkas even more, and gave me heart. We'd do it, yet, despite the difficulties. If we did not, we'd all be miserably dead or even more miserably slave.

Half a dozen dark desperate figures dropped off the last free benhoffs. Before my men could start in prodding with their spears I yelled.

"Do not harm them! They are escaped slaves—welcome them."

Well, we sorted out that little problem. These men had chosen what was, in truth for them, a sensible course, and clambered onto benhoffs to ride after us rather than wander about outside, in the almost certainty of being taken up. I spoke a few heartening words to them and then turned my attention to the group of riders who had joined us.

They were a mixed bunch of apims and diffs—and one diff I recognized at once, now I could see them by the light of a torch bracketed to the wall of the guard tower. I knew him. He was unmistakable.

"Hai, Korero," I said, walking across. "Lahal and Lahal. You are most welcome."

The Kildoi flexed his four arms and his wicked tail shipped over his head. His golden beard bristled. "If I am welcome, Jak the Drang, I would welcome an overflowing tankard of good Thermin ale. Lahal and Lahal. I joy to see you still alive, for I do not forget what passed in Nikwald."

"As to that, the joy was to me. How came you here? These others—" And I looked at them. Well.

Of course I had immediately noticed Korero. But the others—I had told them I was going to Therminsax, and they had shuffled that off, down by that stream outside Thiurdsmot with a crossbow bolt hole in my thigh. Cleitar the Smith still held his hammer, and the head was darkly stained. Dorgo the Clis, his scar livid, spoke for them all.

"We came to Therminsax, because you said so, Jak the Drang." He shook his head, puzzled. "Although why we should do so is a mystery. "But you are in poor case, it seems. We bided our time out there, wondering how best to chop off a few radvakka heads, when you sallied. So—"

"And right welcome you are, Dorgo, all of you. We need fighting men here. And we have ale and wine—the city fathers will bless you and see you have full cups for tonight."

Two men rather in the background, holding zorcas, with a bunch of diffs now moved forward. Dorgo looked and said: "We met these paktuns on the way here. They tell us they are all that is left of an army sent against the radvakkas." He shook his head again and I guessed he was wondering why on Kregen he had come to Therminsax instead of hightailing it for South Vallia.

Among the diffs were Khibils, Pachaks, Brokelsh, a Rapa and a Fristle. They were all hard-bitten professional fighting men, paktuns, mercenaries. One of them, one of the four Chuliks, stepped forward. He looked mightily impressive in his armor and military insignia, his tusks thrusting arrogantly up from his cruel curved mouth. He surveyed me.

"I am Shudor Maklechuan, called Shudor the Mak. I command here. If you wish us to fight for you, I will draw out a contract. Our fees are high, for we are mighty men."

"I might have expected it, by Vox," I said. I'd been having trouble with the city fathers and the khands over similar monetary arrangements. "No doubt you are capable of bearing arms. As to payment, I am prepared to give you a trial period. I see you wear the mortilhead, so you are a paktun. How many other of your men wear the pakmort?"

"Me!" and "Me!" rose from his men. There were thirty or forty of them, and of that number no fewer than ten were real paktuns. There was not a hyr-paktun, however.

The two men I had noticed gentling the zorcas, caring for them, seemed to be arguing away over some private matter. Their fierce whispers were intended for their own ears; but the heat of the matter made them speak louder and louder. Shudor the Mak turned his head and bellowed: "You two arguing again? May Likshu the Treacherous be my witness! Zarado—cease mewling and leave well alone."

The two men withdrew and they did not stop arguing.

116

They were shadows in the angle of a buttress and so I could not distinguish the details of their accoutrements or weapons. The Chulik paktun swung back to me, very grim, very fierce.

"As to a trial period, dom, that remains—"

"I am called Jak the Drang and you call me jen," I butted in, very sharpish, very prickly. "I hold the commission of command from the emperor's Justicar here. I do not doubt you are lusty fighting rogues; but in these evil days one may be forgiven for suspecting masichieri calling themselves paktuns." Before he could get another word in I went on forcefully: "Now take your men and the city fathers will find you quarters. We are in bad case here; but the radvakkas cannot break in. Soon we will sally out and defeat them utterly. In that day I expect you, Shudor the Mak, and your men, to earn your hire."

He took a good look at me, sizing up my mettle. Then he nodded. If I thought this confrontation was over I was mistaken. One of the Pachaks stepped forward. He wore the pakmort. He spoke in that precise, elegant and yet firm manner of the Pachaks.

"We may take nikobi, jen Jak, if the contract is drawn out properly. Our last nikobi was shattered on the field of battle."

"I welcome you, paktun. Your name?"

"I am Logu Na-Pe, paktun, at present tazll but willing to take employment in a good cause—if the cash is right."

"The cash will be right, and the nikobi, Logu Na-Pe."

So I saw them off to their quarters in a comfortable inn and felt a little cheered. They were hard fighting men, all of them, professionals. They were a valuable addition to our forces. But they were few, very few. . . .

There was a great deal to be seen to, well, there always is, by Vox, but particularly so when you not only conduct the defense of a city but also seek to create an army from nothing. So I was kept busy. The saddle animals we had acquired would be useful in a sally; and if the time for the great offensive was long delayed and the fodder ran out, then we'd most likely end up eating these fine steeds. That would be a great pity. But it would be done, that was true, by Zair!

The great advantage of a citizen army is the habit of working together, of order and discipline, ingrained into city folk, as distinct from the wilder and more independent mind of countrymen. We were citizens arrayed against barbarians. Well, if we couldn't beat that illiterate mob outside we had no right to call ourselves citizens, or to inhabit so fine a place as Therminsax. Numbers, solidity, strength; these were our tools for the job, our weapons of war.

Toward morning, wandering back to the imperial Justicar's palace where I had set up headquarters, I passed the inn where the paktuns had been quartered. This was *The Golden Ponsho*. I thought a little quench would do me good, before I turned in, and I might find some of the paktuns about to talk to them and find out a little more of their history. So I went in, ducking my head under the old blackwood beams.

Two men in white tunics sat at a table, their slippered feet stuck out, arguing away. One, I knew, was Zarado. I helped myself to a flagon of wine and sat down near them. A few other paktuns were still drinking; most had turned in.

"Oh, yes," this Zarado was saying. "The Iron Riders are a fierce-looking bunch, Zunder. I know, I know. But I wonder how they would fare, say, against the overlords——"

"I'd like to see it!" burst out this Zunder, a man with dark moustaches, fiercely-brushed up. "By Zim-Zair! I'd relish the sight of these Grodno-Gastas charging the Overlords of Magdag!"

CHAPTER FOURTEEN

News of Pur Zeg, Krzy and Pur Jaidur, Krzy

The flagon halted before my lips. I did not move—could not move.

"May Zantristar the Merciful smile on us! The city is filled with hulus—fambly ready for the reaping. We should never have left the ship in the first place——"

"And whose idea, by Zair, was that? If you'd listened to me we'd be snugly supping in The Fleeced Ponsho again, instead of in some outlandish place at the end of nowhere."

"Me! You were the one who said there was gold flowing out of the rocks in this place! I was for returning to Donengil!"

"And who said we should sign on with those rasts of Maybers? We're a damned long way from home, by Zim-Zair!"

I moved again. I drank. I spilled wine. They looked across and Zarado, his dark curled hair sheening under the lamps, said, "I do not wonder that you are frightened, by the disgusting diseased liver and lights of Makki-Grodno, dom. How came you people to be mewed up here?"

Zunder nudged him. "You great onker! That is the jernu, here, the lord. He was the one telling Shudor the Mak—"

"Oh! Well, I didn't see him—you were nattering away in my ear like two nits dancing in a ponsho fleece."

"Do you call me a nit, Zarado, the sweepings of a Magdaggian gutter? I'll—"

I think they might have wrestled a space then, for it was clear they were good comrades, and continually at odds, one with the other, over everything. And, if no real excuse for an argument could be found, then they'd fabricate one, and joy in the ensuing combat. But I stopped them. I stood up and taking my flagon moved across to their table.

"Lahal, koters," I said. "How came you here?"

I saw their swords now, jutting under the table. Krozair longswords—by their words and their swords I knew they were Krozairs, and not ordinary warriors of Zairia.

By Zair! How I thought of my roistering days on the inner sea, the Eye of the World! My sons were there now; Pur Zeg and Pur Jaidur, both Krozairs of Zy, as was I. I wanted to know of these two—and yet to enquire, to ask the ritual words and forms, to shake hands, would betray me as a Krozair and that would lead to far too many complications.

But I had to know.

"I think," I said, speaking companionably "that you are from Turismond—"

"Yes, jernu," said Zarado. "But you would not know of our homes, seeing this place is so far removed—"

Here Zunder nudged him again. A right tearaway, this Zarado, bellowing his head off without thought.

"You forget, the galleons of Vallia sail the oceans. They have sailed even so far as a place called Magdag."

They both reacted at this, swearing that they'd like to do certain unmentionable things to the Grodnims of Magdag—and then Zunder said, sharply: "And, jernu, you have been there?"

"Aye."

"And to Sanurkazz?"

"Aye."

They sat back. "Well," said Zarado. "You are the first

person we have met since leaving the Dam of Days who knows a little, who shows some knowledge of the world."

This was typical, this regard for the Eye of the World as the center of existence, and the greater outer oceans as being merely the frame. I well understood that. But I pressed on: "I met a man there who said he was a—" I paused, as though searching my memory. "He was a Krossur—no, a Krozair. Yes. Do you know of these Krozairs?"

They exchanged swift looks. I did not think they were Krozairs of Zy; there was something about them, small signs by which a member of the Order of Zy can tell.

Then Zarado laughed in his bluff Zairian way. Disorderly, harebrained, indisciplined, the Zairians. I suppose that very face has produced the mystic Disciplines that make of the Krozair Orders the fanatically disciplined institutions they are. And, I was attempting to bring some of the best qualities of the Krozairs to my Krovere Brotherhood of Iztar.

"What harm is there, Zunder? We will be fighting alongside him before long, and likely all to go down to the Ice Floes of Sicce."

"Or go to sit on the right hand side of Zair in the glory of Zim," I said.

Zunder pursed his lips, let out a sigh, and drank deeply. Zarado merely looked at me. Presently, Zunder said: "So it seems you kept your ears open in Sanurkazz. I, myself, am of Zimuzz."

So that placed him. I turned to Zarado enquiringly.

"Me? Of Zamu."

I know I have a habit of letting rip with a few choice phrases every now and then, in the heat of the moment, and so I said: "I kept my ears open. Also, I may, from time to time, call upon Zair. I mean no disrespect by that."

"If I thought you did," said Zunder, conversationally, "your tripes would be all over the floor before you could spit."

"Aye," said Zarado, quite calmly.

I approved. . . .

We talked a little more, and I intimated gently that I was interested only in their prowess as fighting men for Therminsax. I managed to progress no further in enquiries about my sons, until a chance remark threw up the name of Zy, at which I came quiveringly alert. But to ask outright would be foolhardy, for it was much like a man of Manhattan asking a Borneo headhunter similar questions, and not expecting to be credited with specialist and, probably, partial knowledge.

I had a happy inspiration, at last, for obvious reasons not even thinking of the ploy until Zarado, yawning, said: "By Mother Zinzu the Blessed! I needed that—but now I am for bed. I am not your Pur Dray Prescot, jernu."

The door was opened.

"He," I said. "Is the prince majister of Vallia."

"So they say, so they say. But he is a Krozair of Zy and that is much more important. His sons carry on in fine style—" Here Zunder made a face. "I would not admit this if I was a flagon more sober. I would as lief have joined the Order of Zy—but fate decreed otherwise."

"Ha," said Zarado.

"The welfare of the sons of the prince majister is of very great importance," I said. I saw the quick way they looked at me, and knew my carved figurehead of a face was giving away more than I wanted. Neither of these two had ever seen Pur Dray, Krzy, obviously. "Are they well? Are they great Krozairs?"

"They do well, as you would expect—"

You may imagine how I listened as Zarado and Zunder between them gave me a rundown on the exploits and rogueries of my two sons on the Eye of the World. They lived. They fought the devils of Grodno, they prospered, and their swifters brought back prizes season by season. Zeg, as King of Zandikar, was growing to be a great power on the inner sea. His fleet was becoming a powerful instrument in the eternal struggle of Zairian against Grodnim. So I listened, and eventually, yawning again, Zarado said he was going to bed, or, by Zogo the Hyr-whip, his eyeballs would fall out.

I heard the shrilling of the trumpets from the walls, and so I said: "I think not, Pur Zarado. I think not. The Iron Riders attack. You and your sword may be needed on the walls or at the barricades."

Cursing most fearfully they snatched up their weapons and, clad only in their tunics and slippers, ran out. I was before them. The Iron Riders circled the city, screeching. They swung long weighted ropes, and as they swung them and released, the fiery brands tied to the ends brightened, and sparked, and sprouting flames fell rushing onto the roofs and walls of the city of Therminsax.

CHAPTER FIFTEEN

—◆●◆—

Firebrands

"Water! Water!" The yells bounced into the sky, which, luridly lit by the falling firebrands, pressed down darker than it should. Dawn was not too far off. But the habits of order in the citizenry saw to it that the men appointed by the city fathers to stand their watch at the dawn hour should be awake. Trumpets blew. Men ran with buckets of water. The pandemonium racketed on. People were tumbling out of bed and, half-dressed, rushing to join in the long human chains of bucket-passers and precariously leaning over the parapets to haul that sweet and treacherous water from the canals.

The firechiefs swiftly had the situation under control, for many of the barbarians' brands puffed out in their swift passage, many merely spluttered and died on tiled roofs. Some burned up venomously and caught in combustible materials; and these were attacked with gusto, drenched with water, hammered into black-smoking quiescence.

The attack had come in from the west side of the city where the Letha Brook ran out through a battlemented gate and then, odoriferously, past the vosk-crushing mills and the waste-disposal plants. Downstream all the muck could be washed away from the city. Naturally, the radvakkas had established their main camp to the east, upstream. Their muck floated down to us. In addition, as we discovered with increasing frequency, they threw carcasses and offal and filth into the stream to poison us. Therminsax was provided with wells that produced crystal water, so we cursed the radvakkas, and drank deeply in safety. But with the extinction of the last fires, which took a bit of a hold on the water-mill outside the wall, protected by lesser outer walls and barricades, and a watch being set afresh, I figured that we would have to take steps to unblock the upstream end.

Sleep, then, would have to wait a little longer.

The excitement of the fires had brought the city to life early. As the suns rose with the promise of a fine day, with perhaps a little rain drifting across in the afternoon, perhaps

122

not if the clouds were burned off by then, I paused to watch a group of men attempting to form up in lines. At this early stage I had weeded out all the men of Therminsax who had had military experience of some kind. In the city, to my disappointment although common sense insisted I was lucky to find so many, there were just forty-three men who had once served in an army. There were ten men who had served in galleons, and these lived near and frequented the inn called The Swordship and Barynth. There were, also, over a hundred men who had served in the Vallian Air Service. This, being an imperial service, naturally would take many recruits from the imperial provinces. With these men, then, in the first instance, I had begun.

I had said, speaking forcefully: "I want you to become drill instructors of the most abominable kind. Get the men to march in ranks and files and keep together. If any man complains that you overtax him, or mutters in any way, and you are not able to discipline him yourself, send him to me. I will talk to him."

No one was sent to me.

I really thought, then, that they were under the impression I would personally crop the ears of malcontents. At any rate, the men sweated over their foot drill, learning to keep a dressing and to maintain a steady line. This, as I say, was a beginning.

The men saw me watching them, and a kind of miracle abruptly appeared in their lines. The ranks straightened. They began to march together. The idea of marching in step was well known and practiced; but many of the men with military experience would have no truck with that. They had been paktuns and used to a free and easy life. I had borne down, hard.

Now I stepped across and bellowed: "Halt!"

The ranks ground to a shaky halt, with men bumping the backs of the ranks in front. I started in to harangue them. Briefly, for it was a speech I repeated over and over, I told them they must learn to march in step, to keep their dressing and their distance, and to maintain the different paces as ordered, with an even and regular step, which I had specified out at twenty-eight inches. The figure was not lightly arrived at.

You will recall I had served at Waterloo, where the foundations of my Earthly fortunes had been laid, and I had watched the army, spoken to men and commanders, learned much of the land-side of the Peninsular. The British Army marched with a pace of thirty inches. The French Army with one of twenty-five and a half. While the British marched seventy-five paces to the minute in ordinary time, the French marched at seventy-six. But—the French marched faster than the British. The reason for this lay, therefore, not in statistics.

It was not so much a question of marching faster as of marching better. For what I had in mind for these citizens of Therminsax, accurate and regular marching, all in line, all in step, and all as one body, was vital.

Spending a bur with this body and being properly courteous to the drill instructor with them, one Hargon the Arm, a bluff old fellow with a pot belly, and a fund of stories of his youth when he had been a mercenary and failed—only just missed it by a hair's breadth, by Vox!—to achieve the pakmort, I did feel that they improved. They marched with more of a swing and they kept together. Chalk lines had been marked out on the flags of the kyro to give them their paces and dressing. I bellowed and ran and pushed and hectored, and we all sweated. At the end of the bur I halted them and told them they were coming along nicely and to keep up the good work, and that if they didn't keep together as a strong and ordered formation they wouldn't have to worry so much about the certain fact that the radvakkas would chop them as that I would crop their ears, and that would be far, far worse.

The citizens took turn and turn about to stand watch along the walls and to drill in the open spaces. If any of them thought to wonder how this intensive drilling would help them to fight from the walls, not one ventured to voice the question.

A pungent whiff floated from the warehouses containing hoffiburs and we would have to see them all used up quickly before they went rotten on us. The people were regaining a little of their cheerfulness, and the Vallians, normally a phlegmatic and stubborn but highly independent people when the mood takes them, were of the stuff from which I could fashion a winning instrument of war.

The idea of that could not be allowed to depress me. What I did I did for Vallia, for Delia and, of course, for my family and myself. I made no bones about that. I was a bright devil in the eyes of many people; but I was crass enough to think that I, Dray Prescot, was a lesser evil than the radvakkas of Phu-Si-Yantong. I hope I was right. ₅..

Resuming my walk to the upstream end I found myself, as always, feverishly calculating. Odds and gambles, the certainty of defeat if we sat on our hands and did nothing, the trust I must place in others, the agonizing decisions about delegation of duties and responsibilities. . . . I could not do it all myself. This was an entirely larger operation than that in the warrens of Magdag. I needed men who understood what I wanted, had been trained by me, and who could then train their own men.

And yet—and yet this was altogether on a lesser scale than the warrens. There I had had the services of hundreds of skilled slaves and workers who could fabricate what I needed. Therminsax was well-provided with smiths and with leather-workers and carpenters and trades of that ilk; but, for a start, we were desperately short of iron and steel. Of copper and tin we had bulging warehouses. So, bronze it would be.

The stink wafted toward me as I neared the upstream bridge and gate of the Letha Brook. Rotting carcasses washed downstream now cluttered the iron bars. The filth stank.

"Volunteers," I said. "Volunteers to clear the mess. And bowmen to cover them in case the radvakkas disapprove of our efforts to stay clean."

The job was done. The paktuns who had ridden in brought their bows and crossbows up and we shot off a few radvakkas from their saddles when they ventured too close. The volunteers sweated away in the slime and emerged, panting and odoriferous, with the stream cleared and running sweetly. That would be a daily chore until The Iron Riders saw the uselessness of their efforts to poison us and desisted.

I called a meeting. I did not allow it to be called a Council of War. The city fathers and the civic leaders now well understood that I acted by commission of the Justicar and through him for the emperor. That the emperor was dead was not allowed to confuse the issue. I based the argument on the continuation of Therminsax as a city, and of Vallians as Vallians.

So I outlined what we must do to be saved.

Much of what I told them was very similar to what I had told the slaves and workers of the warrens of Magdag of the Megaliths. We faced a heavily armored cavalry host. We had no cavalry of our own, apart from the almost a hundred ben-hoffs we'd brought in quite inadvertently and the paktuns. Our missile force was limited to around five hundred men who could use the compound bows. Of crossbows we had a small number; but they would have to be discounted, at least from the battle to come although of great use along the walls. And for artillery although the carpenters and smiths were busy building varters and the wheelwrights making them mobile, our standards of proficiency in that arm were almost inevitably bound to fall far below what would be absolutely essential for any traditional use of the artillery arm. So we were thrust back on the mass of the citizens themselves.

In Magdag I had thought we would be fighting from behind walls and in confined spaces of the warrens. In the event we had successfully bested the Overlords of Magdag in the open—and then in a tragedy I still looked back on with fury and regret, had been forced back to the holes and the stinking labyrinth. I'd been hoicked out of it by then, flung by the Star Lords across the Eye of the World, to meet Seg Segutorio. If only Seg was here now! And Inch and Turko and Balass—ah, each one of them would be worth a regiment!

The long room buzzed with talk as, my thoughts for the moment making me fall silent, the chiefs of the city broke into eager, naive, angry, puzzled conversation. One of them said: "We have few swords, jen. We know a little of using spears, by reason of vosk-hunting. But the soldiers of Hamal were beaten by the radvakkas, this you have told us, and they were profoundly impressive warriors—"

"Not warriors," I said. "Profoundly professional, yes. Swods. Soldiers. But they were sword and shield men. We shall beat the radvakkas, as I say, by using a weapon with which they are unfamiliar. It will not work against the Hamalese, and do not forget that in the hour of victory."

Lists had been prepared by the stylors detailing the state of the city's stores. We would have enough, I estimated, just enough; but it would be very tight indeed.

The iron bars in the canals and the Letha Brook were replaced by bronze grilles. All the iron and steel we could discover in the city was meticulously collected up. I showed the smiths a template whittled from wood. The master of the smith's khand, Varo the Hammer, brought up the subject in his turn at the meeting.

"We are making these spearheads, Jen Jak. They consume only a small amount of steel each; but you require a vast number. Yet—" and here he scratched his bristly side-whiskers—"they are main different from any spearheads I have known."

"Before I answer you, Varo, let me ask Rivate the Chisel how he is coming along with the hafts."

Rivate, a dapper little fellow with an eye that could true up a line or an angle to a hair, nodded quickly. "We have produced many hafts to the incredible lengths you ask for,

Jen Jak. The letha wood is of the best quality, as you specified—the trees are being cut down—"

He would have gone on; but I waved a hand.

"These long shafts of springy white letha wood, and these
small sharp steel heads, will make the weapon with which we
will beat the radvakkas. The name of the weapon is pike. The
shafts at the moment are eighteen feet in length; later they
may increase to twenty-two, or be decreased to eleven or
twelve. Just at the moment we must produce them, and train
the men in their use." I stared challengingly at the master
of the carpenter's and smith's khands. "I need sixteen thousand of them."

When the uproar of protestations subsided, I said: "Sixteen
thousand. And the quicker substantial numbers begin to be
produced the quicker we can make a start on thrashing the
radvakkas. The men are already tired of drilling with broom-
sticks."

The question of payment as always came up. I met this in
the same way. "The Justicar is empowered to sign assignats.
The bokkertu is perfectly legal."

They shuffled at this. Each man who signed up in the army
was given an assignat which we all hoped would be collect-
ible. The death of the emperor proved a knotty point; but the
assignats were secured also in the name of Nazab Nalgre and
on lands available in Thermin. More than once I was
tempted to tell them that I had been the fellow to take over
the crown and throne of Vallia—I'd not had my hands on either!—and that I was the emperor and Therminsax the extent
of my empire. I think you will readily see why I did not, and
why I persuaded myself that Jak and Drang could be of more
use than Dray Prescot. Maybe I was wrong; there are those
who say so, but at the time I considered I was pursuing the
correct course.

And that course demanded that I create an impenetrable
phalanx of pikemen upon which The Iron Riders should dash
themselves to destruction.

Plans are usually bedevilled by someone who thinks only
half-logically. I knew I took a terrible risk in thus throwing
all our hopes on this one chance. The Phalanx—well, it had
served me before and, by Zair, it would serve again. But the
chief priest of the temple of Florania—a prissy little man
who devoutly believed in his point of view—had no doubts at
all, that my plans would fail. He gathered his robes about
him and stood up, pointing the forefinger of his free hand at
me.

127

"There sits the man who wishes to cast all our sons down into the bowels of Cottmer's Caverns. The Iron Riders desire plunder. Then let us open our gates and satisfy the greed of the radvakkas, for we are a rich city. We shall, of course, previously hide all our most valuable treasures. When the radvakkas have taken their plunder, they will ride away. Our city will be spared and in a few seasons we will have recouped all our losses." He stared around at the chief priest of Opaz, a spare, ascetic man with feverish eyes and a bad skin that kept erupting in spots and boils. "What say you, brother in Opaz? Are not my words the words of wisdom? Why do we bow the neck so meekly to this wild paktun, Jak the Drang? The emperor is dead and the assignats are worthless. Let us preserve our city."

No one spoke; but all looked at me. I gave a swift glance to the chief priest of Opaz, and saw with that I confess was great relief that he half-turned his shoulder on the priest of Florania. I stood up. I put my hands flat on the table and my old vosk-skull of a head thrust forward, and I do not doubt that my chin stuck out like the ram of a swifter.

"I will tell you, priest of Florania, why we will not open our gates except to march out to fight. I do not like fighting and battles and warfare. I detest and abhor the deaths of fine young men and the wails and agonies of the young girls and of the mothers. You want to open the gates and offer the radvakkas gold and silver, corn and oil and flour, all the good things of Therminsax. And when they have taken what you offer they will laugh. They are illiterate barbarians. But they are not fools. Some of you they will kill at once, as an object lesson. Some, the less fortunate, they will torment until the city rings with their cries of agony, until they are only too thankful to reveal where you have hidden the rest of your wealth. And then they will slay you all, after they have had their sport with you and your women folk. If you want that, priest of Florania, open the gates and welcome The Iron Riders."

He tried to bluster. "You do not know that! They were resisted by the Hamalese at Cansinsax and Thiurdsmot and Meersakden. There are many millers and master bakers in my congregation, devout men, and my power—"

"We shall have scant need for millers and bakers before long," I interrupted, uncouthly. "And if you have had information you should tell us. I know of Cansinsax and Thiurdsmot—what of Meersakden?"

This was a fine city of Sakwara, of which I had heard, containing better than seventy thousand souls.

"The Hamalese were routed by two bands of radvakkas. There are two bands outside our walls. You cannot hope to beat them—"

"I do not hope, priest of Florania. I *know!* They will be destroyed, they will be utterly discomfitted by the Phalanx of Therminsax. And," and here I put a great venom and a horrible evil into my voice and face. "And if you try to play the traitor or speak against the honest burghers of the city, you will be restrained, placed in irons, and cast down the dungeons beneath the Justicar's deren. Is that clear?"

We sat in the council chamber of the deren—the palace— and we all knew that there were noxious dungeons below. He flushed up. I felt quite sorry for him; but he was wrong, so wrong that if he had his way he would open the city to death and torment in forms so hideous he could never comprehend them. But, then, he had had no dealings with The Iron Riders.

The chief priest of Opaz, scratching his cheek, said in a gentle voice: "Sit down, brother, and keep your peace."

With that out of the way we could go on to plan just how we would fashion the killing instrument of victory we planned to hurl against the mailed cavalry of The Iron Riders.

CHAPTER SIXTEEN

In Crimson and Bronze the Brumbytes Form

The days passed. The men sweated and marched and drilled. We had them learning how to march in file, for the organization would be based on the file. I prefer the line; but in this instance the file seemed to be the correct procedure.

The pikes were produced from the manufactories. Also the superb springy white wood of the letha tree, somewhat like ash, was mated to steel heads fashioned with spike, hook and axe, hefty, vicious cutting weapons, halberds. Leather jerkins were wired and sewn with bronze plates to form corselets, and shoulder pieces were artfully fixed at the back to be drawn over and fastened on the chest. The same old arguments went on over shields; but the citizens were not warriors and they were far more pragmatical about the thorny question of shield and no-shield. They had seen the Hamalese and their shields, and although the regiments of Hamal had been defeated, still, it struck the citizens as eminently sensible to have something behind which to stand. The shields, in a very real sense, were to them a continuation of the city walls and barricades. From chin to thigh, the shields were designed to protect a man. Also, springy bronze greaves were made for the lower legs. Now, helmets—the manufacturing capability of the city was fully stretched.

Well, the old vosk-skulls had surged forward under a rain of arrows before; they would do so again.

Vosk-skulls are notoriously hard. Piles and piles of them may be found outside most habitations of men on Kregen. The Vallians had built water mills and by harnessing the power of rushing streams had built trip-hammers that, with difficulty, could smash and crush the skulls to form a fine fertilizer. The vosk-crushing mill had almost burned. Around it were heaped and piled the skulls, hard as iron, waiting to be processed. We took these skulls, removed the jaws, scoured them out, affixed leather and quilted linings, riveted straps, added high brims to protect the eyes and grilled or barred face-coverings. For the nape of the neck overlapping and sliding bronze plates formed the well-known lobster-tail.

I rather liked the look of the resultant helmets. Grim, rounded, well-fashioned and offering high protection, they looked business-like.

Then I ran into a little example of the power of legend and story.

"But we must have plumes!" exclaimed the Justicar. We were watching men being issued with the helmets and relishing the looks of pleasure as the men felt the protection as well as the weight come on their heads. Foreheads must be well-padded. The helmets must sit firmly and yet not too tightly, not too loosely. The brim must give protection from falling arrows.

"Plumes?"

"Aye, Jen. Feathers and Plumes."

Then the Justicar and his council produced the old stories and showed the old books. All heroes had tall and imposing plumes in their helmets.

130

"We are not heroes," I said. "We are sober citizens doing a job of work."

But they wouldn't have it. So plumes were affixed to the helmets by thin bronze strips, and, of course, the majority clamored for that fashion of plume that rises like a giant question mark from the crown of the helmet. I had to give way.

I did say: "If a sword or axe strikes that plume-holder it'll knock your hemlet off—if it doesn't break your neck."

So the Justicar's people, with enormous glee, arranged the tall nodding plumes with holders of stiffened leather which would be cut off or bent when struck. I left them to it, mindful of the thought that in this they showed themselves to be their own men, and increased their importance in their own eyes.

We were distressingly short on swords, and so I could not contemplate, with the scarcity of steel, the mass manufacture of two-handed swords, which would have worked wonders on the iron armor of the radvakkas. Stabbing spears had to be substituted and long knives. Anyway, for handstrokes the halberds and axes would do a fine job—or so I hoped.

While these preparations continued and increased in tempo day by day as the people saw the results of their work, and the men drilled in their files, and the files joined together in ranks and grew daily more solid and regular, I worried over the tactical aspects I must decide.

It was clear to us all in the ringed city that the radvakkas, having plundered the surrounding countryside and being awash with food and wine and good things, were content to sit down and starve us out. They tried their fire-throwing a couple of times further; but our fire service quenched the flames with ease.

We kept an alert watch at all times; the radvakkas made not a single attempt to scale the walls. If they couldn't ride their benhoffs, then they weren't interested. All day they rode about and we watched them in mock combats, in sports, in drunken orgies. All in all, the time passed, and still the tactical questions remained unanswered.

The men in the files would be armored as best we could manage. They would carry pikes and shields. If the Macedonian and Successor phalanxes could contrive that, then so could we. The Renaissance and pike and shot man did not carry a shield—or not very often—but the cavalry charge had dwindled away a trifle by his time from the mailed charge of chivalry, resplendent in the panoply of plate. I wor-

131

ried over our serious lack of missile power. Our five hundred archers practiced religiously each day and the stock of arrows grew. Once the Phalanx had come to grips with the foe then I was completely convinced we would succeed. It was getting them there, and protecting their flanks, that exercised my mind.

Because Europe pushed out into the world, the military institutions and titles familiar to us came into very wide being. On Kregen the Empire of Loh had given the impetus to the terminology with which, so far, I have acquainted you in these tapes. As the Landsknechts handed down administrative ideas and organizations to succeeding armies, so the army of Walfarg that carved out the Empire of Loh left its methods to Havilfar and Pandahem and to Vallia, also.

With the eager help of the Justicar, who delved deeply into th history of Kregen, we reached past the time of Chuktars and Jiktars, of Hikdars and Deldars, back to a time when the organization of warriors was based on the figure six—one of the twin calculating systems of Kregen.

"Twelve men to a file," I said. "With the file leader, the Faxul, in front, where he belongs. A half-file leader, the Nik-Faxul, and two quarter-file leaders, the Laik-Faxuls, each in their allotted stations. And, in the rear, the file-closer, the Bratchlin. He should be a steady man, hardy and stubborn, and, I may add, ready to thump a comrade in front who lags too tardily."

The Justicar pored over his dusty tomes, bashing the stiff pages open in his enthusiasm. The pages were filled with colored illustrations of the pageantry of old, filled with the legends and heroic stories of Kregen—the Quest of Tyr Nath, King Naghan, the Canticles of the Rose City, Prince Nalgre, and many many more.

"I have the utmost confidence in you, Jak the Drang. Where you came from, Opaz knows; but, also, thanks be to Opaz you came to our city. We would have been lost without you."

"Vallia," I said, foolishly touched by his words. "I am concerned for the people of Vallia." I would have to break the news to him about the slaves, and then he and his wealthy friends might not be so kindly disposed toward me.

"Each file of twelve joined with two others, the whole commanded by a Danmork, the center file by a Terfaxul, just so that there is no confusion who gives the orders when they suffer casualties, or form close order."

The Justicar nodded, no doubt thinking of the pageantry of

the men marching shoulder to shoulder, their bright plumes nodding proudly over the serried ranks.

"Twelve files to form a Reliannch," I went on, roughing out the diagrams with paper and ink. "The whole one hundred and forty-four commanded by the Relianchun, marching at front and right, and assisted in command of the second half of six files by the Paltork. Yes, it is a plan almost like others I know of, and yet adapted to our needs. Each Reliannch of a hundred and forty-four men will have its own flankers of medium men, halberdiers and axemen, the Hakkodin, twenty-four of them, with their own file leaders and half and quarter file leaders." I did not smile, but I felt my lips rick. "I shall choose these Hakkodin, these men to guard the flanks, carefully. They will not have a file closer, a Bratchlin, with them."

Slaves pattered into the airy room in a brightly lit tower of the Justicar's deren bringing trays loaded with the superb Kregan tea and miscils and palines. We were not hungry yet, in the beleaguered city. But I had to get my phalanx organized and trained, disciplined, able to march in step and line, perfectly moving as a single gigantic organism. "There will be six Reliannches to a Jodhri," I said. "Eight hundred sixty-four pikemen and one hundred forty-four Hakkodin to a Jodhri commanded by a Jodrivax."

We drank the tea and wiped our lips and then sorted through a list of stores stylors brought in demanding instant attention. Also, a lesser chamberlain reported that a certain butcher was charging ten times his normal prices for meat. I told Nazab Nalgre to send around first of all a deputation from the butcher's khand to reason with the fellow and to bring his prices to levels where the folk might afford meat. If he would not accord with common decency then we'd send around a posse of our volunteer pikemen to make him see sense. The people of Therminsax were one—or ought to be one. I knew enough about sieges to know that those in authority must never be seen to favor any one class over another—save, always, that the fighting men must eat. And, of course, if this damned siege was prolonged, therein lay the rub. Not that this was a siege in the real meaning of the term.

Those illiterate unwashed hairy barbarians outside had no real idea how to prosecute a siege. Had we faced them when we'd been hemmed in in Zandikar, we'd have laughed at them. So we went back to the organization of the phalanx, for, as you will readily perceive, this was my way of obtaining the positions in the phalanx for the men I wanted there.

"Each Jodhri will be one thousand and eight men strong. Six of them, I think, will form a Kerchuri, six thousand and forty-eight men strong." I cocked an eye at the Justicar. Nazab Nalgre was looking pleased that his old legends with their continual references to the six and twelve organization and the names of ranks was once more coming into use. He was a fine antiquary, whatever kind of imperial Justicar he might be. "We may find that unwieldy. But I want two commanders of the Kerchuris appointed, two Kerchurivaxes."

"You have the men in mind, Jen Jak?"

I nodded. "Aye."

He studied my face. I knew that the commanders of the two wings of the phalanx would have to be Therminsaxers. There were many bright sparks anxious to command, although very many of the lesser nobility had already packed up and left long before the radvakkas appeared, and many women and children, also, had left.

"Men of integrity, stubborn, physically strong, courageous," I told Nazab Nalgre, speaking a trifle heavily, I fear, "Men who have a presence, who know they will be obeyed when they give an order. Men who are respected by their fellows."

I merely described the generality of Vallian koters.

"They must be Therminsaxers," I went on. "Otherwise I've half a mind to install that defiant man Cleitar the Smith, for I know him to have discovered he is a bonny fighter when it comes to push of pike. I want Targon the Tapster to handle the Hakkodin." I looked directly at Nazab Nalgre. "Your son, Nalgre, your fine limber young son, Nath. He will command the first Kerchuri."

I brushed away Nazab Nalgre's babble. I was doing him no favor. But Nath na Therminsax, for he was allowed to adopt his father's style for all he had no rank of nobility so far, was a fine young man in truth and, over and above all the qualities I have enumerated, he was quick-witted. "I will make a break with tradition here, Nalgre, and Nath will ride a mount and conduct affairs from outside the Kerchuri. The right hand position—the lynch-pin—will be taken by that pillar of the city, Bondur Darnhan. The second Kerchuri will be commanded by Strom Varga, and the right-hand man will be Jando Quevada." I sighed. "I pray to Opaz they will live through the battle. But the front rank men—well, that is why

134

they are there, why they wear the tapes and the feathers, why they are respected, why they are followed."

Nalgre nodded brightly, seeing only the brilliant nodding plumes over the massed files, the onward surge, the pageantry and honor, seeing his son Nath riding back with the victory. Again I sighed. When honest citizens turn their hands to war they are usually highly practical; Nazab Nalgre, the Justicar of Therminsax, shared the other side of that character, the romantic, the high idealism, the shining honor. He was a man of parts, for the governor of an imperial province, called a Nazab, ranks with a kov. His son Nath might if he wished take the surname Nazabhan. Delia's father had not been altogether a fool in his choice of men to run his affairs, and although he had been sadly led astray in his capital of Vondium, he had appointed sound men in his provinces. Nazab Nalgre was now fully recovered from that mortifying crisis of nerves that had afflicted him after the Hamalese rode out.

Continually, the Justicar moved among the training men, exhorting them to effort, to the acquisition of the skills they must have. The paktuns smiled and quoted the old proverbs about the length of time it takes to make a fighting man; but I put my faith in the innate solidity of the burghers, their strong feelings for their city, their orderly habits of mind, and saw day by day the growing cohesion of the phalanx. Mind you, we carried out most evolutions at this time with the Relianch, the tactical unit. When six Relianches formed and stood shoulder to shoulder in a Jodhri, and we filled the kyros with the Jodhris formed in file, then we could bring them into close order and present a front of four hundred and thirty-two pikes. Drummer boys, four to a Reliance, the trumpeters, sounded the orders, the drums with their solemn and deep blam-blam-berram to keep the step, the trumpets to shrill their commands.

In the manner of these things, just how the name began no one could tell; but folk began to talk of the pikemen in the files as brumbytes. The brumby was—I say was for the animal was thought to be extinct or legendary—a powerful eight-legged and armored battering ram of whirlwind destruction, armed with a long straight horn in the center of his forehead. Something like an elegant rhinoceros, the brumby symbolised the headlong energy of the pikemen. At once I gave orders that the shields should bear a painted and stylized representation of this formidable beast, along with the formation signs. The ordinary brumbyte carried a clear strip across the top of his shield. The differing ranks in the duodecimal system then carried stripes of color to indicate their status, rising from a single stripe—complemented with a single tape on the buff-sleeved shirt and a single feather alongside the helmet plume—to the four tapes and two stars of a Paltork.

The shields, bronze-rimmed and bronze-bossed, were crimson, the imperial color. The First Kerchuri carried a broad brown chevron and the Second a brown ring upon the crimson.

All main plumes were of crimson. The tails were colored Jodhri by Jodhri. As I said to the officers: "We present a solid mass, a devastating avalanche of crimson and bronze." Then, because these things matter, I added: "But the brumbytes may decorate their kaxes in any way they wish, so long as they do not destroy either their effectiveness or their suppleness."

The brumbytes sang as they marched to the beat of the drum, manipulating their pikes with growing confidence, although you may be sure there were some horrendous tangles at first. When a fellow tried to make a right turn with his pike horizontal—well, the imagination does not boggle, but he became highly unpopular with the brumbytes in the files near him.

Colors, flags, standards, were carried; but these would only be a hindrance after the onslaught and arrangements were made for them to pass to the rear. Each Relianch had its color, of course, and a grave variety they made, all based on the imperial crimson.

One evening when I was at last beginning to think we were in some cases to march out, Archeli the Sniz reported to me, allowed immediate access as I had ordered. He was a sly, prying little fellow, recommended to me by the Justicar, and I had set him to spy upon the chief priest of Florania.

"Jen!" he said, speaking quickly. The gathered city fathers and officers looked up from their work at the long tables. "The cramph has been in communication with the radvakkas. I did not know what he purported—but now I know he means to open the Gate of Aman Deffler to them. And, Jen, the task was difficult—"

"Yes, Archeli. It was. Go on."

"Tonight, Jen. Tonight he means to open and let them in."

CHAPTER SEVENTEEN

The Battle of Therminsax

The fuzzy pink moonlight washed over the stones of the wall and deeply shadowed the buttresses. Moon blooms opened their petals greedily to drink of the light. The silence drifted with a little breeze, broken only by the occasional sleeping growl of a ponsho-trag. We watched the lenken gates. The Gate of Aman Deffler was the nearest gate to the Temple of Florania. The idiot intended to open up and let the radvakkas in. I had collected the Hakkodins, the halberdiers and axemen, and now we lay in wait.

Presently footsteps sounded pattering along the flags. Dark figures moved on the ramparts, for here the gates fronted an open pasture and no suburbs had been built up against the walls. The watch, alerted just in time, made no resistance but fled. I did not want good men killed. The gates swung open, carefully greased by these deluded followers of Florania.

Crouched in the shadows, tense, I saw the oncoming mass of Iron Riders. I gave the sign.

Up on the walls the watch returned and with them bowmen and the paktuns. Down below my Hakkodin moved forward. We let perhaps a hundred radvakkas in, surging confidently forward in their iron. Then the gates were shut, the way cleared by lethal sweeps from axes and halberds, the opening bolted up.

Then we turned on those Iron Riders who had ridden in.

By Vox! The pent-up fury of the citizens was wonderful to behold—wonderful and horrible in its revelation of the fury honest men feel when their lives, their livelihoods and their loved ones are threatened. The axes cleft mail, the halberds swung with irresistible force. The Iron Riders were swept from their saddles. They stabbed with their spears and swung with their swords; but the devils of my Hakkodin were everywhere, swarming all over them. In a matter of murs the carnage was over, the savage sounds of steel on iron, the shrieking commotion of men in combat stilled.

Panting, his halberd a shining brand of blood, Targon the Tapster confronted me.

"Hai, Jak the Drang. Now you have seen!"

"Aye, Targon. Now you understand the radvakkas are merely mortal men—"

"By Vox! When you leaped on them I almost felt sorry for the benighted devils." He laughed, the reaction setting in. "Although, I swear by the Invisible Twins, you are a greater devil than any of them."

"Clear the mess away," I said, intemperately. "Carry all the iron to the workshops. Take the unhurt benhoffs to the stables and you do not have to be told what to do with the poor animals who have been injured." I looked up at the walls. "Hai! Have they gone?"

"Aye, Jen. We saw them off and emptied a few saddles."

"Shudor the Mak!" I bellowed. "Take your men out and cover the working party. Bring in everything of value the cramphs of Iron Riders have left us."

Shudor, who had signed a contract and accepted good red gold for the services of his paktun band, obeyed. We wasted nothing in besieged Therminsax.

Then I went off to have a few words with the priest of Florania.

The Justicar and the city fathers met in solemn judgment. Everything was done with strict impartiality and adherence to the long-established customs of the bokkertu in Vallia. But the evidence was so strong that the verdict of guilty was the only one possible. So I, being squeamish, left the matter in the hands of the city fathers of Therminsax, whose city would have been betrayed by this misguided man. What they did I will not repeat; but the example, I felt reasonably confident, would deter any other poor deluded wight from plunging so foolishly into an act of treason.

As for his followers, they repented at leisure.

I went to find the two Krozairs, Zarado and Zunder. As always, they were arguing, this time about the relative merits of the halberd and the axe, and so I was able to say: "I have noticed your swords, koters." I called them koters in the Vallian way, for koter, being a word of similar meaning to gentleman, covered our transactions. "I fancy I would like to have the armorer make me one up in like fashion."

They laughed, and showed me their Krozair brands. In Therminsax there were the usual number of smiths any place would need; of armorers there was but one, Ferenc the Edge, for it was said he could hone a blade like no one else in all

Thermin. He had been kept busy, grumbling about letting blacksmiths into the high mysteries of his art. I had simply told him that any self-respecting blacksmith could put a good edge onto a scythe or sickle, that I had shown the women how to fashion the scaled bronze kaxes, and to pitch in with a will. Now the two Krozairs showed me their swords, and I took them off to find Ferenc the Edge. With me I took an armful of the radvakka swords.

"Now, Ferenc," I said, in the heat and smoke of the armory. "These two monstrous swords. You see them."

"Aye, Jen," quoth this Ferenc the Edge. "And mighty unhandy they look. The handle length is impossible. And there is a curve, if I mistake me not, in the blade—"

"Good man!" I exclaimed. "The curve is of the most subtle, being more of a rise of the cutting edge to the center point. You will make me a sword like this from these radvakka weapons."

The Krozairs fell about laughing. "It takes skill—" And: "You'll cut your legs off, if not worse!"

But I insisted and left Ferenc to it, with a promise that he must make the blade superb and if it snapped across in battle I'd stalk back and stuff the shattered end up where it would do him no good at all.

But I knew, sadly, that however fine Ferenc's work would be, the blade he would forge would in nowise compare with a true Krozair blade.

More days passed and our preparations drew on. We made thousands of bronzen caltrops. Chevaux de frise were constructed and husky youngsters, fleet of foot, were trained to run with them and drop them in position, to pick them up and run again, to the shrill commands of stentors. The benhoffs we had taken were added to our cavalry force, and we could field almost two hundred now. Our five hundred archers were now at the stage where they could loose accurate volleys with an expertise that, while it would provoke Seg to a chuckle or two, would for all that do pleasant mischiefs to the radvakkas.

I was not concerned to choose an auspicious day for the sally, a holy day or a day sacred to some god or other, not even Opaz. I would choose the right day for my brumbytes. As it turned out, the right day dawned on the morning of Opaz Enthroned, which was a good omen. Normally, the long chanting processions singing their eternal "Oolie Opaz" would wind through the streets. I gave the countersign as

139

Oolie Opaz and told the people that that would suffice on this day.

Truth to tell, the sally could not much longer be delayed. Our food was now in sure sight of running out. We had trained to a pitch and now we needed combat to temper our arms. And, as you may well imagine, I was overtaken by the most profound panic of indecision. How could we face the ponderous onrushing might of The Iron Riders? Would not all our careful plans be rendered useless? Our hedge of pikes swept away? Would the burghers change into hardened brumbytes, and stand, and win?

Ferenc the Edge found me, his squat face glowing and smudged with black. He held out the sword.

"Here, Jen Jak. And may Opaz have you in his keeping, for I have tried to swing the blade and took a chunk out of my leg, may Trip the Thwarter take it." He handed me the sword and I felt a rush of nostalgic onkerishness envelop me as I wrapped my horny old fists around the handle. Ferenc eyed me. "Go in good spirit, Jen Jak, and, by the Blade of Kurin, as my clients say, I wish you well."

With the sword in my left hand I took out the assignat I had prepared and handed it to Ferenc. When he saw the sum I had written and which had been countersigned by the Justicar he whistled.

"You put great store by that monstrous brand."

"Aye. Now go and take your place. Every man must play his part today." And I added: "And may Vox send his aegis to give you comfort."

Whatever happened today, from henceforth it would be known as the Battle of Therminsax. That was inevitable.

The temples crowded with brumbytes and Hakkodins, seeking a last measure of comfort. The women bore up marvelously; but I understood their agonies. I held a last order group with the two Kerchurivaxes, Nath Nazabhan na Therminsax and Strom Varga na Barbitor, and with the Jodhrivaxes. They knew the plan. To dignify what we purported as a plan must be overstating it. We intended to march out, form phalanx, and smash the radvakkas.

Even a well-disciplined phalanx will trend to the right so as instinctively to bring the shields around to face the enemy. To give a little added protection to the right flank we would march out across the open plain with the Letha Brook on our right. The Hakkodins would flank us. If we did go right we'd find our feet getting wet. So I had a private word with Bondur Darnhan and Jando Quevada, the two right-hand men.

Briefly, I told them that the direction of the two wings depended on them—they knew that, anyway; they'd drilled enough times—and that they were to parallel the Letha Brook.

"Put your heads down, your pikes level, your shields up—and go straight in. And tread warily over the clutter on the ground."

So, dutifully, they smiled at the feeble joke, and went off.

We marched out.

The army of Therminsax marched out.

The two Kerchuris marched. The Hakkodins flanked them. The cavalry and archers took post on the rear flanks, awaiting immediate orders.

And I got the jitters. Were twelve men enough? Was a phalanx twelve pikemen deep thick enough? Ought I to have made it sixteen, like the Macedonians? The pikes projected past the front ranks, forming a multiple hedge of steel; but I could have lengthened the pikes, made five or six project. I looked at that impressive array, superb in bronze and crimson, marching with a swing, with the drums rolling, and I felt the icy shivers of dread.

So much to gamble, so many lives. . . . It is imperative if you are to gain an insight into that formidable and splendid array to grasp something of what it was like to march as a brumbyte in the files. A heavy helmet weighs down your head and the metal visor obstructs vision. You grasp an eighteen foot long pike, and you hang your shield around on your left shoulder, trying not to let it slide away to the side. You are aware of your bronze-scaled kax pressing on your chest and back. You clump along, in line and file, as you have been trained. The man in front is old Nath, a good fellow if a boaster, the man to your rear is old Naghan, who always wants to tread on your heels. The men on either side you know, have worked and trained with. The dust rises. Your nostrils sting, your eyes want to run with water. The breath clogs in your throat. And you must grip your pike firmly, held aloft until the moment comes when the trumpets shrill and down go the pikes, level, and you increase pace. Then you can hear and see practically nothing as you just press forward until—but then, you have not yet experienced that fraught *until*. All the training and practice in the world, even charging solid wooden fences, cannot really prepare you for the hideous reality that will follow when that *until* becomes fact.

141

Solid, compact, compressed, shield locked, pikes all slanted, the phalanx moved out.

One of Shudor's paktuns had got himself killed and so I was able to buy his zorca, at an impossibly inflated price, from the band. Gold had to be paid; assignats were of no interest to the mercenaries. So I rode a zorca and was clad in a bronze kax of the same kind as those worn by the brumbytes, wearing a vosk-skull helmet with the bronze fittings, carrying a long spear, a shortsword and a broadsword from the rad-vakkas—and with the Krozair brand scabbarded over my back. The scabbard had been made by the handmaidens of Nazab Nalgre's wife, the quiet and soft-spoken Lady Felda. From the saddle hung down a steel axe, short-hafted.

Naghan ti Lodkwara and his Hawkwas, riding the benhoffs we had taken, formed a small guard reserve. And I become aware of a monstrous shadow at my back, and turned, and, lo! There rode Korero, bearing an enormous shield. He met my eyes and he looked abruptly shifty.

"Why do you ride there, Korero?"

"You have given me no place in this phalanx, Jak the Drang. I remember what I remember. This shield is large enough for the two of us."

All I could do was say: "You are right welcome, Korero the Shield. But guard yourself, you hear?"

As I swung back to check the progress of the phalanx I found myself muttering darkly: "What in the sweet name of Opaz will Turko the Shield say?"

Cleitar the Smith rode with us and he carried the standard. This was a large banner of crimson with the yellow saltire of Vallia, and, in the hoist, the crimson and brown of Therminsax arranged in their insignia shape. Dorgo the Clis and Magin rode with us. Also, we had a truly enormous brazen trumpet blown by Volodu the Lungs, a barrel-chested, square-faced rogue with a penchant for ale of any quality and in any quantity.

The brumbytes were signing as we advanced out across the open plain by the brook. Where they got the spit from, Opax knows. They began with refrains like "The Maidens of Vallia" but as we advanced and saw the mailed cavalry riding out and forming to meet us, the songs grew more wild. A couple of times each Kerchuri was singing a different song; but as we drew forward to the place I had marked, everyone was bellowing out "The Salvie on the Slippery Slope." I did not think the ladies crowding the walls of Therminsax could make out the words, even if they might hear the tune, and

142

that was just as well. It is a marvel how decorous, seemly, orderly townsfolk will transform themselves in moments like these into the wildest spirits imaginable.

The stentors blew their trumpets and the shrill notes halted the phalanx. The radvakkas trotted out, ominous and deadly in their iron. The lads with their caltrops on quick-dispensing rods ran out ahead and strewed the ground. On the flanks the chevaux de frise were positioned, ugly trestles armed with spikes, protecting our flanks. The lads assigned to this duty, fleet of foot, collected at the rear of the phalanx, out of the way.

We halted, all the pikes upright, and the banners and standards moved to the rear.

I wanted—how I wanted—to leap off the zorca and grasp a pike and so stand in the front rank. But I had a duty and that duty chained me here, in command, ready to hurl the weight of our attack where it was needed. A phalanx arrayed so deeply and with shields locked can go straight ahead. It is designed to go straight ahead over anything. To wheel, to form, to go sideways, is so difficult that it is barely attempted. We had carried out experiments, and had some success, but usually the phalanx fell into complete disorder. I had chosen to march out with the phalanx facing the main camp of The Iron Riders.

We would go ahead.

But, all the same, despite that, my place was where I was.

And, all the time, I continued to marvel at the way in which the solid citizens of Therminsax had transformed themselves. From a witless bunch of scared loons—with the exceptions of those men I had seen and noted—the burghers now stood calmly in their packed files and ranks awaiting the onslaught of the dreaded Iron Riders. The transformation was exceedingly marvelous, and I felt a warm and choking affection for these brumbytes sweeping over me.

The jitters persisted. Ought I to have provided baldachins, canopies of cloth to hang from the shields to protect the legs? As I lifted in the stirrups and peered ahead at the advancing Iron Riders, I had to make a fierce effort to banish worries like that. The Phalanx of Therminsax had been forged. It existed. It was. In only a few murs it would be in action, in its first action. Everything was going to go splendidly. It was. I had to believe that, believe utterly and with the fanaticism of the doomed.

Dust puffed from under the iron hooves of the benhoffs. The radvakkas had no doubt been astounded to see the gates

143

open and an army march out. I hoped that they would regard us as just another army like those of Hamal they had destroyed in the outright violence of their charge. They had no doubt tumbled out of their tents shouting with glee, arming in all haste, snatching up sword and spear, leaping into their saddles. Being barbarians they would all race to be the first. Their chiefs would, because they were chiefs, be able to control a few of them close at hand. But the mass would dig in spurs and set off.

This they did, and so they came down on us like a spuming unformed mass, bunched as they closed, riding knee to knee. The front ranks tended to draw together, followed by a whole tail of furiously galloping riders.

"What a sight!" said Cleitar. He shook the great banner. In his right hand he grasped his massive hammer, and the head was newly fashioned into a piercing spike at one end and a crushing hammer at the other.

"Very impressive," observed Korero. He sat his benhoff alongside my zorca, but I knew he would haul out to the side and rear when the heat grew. He had no fear of arrows, for the radvakkas were in too impatient a mood. They just clapped in their spurs and charged.

Our own archery rose from the flanks. I had not stationed archers to the front, for I did not want bowmen running back through lanes left in the files, with the subsequent movements to fill the gaps and possible dislocations. The phalanx waited like a solid rock against the pounding of the breakers.

The Iron Riders hammered on. At the last moment the bowmen retreated behind the bristling spiked trestles and continued to put in a raking discharge. Any moment now—the noise of the thousands of hooves bellowed to the sky. The dust rose. The twin suns glinted from iron armor and steel weapons. Instinctively I tensed and then relaxed as the forces met.

Bedlam. Sheer awful bedlam. The noise blattered away as if insane imps of hell were beating drums through Cottmer's Caverns. The smashing impact of those superb riders against the steady ranked lines of brumbytes rocked on, rocked in equilibrium, rocked back. I saw a few pikes splinter and sprout skywards. I saw the long level lines of pikes holding, stabbing, transfixing man and beast. The phalanx held. Not a man yielded an inch. The Iron Riders rode into that bristling wall of steel pike heads and were ripped from their saddles, slashed into the ground, brought to a grinding dusty bloody halt.

144

We lost men. I sorrowed for that. But only a few, a very few, and particularly in one relianch where the front ranks went down under a collapsing tangle of benhoffs. But the brumbytes in rear moved up, stabbing and thrusting, and the cruel steel pike heads forced a clearance, and the line held.

The overlap of the radvakka charge lapped around our flanks. This was where danger threatened. But the very vehemence of their charge carried them spurring on. Those who tried to rein inwards were stopped by the chevaux de frise, and by the archers who shot lethally into them, and by the Hakkodins who slashed with axe and halberd and dragged The Iron Riders from their tall saddles with spikes and battered them into the ground.

On the right flank a mess of benhoffs floundered into the Letha Brook and were dealt with in water and blood.

I saw the recoiling movement. The Iron Riders following up their first ranks had either crashed headlong into them to add to the confusion, or drawn rein and wheeled away. Groups of radvakkas pirouetted about the plain. They would gather for another charge, of that I was certain. Again uncertainty hit me. Now? Or give them another charge and then? So I waited, confident in the cool heads and high courage of the brumbytes.

The front rank men knelt and thrust the butts of their pikes into the ground, their shields facing front and locked. The second rank men thrust forward under arm, over the shoulders of the front rank. Farther back the two handed over-arm grip was used. All in all, to face that bristling pike-hedge would take a great deal of nerve and courage.

Of nerve and courage and sheer stubborn pride the radvakkas were plentifully provided. They gathered and charged again. And, again, they were piked to a bloody standstill.

Now!

The rear rank men, the Bratchlins, were yelling and stretching out their empty hands. Men bearing fresh supplies of pikes scrambled forward. As the front rank pikes were broken so the files passed up fresh, levelly, as they had trained. There were no spikes at the butt ends, and no reversing the pikes as though they were mere nine-foot spears. I gave Volodu the Lungs the order.

He blew the "Prepare to advance."

Immediately the front rank men stood up. The pikes came down level. The brumbytes took a grip on their shields, their pikes, on themselves. I nodded to Volodu.

He blew with scarlet and distended cheeks. "Advance."

All the other stentors took up the signal. With ringing trumpets and with the thundering rataplan of the drums bellowing the files on, the whole phalanx advanced.

With helmets bent fiercely forward, with glaring eyes, with clenched teeth, the brumbytes advanced. The level rows of pikeheads glittered. The tramp of bronze-studded boots hammered the ground. Careful of the scattered caltrops that had brought down many a poor animal, of the corpses strewing the ground, treading small, the men advanced. When the phalanx had cleared the cumbered ground, and ahead pirouetted an astounded cavalry, and the main camp of The Iron Riders, Volodu at my nod signalled the "Double, Advance, Charge!"

The whole phalanx broke into a double march, a furious yet steady pace, almost a run, that carried them over the ground and scattering the remnants of the radvakkas to our front, brought us up to the leather tents of the camp.

The "Halt!" brought them up with their pikeheads ripping into leather.

Here the Hakkodins went to work, with the cavalry who now came up. The destroyed the camp. During that enjoyable work the phalanx turned about. This was accomplished with a smartness of drill I admired, for I saw how the taste of action had sharpened the men up. Trumpets shrilled. The Second Kerchuri remained fast. The First moved off. All pikes were vertical. When the First had cleared the Second, the whole Second Kerchuri left-faced. Rank by rank they marched to the rear of the First. When each file was exactly aligned, the trumpets blew again, the Kerchuri halted and faced front. Twenty-four deep, we set off back to the city.

Strom Varga, commanding the Second, cantered over to me.

"Yes, Strom. Nobly done. Be ready instantly to halt your Kerchuri and turn about. Or to face either flank."

"Quidang, Jak the Drang." He cantered off, perfectly composed. The evolution would be tricky if some wight forgot to hoist his pike before he turned. Drill and discipline—resent them though the soldier might, they helped to keep him alive on the day of battle.

So we marched back in triumph. Had we possessed a good cavalry force we would have ridden in a bloody pursuit. As it was and in a way very satisfying to me although regarded askance as less than dignified by the citizenry, we were accompanied back by a whole clamoring host of freed slaves. Radvakkas maneuvered some way off. But we did not march straight back, for the ground was cumbered. That led to a tidy old mixup in lining up for the gate; but I told Volodu to signal "Relianch." Then the brumbytes sorted themselves out and marched in in good order. The gates were closed. I breathed in deeply. I had struck out one good resounding blow. But the pikes of my men, my sturdy brumbytes, were crowned with the laurel wreaths of victory.

So we celebrated.

The next morning there was not a radvakka to be seen. All the tents unburned had vanished. The cooking fires were cold.

The Iron Riders had gone.

Therminsax had been saved.

CHAPTER EIGHTEEN

Nath Nazabhan

Over the next period of my life upon Kregen I had best tread lightly. Much of what immediately followed stemmed from the facts surrounding the besiegement and Battle of Therminsax. While I had been mewed up there and in the period following when with a choice band we traveled from city to city along the old frontiers and pressed on into Hawkwa country, many great events had taken place in Vallia.

My orders from the Star Lords, to be obeyed, necessitated the complete overthrow of The Iron Riders. So I took the matter.

To accomplish this in a short time was patently not possible, lacking a plentiful supply of infantry capable of standing against the armored cavalry charge, and lacking a powerful cavalry of our own. With that choice band—a group that grew together in times of adversity as well as of success—we moved from city to city instructing, exhorting, demanding in the name of Vallia. Where the radvakkas were too strong we bypassed the place. Then, in the fullness of time, we would return and cleanse one more spot of Vallia.

The Iron Riders were slow to counter our measures. We had to make absolutely sure that each province and city we liberated was capable of defending itself against further attacks. With a strong cadre from Therminsax, by expertise that grew with every fresh successful drill no less than encounter, we developed speed in our methods. But, all the same, it was a lengthy business.

To arouse a nation to arms is one thing; to train them to win wars is another.

Our first task which we successfully completed was to clear Thermin back westwards to the Great River. On the day we reached The Mother of Waters, I recall, we looked across and saw on the right bank a massed group of totrix cavalry, wearing the checkerboard ochre and umber of Falinur. I suppose, thinking of it, it was fortunate that a bridge was not nearby and the river ran broad and deep here. A smashed and routed band of radvakkas lay in our rear, and we were still more concerned with them than with the rebels over the river. For, make no mistake, rebels they were, Falinurese who had sided with Kov Layco Jhansi and taken up arms in his struggle for the imperium. His kovnate province of Vennar marched with Falinur to the west. Beyond him lay the long range of heights known in their northern sections as the Black Mountains and in that immense amphitheatre to the south, the Blue Mountains.

No good sitting dreaming. We had work to do to the east. Sitting there with the standards and banners about me, I gave the orders, and the cavalry moved out, and the phalanx swung into their dwabur-consuming stride. Oh, yes, these days we marched about the country as a phalanx, made up from men of many tiny villages as well as towns and cities. We trained as we marched, and we picked up fresh recruits every day, it seemed. Mind you, our strength as yet was short of a complete phalanx, and I intended to regularize the numbers out logically. We had almost a full Kerchuri with us, of which four Jodhris were fully trained. Despite my powerful arguments that he should stay with his father and in his city, Nath Nazabhan had elected to march. He was the Kerchurivax. A fine man, a fierce and loyal fighter, he did much to lighten the hearts of the brumbytes, despite his strict adherence to the codes of discipline we enforced.

And, believe you me, the discipline in the phalanx was strong.

We cut south following the river and opened up Eganbrev and then swung sharply east in that broad double-hook of She of the Fecundity and so cleared our way through Aduimbrev. I am making this narrative abbreviated here. We successfully liberated Thiurdsmot and Cansinsax, and, by this time, we had four Kerchuris with us. They amounted to twenty-five thousand men. We had a cavalry arm, also, by this time, mounted on totrixes and nikvoves, and these were organized in the usual system, squadron and regiment. They were all heavily armored cavalry, with kax, spear and sword. In addition we possessed a small scouting force of zorcamen. Gathering men and animals together from everywhere, we at all times observed the proprieties and I signed countless assignats. Well, that is a lie my staunch comrade Enevon Ob-eye would strongly object to.

Enevon—One-Eye Enevon—served as my chief stylor, and he kept scrupulous accounts of every assignment we issued, as well as the army lists. He was from Valka. He had seen me and opened his mouth and I had run him into my tent under the crimson and yellow flag, and cautioned him. He called me Jak the Drang.

He'd been on a trading mission and become caught up with the revolts in their various places and phases and so could give me no late news from Valka.

That reminds me of the day we marched into a ruined town having driven off a wispy attempt by a handful of radvakkas to halt us and found in a tumbledown barn the sad remnants of an airboat. Well, between us, we patched the thing up. So we had ourselves a flier. I called Korero to me. His great shield, and often two shields at once, had interposed between me and the arrows and sword-strokes of the enemy. I looked sternly at him.

"Korero the Shield. You can fly an airboat. You will fly to Valka. You will enter the Heart Heights and there perform a certain function."

He did not want to go. He was from Balintol, a weird, exotic place, if ever Kregen sprouts such mysterious lands, by Vox. But he could fly and he could read a map and he was of great heart and courage. I entrusted a sealed message to Diela into his four capable hands—not forgetting his equally capable tail-hand—and saw him off with many Remberees.

To finish that story anachronistically, as is not my wont, he returned in the fulness of time, finding us easily enough by reason of a burning city and radvakkas lying strewn in their own blood, and reported that he had seen the Princess Majestrix of Vallia, whom men now called the Empress of Vallia, and that she had opened the letter addressed to her by Jak the Drang and had read, and grown pale, and pressed the paper to her heart, and had then treated Korero the Shield with great kindness.

"She was well?"

"Aye, Jak. She commands an army there of the bonniest fighters I have seen in a long time. They are re-taking Valka for the Strom of Valka—wherever he may be, for men did not know."

I read Delia's letter in answer to mine. I cannot repeat its contents; but it was as Korero had reported with his sharp eye. Valka was being won back from the mercenaries who had thought the Prince Majister's stromnate easy pickings. She understood I could not join her for the moment; she would join me when it was possible, although she sounded a warning note. Her thoughts were with Delphond and the Blue Mountains. As to Zamra and Veliadrin, our people resisted there; but waves of aragorn and mercenaries from all over, drawn by the news that Vallia was in turmoil and there were easy pickings, were flocking in like warvols.

And that reminds me that I had continually to remind my great-hearted brumbytes that they might overtopple mailed cavalry; but that they could not go up against the iron legions of Hamal. The information was not welcome; but I pressed the point and, also, against possible evil, increased our missile force. We were a national army—or almost so. We had a few mercenaries in our ranks and could pick up more as we progressed. We had a detachment of Bowmen of Loh—and none of them had served in the Crimson Bowmen. This corps I did not resuscitate, having strong ideas on the subject of what I intended in that direction.

Time had flown by and we were well into the North East—well into Hawkwa territory. Now the campaigns we waged changed in character. There was no longer the pressing need to recruit and train men to form phalanxes. We marched and we were the phalanxes. As we liberated areas and towns and cities we destroyed the bands of Iron Riders who opposed us, and rolled up in a receding tide those who fled. The operations took on more and more the guise of campaigning warfare. Gelkwa was freed. With the pikeheads of the host slanting against the suns at my back I appointed a Hawkwa noble, Strom Hafkwa, to be the new Trylon of Gelkwa. He accepted; but he did ask: "By what right, Jak the Drang, do you do this thing?"

I relished the moment for its parallels.

I pointed at the phalanx, at the serried files and ranks of pikes.

"There is my mandate."

Of course, I then added that I bore a commission from an imperial Justicar, and was using that to ratify my actions. He was one of those—and there were many of them as there had been many to sing a similar tune in Djanduin—who raised the call, cautiously at first but with growing volume, that we should all march to Vondium and chuck out this traitor Seakon and install me, Jak the Drang, as emperor.

I smiled.

"One day, one day, perhaps. But I seek no personal aggrandizement." That was true, by Krun! "First we must cleanse all Hawkwa country of the radvakkas."

The Hawkwas clustered about in this moment, as a new Trylon of their province was installed, nodded. They said, in effect, and I do not repeat their words: "Much favor is yours, Jak the Drang. All Hawkwas will stand in your debt, for you do not impose alien rulers on us when you might, seeing you have the strength. We accept your rulings." That is more or less it.

I took some pains to make sure I did not come into contact with any who might recognize me from those hectic days I had spent here previously. That was unlikely, really; but it was a chance I was not prepared to take—not just yet.

I think, now, that Korero the Shield put two and two together and came up with the right answer. But he respected my wishes and kept his own council. Also, Nath Nazabhan knew. It popped out one day, and enquiry determined that his father the Justicar had told him, so that he would mind his manners with me. I smiled—again, I smiled.

"Then you have kept silence, Nath, and will continue to do so. But I can tell you that an imperial province lies in your hands once we have this mess sorted out."

And then he surprised me. He said, this tough, limber young fighting man: "I follow you, emperor, for two main reasons. One is to clear Vallia and to flex my arm against her enemies. And the other is because of yourself."

I did not pursue the matter, as we turned to details concerning the new swarm of irregulars who now followed us as we marched. Nath had been promoted to command a phalanx, the other being in the hands of Nev who was a Therminsaxer and who had risen through the ranks being a man of exceptional ability. He had once been known as Nev the Bottle; but now he never touched a drop and my orders said he was now Kyr Nev ti Rendonsmot, a title taken from the town where he had been instrumental in holding his Jodhri firm against almost insupportable numbers, and then of advancing at the double and flinging The Iron Riders back in confusion.

Yes, yes, there were many battles and many campaigns and sometimes the arm grew weary and the brain dizzy; but we persevered, clearing Vallia of the radvakkas.

The irregulars, and I call them that only because they were not as yet integrated into the army, posed problems. Men of Vallia from farm and town, they followed us. They aped our ways, and built themselves shields of wickerwork, and carried long spears, and perched vosk-skull helmets on their heads. On more than one occasion they raced in with a whoop and a yell on the flanks of the radvakkas and materially assisted us in the victory. I had issued orders that the irregulars were to be given the full assistance of our ambulance and medical services, and the doctors with us attended to the irregular wounded in the same way they attended the brumbytes and the Hakkodins. Although we had provided an ambulance and medical service from the very beginning, and little enough they had had to do on that never-to-be-forgotten day of the Battle of Therminsax, the fact remained that once the shields locked and the pikes came down, our men suffered relatively few casualties. This heartened everyone.

So many vivid and burning memories of those days of marching and campaigning and battling rise up before me now as I speak. Would that I had the time and a thousand cassettes to speak of them; but always my thoughts pressed on feverishly to the accomplishment of what I had set my hand to, the liberation of Vallia and then the return to Delia and the surcease from strife.

When men march together and fight on from year to year they change, their characters alter, in subtle and gross ways they become different men from those who set out. The histories of Napoleon and Alexander demonstrate this with stark and pitiful clarity. We were not troubled by desertion. If a man did not wish to march with us, then he was free to leave. We were, after all, not a conscripted army but a national army of liberation, fired by the zeal to cleanse our country. So I deliberately instituted a policy of maintaining a turnover in the files. By this method men would be sent home as others pressed forward, after training, to fill the gaps. I did not wish my little army to become tainted, sour, as happened to other armies of the past.

One bright day after a smart little dustup when a wing having advanced perhaps a little too far against two strong bands of radvakkas, and having formed a schiltron, pikes out, to resist, was smartly relieved by a cavalry charge in the flank of The Iron Riders, I looked up into the air and saw a flier circle and land nearby. We used our own single flier to recce; I daresay that was the only airboat for a thousand miles or so. And, now here was another. She bore flags the colors, gray, red and green, with a black bar, and so I knew she was from Calimbrev, that stromnate island south of Veliadrin, and also I knew who this was who came leaping over the coaming and racing over the torn-up grass toward the group of riders about the crimson and yellow banner of Vallia. I'd have known that slender, smooth-faced, respectable young man anywhere.

If he yelped out my name before my gathered officers. . . .

But in those hectic days we had spent together in the Kwan Hills and Gelkwa, and, as well, in that harum-scarum chase from Drak's City in Vondium, something must have rubbed off on him, for as he came running toward us, waving his arms, almost tripping over his rapier and clanxer—I half-smiled when I saw his armory—he bellowed out: "Jak! Jak! It's me!"

Mind you, young Barty Vessler, the Strom of Calimbrev, still shouldn't have yelled any name. It was lucky for him I was using the same address alias as before, except that I was not Jak Jakhan but Jak the Drang. I urged my zorca out front and center and then hauled up as Barty arrived, red-faced, panting, overjoyed. He was a supple, bright, eager young man, filled with ideas of nobility and chivalry a little rough-hunting with me had not knocked out of his noodle.

"Barty!" I said, speaking warmly, for I felt pleasure at the sight of him. "Strom. You are right welcome. Lahal."

"Lahal and Lahal, Jak. I am here. I will fight. I have heard—Del—that is, a message—" He floundered.

I lowered my voice. "I am Jen Jak the Drang. See me in my tent in a bur. And, Barty, for the sweet sake of Opaz, keep your trap shut."

He nodded, and that wickedly sly grin of the ingenuous at their awed realization they are involved in skullduggery passed over his smooth, polished face, making him look like an apple set out in the front of the greengrocer's stall.

"Quidang, Jen Jak the Drang!"

Names, names. . . . They conceal and reveal all, and can sometimes lead to very messy deaths. . . .

Before I could see Barty the aftermath of the little action had to be tidied up. The Kerchuri that had advanced with somewhat too great precipitancy had done well to form their schiltron, in this case a circle of bristling pikes, and resist successfully until relieved; but I wanted a word with their Ker-churivax, stubborn old Nalgre ti Fomenoir. He would shake his head and agree with what I said and then, the next time, would as lief lead on his Kerchuri in that hard, heavy, pounding advance, the brumbytes all advancing with helmets forward and pikes thrusting. We had become used to charging forward and hurling down all who opposed us. We must not become complacent.

And, after Nalgre ti Fomenoir had been spoken to there was the matter of the Love Story to be attended to.

A certain brumbyte had become enamored of a little lady in one of the towns we had liberated. A fine girl, strong and well-built, she had captivated this pikeman, Nath the Achenor. When the army marched out, Achenor could not bear to part with his lady love, fair Sarfi. Equally, he conceived that his duty lay with the phalanx and he would not desert. So—so the pair of them stood before my tent and I glowered on them.

They stood to attention with their bronze and vosk-skull helmets gleaming, the barred visors lifted, the crimson plumes lofting. They held their pikes at the regulation position, vertically, the heads stained with blood. Their bronze kaxes shone, and Sarfi's had been cunningly adapted so as to fit her interesting shape. Their shields rested on the ground, leaning against their left legs. I looked at them, this pair of brumbytes, one male and the other female, and I sighed and wondered what on Kregen to do with them.

"So, then, Sarfi, you fancy yourself as a Jikai Vuvushi?"

"No, Jen. I am a brumbyte and I march in the phalanx."

"She carries her pike with the best, Jen," broke out Nath the Achenor. He threw her a swift, fond glance, and then snapped back to glare to his front. "I love her dearly and she loves me and we will not be parted."

"I do not argue with that. I believe she is trained, for your Relianchun would not have tolerated anything less."

"She is well-trained, Jen."

I did not say that I had spoken to Relianchun Anror ti Aventwill, the commander of their Relianch who was due to be promoted to Jodhrivax. I looked on these two love birds and I said: "You will return to Sarfi's home. There, no doubt, you will be married and begin to raise fresh brumbytes. That is your concern. I request—request and do not order—that you drill and train the younger men of the town in our methods. You would have made Laik-Faxul very soon, Nath. You have the training. Make sure it is not wasted."

Nath the Achenor started to argue, clasping his pike and shield, saying that he did not wish to leave the phalanx. But I pointed out to him that the phalanx was no place for a girl. Mind you, that was a long time ago and things changed on Kregen, as you shall hear.

So the pair of turtle-doves were sent off, trailing their pikes, unhappy at the moment to leave their comrades. I would not forget the phalanx and what we had achieved. Then I went to find Barty Vessler.

Barty brought news of my daughter Dayra.

He did not know she was Ros the Claw, he had not seen her, brilliant in her black leathers, her lithe feline form very quick, very deadly, he had not witnessed the slashing destruction wrought by that cunning curved metal-taloned glove upon her left hand.

As ever, after he had failed to halt the invasion of his stromnate by the aragorn, Barty had gone seeking Dayra, for he was passionately enamored of her in his refined, elegant and chivalric way. He had found Delia in Valka, who had no late news on Dayra, and had been told of my doings and whereabouts. So he was here, panting on the trail of Dayra, and with information he had picked up that did, in very truth, give a lead.

"For," he said in his light, quick way, "I ventured up to Vondium and, Jak, you will be interested to know that Drak's City held out for long and long—"

"You did?" I exclaimed very stupidly. Then: "Well, that warren could hold an army at bay. Who took it in the end, Layco Jhansi or Phu-Si-Yantong?" Then I had to run over a little of the influence that Wizard of Loh exercised, and of his part in the calamity that had befallen Vallia. It seemed to me that secrecy about the Wizard of Loh was no longer necessary. His acts were plain, carried out by his tools, the chief of whom, as far as I then knew, were the Hamalian Army in his pay and the malevolent Hawkwa party under Zankov.

"The Hamalians control the city with Vallian puppets to make the thing look right. It sickens me. The Hawkwas have fallen out with the Hamalians. Drak's City burned—a good deal of it, like the city—but everything is being rebuilt at a prodigious speed. And Dayra was there; but she was entangled with a bunch of mercenaries—masichieri, most likely. They infest everywhere."

"And?"

"I heard that she had been insulted and had dealt with the

155

masichieri—there was talk of her slicing them up, which puzzled me. Anyway, she left."

It did not puzzle me. The thought of foul-mouthed, sly, treacherous masichieri insulting my daughter did not, thankfully, cause me more pain than it ought, for I was well aware that Ros the Claw would, indeed, slice up any oaf who thought she was easy prey.

"They meet at a place called Olordin's Well. I came to you because—" Here Barty paused, and colored, and looked away.

I had not given him my blessing in so many words; but I had come to an appreciation of him, so I thought. I said: "I am unable to leave the North East until all The Iron Riders are dealt with. Dayra can look after herself. As soon as I am free I shall go to Olordin's Well."

With the courtesy that was also a useful arguing tool, Barty let that lie and we talked of other things. He would return to the subject, that was sure.

With Barty's late information and what we had learned elsewhere, the picture of the present state of Vallia emerged. It was unclear—the condition of the southwest remained obscure. But the North West—not so much a geographical location as a combination of provinces, always staunch Rakker country—had combined even more strongly and under the leadership of Natyzha Famphreon, the Kovneva of Falkerdrin, had declared themselves independent of the rule of either Hamal or Layco Jhansi. Now Jhansi fought campaigns along his northern borders. His tilt at the throne had not succeeded; but, at the least, he had taken the pressure off the Blue Mountains. Barty shook his head at my enquiry about the Black Mountains, Inch's kovnate.

"They have been engulfed, Jak. I heard that a strong mercenary army swept through. Some of the Black Mountain Men have moved south to join the Blue Mountain Boys, and they hold out there—or so it is said. But who can believe anything these days?"

The large island of Womox off the west coast had elected itself a king, and severed communications. Womoxes still served other masters in Vallia and elsewhere, as you know; but this was just another indication that the Empire of Vallia was falling to pieces. Certainly, events had not turned out as Phu-Si-Yantong would have planned or wished.

As for the many islands fringing the coast of the main island, anything could be going on there and probably was.

Those provinces which had previously been held by nobles

156

who had refused to take up an alignment, and there were plenty of them, like the high kovnate of Bakan to the north-west of Hawkwa country, had been ravaged by greedy neighbors or invaded by hordes of aragorn and mercenaries. Flutsmen roamed the skies of Vallia, these days, and that was good for no one.

As for what was going on north of the massive barrier of the Mountains of the North—that was as remote as the probable carryings on on any of the seven moons of Kregen.

For our part, the officers and men around me, we more and more considered ourselves as representing the true Vallia. As I was told by these choice spirits: "The Empire of Vallia has been destroyed and no one can deny that. Now the island and islands are cut up, fragmented, separate. We are the true Vallia, the continuation of the old, and under our banners march men who are true to you, Jak, and to Vallia."

If this was high-flown stuff, then that was sometimes the way of your bluff Vallian—as of any other of the peoples of Paz on Kregen, so it seems—but they remained for all their quoting of poetry and singing of songs just as slippy at slitting a throat or two.

Phu-Si-Yantong was a mere crude conqueror; if he was a sorcerer also, the protections afforded me appeared to be working so far, praise be to Zena Iztar. Layco Jhansi knew very well that his only pretensions to the throne lay in the swords of men he could hire. The Racters had withdrawn and, as so often before, bided their time to strike. Anybody else who sought to become Emperor of Vallia could only be a mere adventurer. This Seakon who now occupied the throne and wore the crown and grasped Drak's Sword was just such an one, a successful one. From what Barty said it appeared the Hamalese sustained Seakon in power. What, then, of the aspirations of Zankov?

Barty seemed to think Zankov led the Hawkwas; but I was not persuaded of that. After the disappearance of Udo, the lead in Hawkwa affairs had been taken by Nankwi Wellon, the High Kov of Sakwara, and we had had a right little flare-up with that prickly personage. He had been downright indignant that The Iron Riders had been swept away by, as he put it, a rabble of southerners. At our interview, when he had put on airs and graces, being the kov and very condescending and mighty with it, I had had to cut him down to size very smartly.

A kov runs a kovnate province; a high kov runs a province which contains a diversity of races each with its own separate organization—the kind of set-up I had had trouble with in Veliadrin with the damned Qua'voils. In Sakwara there were two other powerful groups, one of Brokelsh and the other of Rapas. They were barely tolerated; but they were allowed to live their own lives. The Iron Riders had wrought horrifically upon these communities of diffs, and their numbers had been reduced by better than eighty percent. The carnage had been colossal, obscene, not tolerable.

The Hawkwas with me showed the Hawkwas of Sakwara very clearly where their sympathies and loyalties lay. It crossed my mind, perhaps pettishly, that Sakwara might do better by being divided into a number of smaller provinces, vadvarates and trylonates, perhaps.

In the event, the High Kov Nankwi Wellon had to accept the situation. He remained the high kov. We had cleared the radvakkas from his territory and we left him to rebuild as we pressed on into the Stackwamores, clearing the country out of pockets of Iron Riders. And then, of course, the radvakkas began to coalesce, even to forget inter-band rivalries, and to join together into one mighty horde.

What, you may ask, in all this of that scheming little bitch, Marta Renberg, the Kovneva of Aduimbrev? What, indeed! Well may you ask.

After the fall of her province of Aduimbrev she had gone hot foot to Vondium to berate, to argue and finally to please—if I read the situation aright—with the Hamalese. She would want them to reinstate her with their iron legions, and they would want to leave well alone and not tangle with the radvakkas. If she returned and claimed Aduimbrev back she would find a very different situation, and one she would not like. I did not particularly look forward to that meeting. To be truthful, I detested the very thought of that coming confrontation, by Vox!

For the talk throughout the army now, in the phalanxes, in the Hakkodins, in the cavalry and archers, was all of marching to Vondium in a mighty host and there proclaiming Jen Jak the Drang Emperor of Vallia. The irregulars, too, were of the same mind. They knew on which side their bread was buttered. I merely made myself smile lazily when the subject came up, saying to them tsleetha-tsleethi, all in good time.

The irony of my devotion in clearing out The Iron Riders from Hawkwa country was not lost on me. The Hawkwas were fully aware that we could have marched on Vondium—no one really believed the Hamalese swods would stand against the phalanx no matter how many times I warned them—and so they regarded me with great favor in that I used the army to clean up their country. I did not mention the Everoinye; but if ever a situation deserved the irony of history, this one did.

The campaign persisted and gradually the great day of the final reckoning approached. We were apprised by our scouts and our two fliers of the positions and strengths of the radvakkas. We marched up, the dusty columns with their slanting forest of pikes trudging over the land, pressing closer and closer.

Having cleared the center of Hawkwa country, the South, East and West Stackwamores and the other provinces, we marched north through Urn Stackwamor. Ahead, far far ahead, the icy pinnacles of the southern ranges of the Mountains of the North hove into view. We trended eastward, toward the coast, aiming to pin the radvakka horde against the River Sabbator. The river ran down into the sea opposite the island of Vellin and separated Urn Stackwamor from the trylonate of Zaphoret to the north. In this part of the country there were many Peel towers, stark and angular against the sky. The people had resisted stoutly and many of the Peel towers lay in ruins, for the radvakkas had dealt sternly with the people. Food was not too hard to come by; but the host consumed vast quantities, and I knew that we must finish this thing quickly. Assignats might be written but they could not produce food where there was none.

Barty said: "I am no coward, you know that. But I cannot wait any longer. I do not understand your so tender regard for the Hawkwas. By Vox! We suffered enough grief from them. I must be off to seek Dayra."

"Go with my blessings, and may Opaz fly with you. But I must finish what I have set my hand to. I will see you at Olordin's Well. I shall come as soon as I can." I stared at this slender, easy, well-mannered young man. I sighed. "And mind you take good care of yourself, Barty Vessler. My daughter is, I am sure, highly demanding of any man."

He grew red in the face, and stammered, and swore all manner of high-flown sentiments. Barty Vessler. Yes. Well, I stood to see him off as he observed the fantamyrrh boarding his flier, and we shouted the remberees. He took off.

And I, somewhat savagely, I confess, set my army in order and gave Volodu the Lungs the order to blow the "March" and we set off for the final battle against the mailed might of The Iron Riders.

159

CHAPTER NINETEEN

———◆◆———

In the Name of Jak the Drang

That army was superb. There is no doubt of that. They had marched and fought and sung together. Each part knew its duty and did it and more. The Phalanxes, for there were two full phalanxes now, slogged forward in the center, with archers and Hakkodins in the intervals and flanking. The cavalry trotted on the wings. Like an enormous tide of bronze and crimson we advanced. And, too, by now many of the brumbytes had acquired iron armor to replace the bronze. But we continued to use the old vosk-skull helmets, often with iron instead of bronze fittings. We functioned like a cutting machine. We would go through anything.

So the brumbytes said.

The Iron Riders had gathered. They were all here, for they well understood that this was the final reckoning. In one single gigantic horde they would meet us and this time they would crush us utterly, once and for all.

And although the radvakkas were illiterate barbarians, they had learned. They altered their tactics. It was a development long overdue and one against which I had given thought and planned with my officers and men. The army marched forward, singing, confident, ready to sweep away The Iron Riders in this last climactic battle.

We were all chosen men. The word "Legion" carries the connotation of selection. We were the Phalanx, and we were selected from the best. The swarms of itinerants and irregulars hungered to join our ranks. So we marched forward with the crimson banners flying and the bronze and steel gleaming, with the drums blamming their thrilling rataplan.

Ahead the long long line of radvakkas came into view.

At once Nath said: "Hai! The rasts try a new trick."

The Iron Riders did not charge headlong at us the moment they could. Instead, they hung back, pirouetting out there across the plain, with the glinting thread of the River Sabbator at their backs. The wagon leaguers and the camps occupied a vast area of the watermeadows. The twin suns shone.

The banners flew and the trumpets pealed. The Phalanx halted.

I say Phalanx; against this moment we put into practice the plans we had developed. File by file the Relianches moved into open order, the Bratchlins standing fast and the files marching back to turn and come up behind their neighbors, thirty-six men deep. Into the intervals stepped the archers. The evolution was completed smoothly and in good order—and only just in time.

The Iron Riders in clumps and groups swept toward us and retreated and as they curvetted so they loosed a rain of arrows.

At this early stage most of the shafts fell short. Our trumpets blew "Shields" and up went the crimson flowers, like a field of roses, ready to resist the falling arrow storm. Our archers loosed, careful, aimed shots, from standing or kneeling positions that took a toll of the galloping radvakkas. For their part, The Iron Riders attempted to press in to the range at which their short bows might reach; but the compound bows of our archers outranged them handsomely. As I have said, one does not fire a bow. Kregans have a word which roughly approximates our terrestrial word firepower. Now Nath half-turned in his saddle, laughing, gleeful, raking me with the demand in his bright eyes, already triumphant.

"See, Jen Jak! Their dustrectium is pitiful! Let us close ranks and lock shields and advance."

"Their attempt to prepare the mass is, indeed, not worthy of our preparations to resist. Mayhap they have another cast hidden from our view. Let our bowmen empty a few more saddles, Nath."

On my other side Nev fidgeted astride his zorca, anxious to bring his phalanx into action. But I made them wait. I needed the radvakkas to appreciate that their new tactics were failing them, and to gather, once again, for the headlong charge that, I fancied, this time they would make with the final fling of desperation.

Well, the story of that old battle is there for all to hear in the song that was made. The "Black Wings over Sabbator," it is called. This is a typical Kregish reference to the incident where a fleeing formation of radvakkas, circling, came across one of our ambulance units tending the wounded of both sides and simply rode across them, slaying friend and foe alike. That was after, at last, I gave the signal, and we closed ranks and locked shields and with helmets fiercely bent forward, plumes nodding, and pikes levelled in a lethal hedge of steel, we advanced at the regulation double pace. The moment was judged nicely. We caught The Iron Riders just as their chiefs had finally collected the scattered bands into that fearsome armored host with which they had so often ridden to victory. We hit them as they formed, before they had even put spur to benhoff. We hit them and the pikes bit and the halberds slashed and we rolled them up and crushed them and destroyed them utterly.

Pinned against the Sabbator they could only stand among the tents and wagons and fight until they died.

Our irregulars swarmed in. Our archers picked off any who sought to flee. Only that one formation which so mercilessly razed the ambulance unit escaped; and subsequently they were pursued and brought to justice. For, believe me, that is how the army viewed the situation.

Relianch by Relianch, the brumbytes came back out of the line, pikes tossed, formed, intact, ready to face anything.

As I say, and no doubt will continue to say, by Vox, that was an army.

That it was wildly anachronistic meant merely that it gathered the more honor. Of glory I will not speak. But I had, with the full co-operation of Nazab Nalgre, instituted valor medals, phalerae, and these were worn with pride.

In the history of those skirling days kept by Enevon Ob-Eye the battle was recorded as The Battle of the Sabbator; but men usually refer to it as the Sabbator. It was a famous victory—and, thank Zair, our casualties were less than minimal. On the aftermath of the action I looked up, and there, floating over the Phalanx soared the gold and scarlet Gdoinye.

I put a hand to my helmet and hoisted the barred facemask, and stared up narrowly. The raptor swung about, and glided down and then, as though satisfied, flirted his wings and soared away.

The very next day I said to Nath: "You are in command of the army now, Kyr Nath. Nev will support you loyally. Appoint whom you wish to command your phalanx in your stead, although I think we both favor Kyr Derson. Conduct the army back to the southern borders ensuring that the whole country is free. Then you may disband and send the men to their homes. The work of rebuilding is pressing."

"But—Jak."

"I have business elsewhere."

"Where, by Vox?"

I looked out of our tent and saw the brumbytes. Four full

Kerchuris we had now, and their crimson shields no longer bore the brown of Thermin. They were an imperial host, bearing yellow insignia on their crimson shields. I felt the wrench at parting. As I had said to Barty: "The organization is so simple even the dullest oaf can understand. Twelve pike men to a file, twelve files to a Relianch. Six Relianches to a Jodhri and six Jodhris to a Kerchuri. And each position of command from a Laik-Faxul to the Kerchurivax, is linked in a chain. The rank and function are inseparable." When you spend a part of your life building anything at all, when the time comes for the dismantling, regrets creep in, nostalgia, all the silly unmanning emotions that, I suppose, in some measure indicate the value of what you have wrought.

So I said to Nath: "I shall probably end up in Vondium; but I do not know."

"Then—"

"Command the army well. Make sure we have the whole country cleared. Rebuild. Your father will advance money. As far as the borders are concerned—"

"Layco Jhansi is a traitor!"

"Aye. And he is kept in play by the Racters north of him. Let the brumbytes go home, Nath. And the Hakkodins and archers. As for the irregulars, they will melt away now the fighting is over."

So I took my leave. The island of Vellin to the east ought to be cleared, always assuming radvakkas had fled there; but I doubted that. The Gdoinye would not have let me go if my work was unfinished. The actual leave-taking turned out to be highly emotional, and my plans to slip away were frustrated. There was a full-scale parade and review, with the trumpets blowing and the drums beating and the banners flying. The army marched in review—and the sight of the solid masses of crimson and bronze, with the pikes all slanted together, affected me profoundly. This farewell was, after all, worth my own embarrassment.

Korero the Shield said, as I saddled up: "You do not seriously think I would let you ride alone?"

The others of that choice band who, even though the country was cleared of radvakkas, still had no homes of their own, said much the same. Cleitar the Smith, who bore the banner of Vallia, may have had a home; but he had no wife and children to go home to. Dorgo the Clis was now so habituated to fighting with me that he was amazed I could even think of sending him away. And this was so of the others, valiant fighting men I had led in battle, who formed a kind of reserve guard cavalry. Mounted on zorcas, we rode south in a bunch, with calsanys with us loaded down with provender and weapons and, I confess, with gold. Gold might be very needful, for I had no idea of the kind of situation we were riding into.

It would be useful to point out here that so much plunder was recovered from the radvakkas that, of the raw gold alone, we were able to repay many of the assignats, and I appointed a corps of stylors to catalogue each item of treasure and make our best efforts to return it to its owner. This was justice of a very rough and ready kind; but, at the least, we did not take everything for the army, as—we all know— many would have done.

The depreciation in the value of money which afflicts civilizations from time to time posed a threat which I was concerned to prevent. Armies cost money and the land will provide only so much. With the troubles that had dismembered and disrupted Vallia reducing production drastically, pretty soon the people of the empire would wake up to find themselves poor. The aragorn and the slavers did not help, for their depredations might remove thousands of hungry people; but they created so many terrors that in many areas the land had not been worked properly since the first invasions.

As we rode south we saw evidences of that. More and more I felt the claustrophobic effects closing in on me. We were a band of fugitives where we rode, leemsheads, outlaws, shunned by the people of the villages, with the gates of towns slammed in our faces, with the campfires of armed hosts at night to warn us off. This land was torn with anger and terror and evil. And these were the broad rich central provinces of Vallia! Truly, an emperor would weep to see how sadly fallen away was his patrimony.

The iron legions of Hamal were a different proposition from The Iron Riders. I developed a scheme. The countryside was infested with brigands, drikingers who waylaid any and everyone. In a brief and bloody encounter with one such band my choice spirits discomfitted them—rather roughly, I must report. We told the drikingers that if they wished to live they must confine their depredations to waylaying and slaying Hamalese, aragorn, Flutsmen, the mercenaries and masichieri. They were to leave the honest folk of Vallia alone.

"Any by what right do you imagine you can make us?" demanded their leader, blood streaming down his reckless face, held by the elbows and forced to stare up at me.

"Do the Hamalese not contume you? You are held in contempt by them. You are nithings. Yet you are Vallians. You were not always drikingers. Very well, then. Men call me Jak the Drang. I tell you that I shall utterly destroy the Hamalese and all the vermin who infest our country. Have faith in Opaz. The evil days will pass."

Such were my words, or roughly what I said, over and over, to the men we encountered in our travels. And, on that occasion and, subsequently, on every occasion no matter that I did not much care for it, one or other of my choice spirits would sing out: "Aye, hulus! Remember, this is Jak the Drang, who is Emperor of Vallia, and will sit on the throne in Vondium and take Drak's Sword into his hand. Remember and tremble at his name."

Well, as we neared the capital, we found the name of Jak the Drang had gone before us, and men were ready to heed my words. The scheme I put into operation demanded that the women and children of these rich lands remove themselves to the North East. Reports reached me regularly from Nazab Nalgre and the other nobles in Hawkwa country, all of whom now called me emperor without affectation. Their borders were secure. Their first harvest of the new season was a bumper one, producing the plenty of the land in abundance. This operation in two ways to help us, for the people who traveled to the North East left their own shrunken fields to enter a land where they could eat their fill, and Nalgre and the others forwarded on food to us as an earnest of our good intentions. And, in a third and altogether more profound way—if anything can be more profound than the state of a man or woman's inward constitution—the news of what had been achieved in Hawkwa country circulated.

At the name of Jak the Drang these miserable cowed people, living in fear of the Hamalese and the mercenaries, took heart. What had been achieved there by Jak the Drang might also be achieved here. The process took time. More than once we were forced to enter the open field and battle bands of masichieri—it was mostly them—in defense of a group of people. But our name and the report of our deeds spread.

When the Hamalese sent a force against us we melted away.

When we ran into real drikingers, bands who had been bandits before the troubles, they were dealt with in a proper and summary fashion. The bands who roamed the countryside now were death on wheels to the invaders of their country, and full of concern for native Vallians. We gathered more people, of course, in our peregrinations until we moved in a tidy little force, daily growing in strength, never halting in one place, but clearing up a spot of trouble and moving on.

The canalfolk were a tower of strength. The vens and venas, the vener, proved themselves fully alive to the peculiar advantages and possibilities of the canals, and long strips of narrow boats carried the refugees into the North East. Of course, occasionally, a caravan was stopped. Sometimes there were tragedies. But gradually, as the season passed over, we cleared the lands of most of the women and children. The task was colossal and, of course, we could never fully complete it. There were just too many people in these lands around the capital.

But we cleared so many that the Hamalese were forced to resort to setting guards on the farm people remaining. The fields were being left unattended, and no crops grew, and the food was going to run out—and soon. The hordes of rasts who had burst into Vallia and eaten of her goodness stored up in barns and warehouses would go hungry—unless they chose to leave.

I suppose—indeed, I know it to be true—that the Dray Prescot who is me was not the person in those days called Jak the Drang. Jak the Drang browbeat bandits, harangued lords and nobles, had no hesitation in dealing with the utmost ferocity with murderers and rapists and those who had battened on the misery of the people of Vallia. The name of Jak the Drang was whispered—in fear by his enemies and in pride and exultation by his friends and comrades.

But—it was hardly me, hardly the new Dray Prescot—although to be truthful, there was a damned lot of the old intemperate Dray Prescot in Jak the Drang.

When we reached Olordin's Well and found the little hamlet a razed wreck, without hair or hide of a soul, I admit I raved and ranted and was like to have done something exceedingly violent—which is against my nature—when Barty, who with a few friends had been waiting nearby, came running up. He had fliers and provisions and friends; and he reported that Dayra must have been at Olordin's Well but had long since departed.

I said: "Bear up, Barty. That young lady can take care of herself exceedingly well." Almost, I told him of Ros the Claw. The tiger-girl, the kissom chavonth-maiden in the black leathers.

"I believe she can, Jak." He eyed me. He was still the same elegant refined young man; but a little of the roughness of life had him. In a lowered tone, he said: "If she is anything like her father, then I feel sorry for anyone foolish enough to offend her."

"There is a task we must do, Barty." I told him of the scheme, and he burbled that, by Vox! he liked the sound of it. "The food has to be grown, say the Hamalese, and the Vallian farmers must grow it. We are seeing them safely away. But some, the rasts from Havilfar mew up, set working in the fields from dawn to dusk, alongside their slaves, put guards to watch and to whip. There is such a farm near here. We have sent out a call and the men will come—"

"I know, Jak," said Barty. "Your name carries much weight in these troublous times. The men will come."

The men did come, stealing by night from their fastnesses in the recesses of the forests or in the hills, for although Vallia is fertile and well-settled, there is still a great deal of it and many wild places remain untenanted save in times of turmoil. The men came and we made a descent on the guarded farm and freed everyone Vallian there, free man and slave alike, and the women and children joined the procession of narrow boats to the North East and the men joined one of the growing number of resistance bands. We laughed and counted it a victory.

It was around this time, when things were going well if slowly for us and I prepared to visit Valka, that an incident occurred whose importance I had no way of knowing at the time, although later on it was to play a vital, a decisive, part in ensuring my hide stayed around my flesh and bones. Our band had freed a group of villagers and we had seen them off and we were in camp. A group of locals—peasants, they might be called in another context—who gave us surly looks and refused help were found to have actively co-operated with the Hamalians. They had sided with the Hamalians against their own kind. When they discovered their error and tried to escape they were arrested.

Now people will always be found who will collaborate; by Zair, it is a matter of weighing evils. Some of my hardened old blade comrades, and Dorgo the Clis vociferous among them, were for stringing up the guilty ones forthwith.

It fell to me to harangue the mob, there in the erratic dramatic sparkle of the campfires. I told them many of the things you have heard me say before. Human life is sacred, diff and apim alike. These were deluded people; yes, they had betrayed good folk to terrible fates; but vengeance for the sake of vengeance destroys him who so callously metes out retribution without thought of the deeper motivations. We would not slay them. They would be set free, and in the shame they would feel they would hew to the path of justice henceforth. Well, even then I was not quite naive enough to believe all of them would never sin again; but for the salvation of a few the many must go pardoned. It was a hard dialectical struggle; but in the end, and because it was Jak the Drang who spoke, my view prevailed.

A small group of people vanished out of the firelight into the shadows as my men, still a little reluctantly, released the prisoners.

That group who vanished so smartly did not belong to my people; but they were gone. They had looked hardy. So we moved on from that area, and I delayed my visit to Valka, until we had established ourselves in another place, where we began at once to cause mischief to the aragorn, the masichieri and the Hamalese.

Then, I borrowed one of Barty's fliers and flew to Valka.

CHAPTER TWENTY

Fire Over Vallia

"No. I think the plan to be not a good plan. I do not like it. And, yes, I have been away to—away to where I have promised to speak to you of and will do when this mess is cleared up. But, as to your plan, no, my heart—in this I am not with you."

She looked at me. I braced myself up and returned the look. It is hard to cross my Delia—hard! It is nigh impossible. But, in this, I remained adamant.

"We are safe here in the Heart Heights," she said, and she crossed to the wall of rock and stared out and over into a vasty dim blueness separating this mountain fastness from the far peaks. "We resist the aragorn and the mercenaries, the Flutsmen and the masichieri. We drive them back. Soon, we shall retake Valkanium and the war will be won. I am no longer needed here."

"That can never be so—"

"You know what I mean! I shall return with you to Vallia and together will we eject the Hamalians—"

"I do not fight a war like this one. It is not even a proper guerilla struggle—well, more or less. It is dark and unpleasant. I prefer you to stay here and, by Zair! even here you risk yourself every day, for I know—"

"And since when have you, Dray Prescot, ever been prudent?"

I rubbed my chin, abashed. Then, stoutly, I said: "You would hardly recognize me, in these latter days. For Dray Prescot treads mighty small where once he—"

She laughed. The suns sheened in her hair, making those outrageous chestnut tints shimmer and shine. She clapped her hand to her slender waist, and half-drew her rapier.

"Dray Prescot? Aye, he lags well to the rear. All one hears these days is the name of Jak the Drang."

"Oh," I said. "Oh, well, he is a rascal, to be sure."

So we wrangled. I did not intend to stay long, but one thing and another retained me in Valka. Tom Tomor and Vangar fought their wars of liberation in Veliadrin, and my Pachaks were on the verge of clearing Zamra; but the days were hot with the sounds of strife. Drak had gone to Faol to search out the Manhounds, Melow the Supple and her son Kardo, who was the true and trusted heart-comrade to Drak. Shara, Melow's daughter, twin to Kardo, was, I understood, with my daughter Lela. And where she was—

"The Sisters of the Rose, my heart. Lela is much occupied with them in these times. From her I learn much of conditions."

"Lela and Shara did not go with us to Aphrasöe," I said and I know my voice sounded grim. "That must be rectified soon. I do not wish to look forward to what must follow else."

"And Barty Vessler?"

"Dayra is looking after herself. She is well able and—"

"Oh, aye. She learned well with the SoR—so well that she spurns us and goes her own ways." My Delia sounded hurt and more than a little bitter, which struck me with agony.

"So you finish your work in Valka. I will work on in Vallia. I called in on Forli and scouted MichelDen hoping to find Lykon Crimahan and report on his success. But there was no sign of him and the kovnate was still infested."

"He came on here, dejected, and now he is in the north, trusting that when we have cleared Valka and the islands we will march on MichelDen for him. His trust is not misplaced."

"Something may be made of him, yet. But I must play all the time on Vondium. Farris is flying back with me, eager to take over in Vomansoir. The people will welcome him—the fighting bands that remain, for we have made a clearance there."

"You take Farris and you will not take me!"

"No."

Down below in the shelter of the next terraced rocky wall a pastang of Valkan Archers marched out to take up their sentry posts. Delia had worked well in Valka. Those regiments of ours so treacherously sent to the north of the Mountains of the North had not been heard of. I could only trust they continued in existence. Of fliers all Vallians were pitifully short, and the Flutsmen still roamed, reiving and murdering from the air.

Around the capital, Vondium, I was drawing the net in tighter and tighter. I say I—I mean Jak the Drang. From Vomansoir we had extended to Rifuji and Nav Sorfall immediately to the east. Naghan Vanki, the old emperor's spymaster, had gone to ground and messengers from Jak the Drang sought his active assistance. The capital of Vallia, Vondium the Proud, was surrounded by imperial provinces, as seemed only wise. To the west of the Great River lay Vond, and to the east, Hyrvond. The river ran a long east-west reach here and to the north lay Bryvondrin. In all these imperial provinces the emperor's Justicar had been foully murdered, and men had been in despair. Now the infamous bands of Jak the Drang brought a new resistance and a fresh hope. The net drew in.

We went in presently to sit down to a sumptuous repast, by the reduced standards of the Valka of those days. But there was food and the rations were evenly spread among all.

Delia saw I meant what I said, and contented herself only by saying: "You will take a force of Valkans with you? Some of your Freedom Fighters, old blade comrades—"

"I have but Barty's voller, and that will take a bare fifty."

"Then take fifty fighting men of Valka, for they thirst to battle alongside their strom."

I cocked a cautious eye at her. Her color was up. So I knew what she intended. Slowly, I shook my head.

"You need all the fighting men here, my heart. And I find men who were stylors and farmers and cobblers and a thousand other trades springing up overnight into warriors." She

170

had listened enthralled to my story of the Phalanx. "And, sweet schemer," And that bit of sickly-sweet sarcasm aroused her, by Vox! "I do not want another stowaway as—"

"You knew all the time, then, before we fought at the Crimson Missals!"

"Mayhap I did. But you are essential here. Do you not think the Freedom Fighters of Valka relish battling alongside their Stromni?"

She lowered her eyelids; but she was mightily put out.

"And," I went on remorselessly. "You are not to venture yourself so. Do not go to froward into the battle."

"If I go froward it is because of—" And she stopped, and bit her lip, and so we gazed on each other.

When the time at last arrived when I could tarry no longer and I forced myself to tear myself away, that same Dray Prescot who was Lord of Strombor and Krozair of Zy, besides being Strom of Valka and, now, for his sins, some kind of Emperor of Vallia, she handed me a rolled bundle. It was scarlet. I knew what it was.

"I go back to being Jak the Drang."

"I know. Yet, at the end, methinks you will fly your own battle flag, that famous tresh men sing of, the battle standard Old Superb."

I took the flag. My hands brushed hers. So, for a space, we clung together. Then, with a stony face and a bursting heart, I went out to Barty's voller, and called the Remberees, and took off slanting into the morning blaze from the twin suns, from Zim and Genodras, the Suns of Scorpio fiery and glorious over the face of Kregen.

I did not unroll the flag. I stowed the tresh away, Old Superb, and wondered when, if ever, I would fly that battle banner above the hosts of liberated Vallia.

Looking back now I can see more clearly and understand many things that puzzled me at the time. The very completeness of the clearance of Hawkwa country, the repulse of The Iron Riders, impressed all who heard of it. The Iron Riders had shattered army after army of the Iron Legions of Hamal. And then a new army had arisen from the very people of Vallia themselves, a young, brave, confident army, and had routed the radvakkas utterly. No wonder men talked with bated breath of the accomplishment. All those months of labor had borne mighty fruit. The time had been well spent. No one sought to enquire into the character of that new Vallian army, to wonder how it would perform against the Hamalese. It had won. The laurels of victory crowned its spears.

And—the man who had accomplished this, the notorious Jak the Drang, had aroused the countryside, was gathering a host against Vondium. Then arm, friends! Gather yourselves for the final struggle—once the capital is Vallian once more then the rest of the country must follow.

I did not miss, also, the interesting if ironical fact that this had been made possible by those very people who had once sought so violently to free themselves from Vondium, to become independent within the empire. There were strong forces of Hawkwas who persisted with the old and, in my view, fallacious dream. But the hosts of the North East marched with Jak the Drang for a strong and comradely and united Vallia.

Mind you, I did not share the view that with the repossession of Vondium our problems would be solved. The vaster reaches of the island empire would remain in non-Vallian hands. But, I did admit, if not the end of the affair, then the capture of Vondium would signal the end of the beginning.

Delia had proved herself her usual self in her packing of the flier for the return journey. Among the contents of the many wicker hampers, beside food and weapons, were lengths of scarlet cloth. . . .

Farris, the Lord of Vomansoir, piloted for some of the time. We had much to say, one to the other, yet the words were hard to come by. . . . He welcomed my news of the recent events in his province. He had fought most valiantly in Valka and I in Vomansoir, so we were well quitted.

"Once we march into Vondium, majister," he said. "Once the people can look with renewed hope to a strong central power—"

"Not majister, Farris. Jak the Drang. And a strong central power as you put it may be a mischief in itself."

"You do not believe that!"

"Sometimes I do not. But, sometimes, I wonder. All I want to do is let Vallia alone. To let the people lead their own lives as they wish, happily." Then I was forced to add, to make absolutely sure Farris understood: "And we shall free all the slaves. It will take time and it will be a messy business; but I am resolved."

"There will be much opposition—vigorous and violent opposition. But you know that."

"Aye. I know that."

During his sojourn with my people in Valka Farris had

seen much of our ways, and understood much more clearly the way we thought Vallia should go. That we were right was a guiding principle; and we recognized the pitfalls in this kind of blind arrogance and arrogation of superiority. But the sights and smells and sounds of the slave bagnios reinforced our determination to go on, in humility, believing that what we did, in very truth, the right course.

"The men who were once slaves fight right stoutly in the new forces of Vallia," I told Farris. "They fight because they have been promised their freedom." However despicable a device that may be, I tried to think that in this case it was genuine, that the stalwart brumbytes, those ferocious Hakkodins, the prowling fighters of the bands closing now on Vondium, would not be betrayed. Then I would brighten. Anyway, I would say, who was there who would force them back under the yoke of slavery when they had formed an army, had seen what free men might do, had found themselves as men? There would be farms and workshops and goodly livings for them in the imperial provinces alone.

Taking Farris north to Vomansoir I dropped him off near his own provincial capital, that was, so the rascally leader of the bands of Freedom Fighters outside the city informed us, due to the fall on the morrow. I stayed to watch and in the event to fight. The men surged forward to the attack yelling: "Vallia!" and "Jak the Drang!" and we burst in. The people rose. The Hamalese fought and, not always but more often than not, defeated the vicious bands of Freedom Fighters who sought to oppose them directly. But we chivvied and harassed them, and drove them into the fortress, and mewed them up. It would only be a matter of time, and the Lord Farris expressed himself as highly pleased.

As to the men and women who had resisted so stoutly, only to have their erstwhile lord return at the penultimate hour, they welcomed Farris, as I believed, because he was known as a just and enlightened lord, to whom any man might turn in distress in the sure knowledge of sympathy and ready assistance. So I said.

It was left to a one-eared, dog-toothed rogue to say to me, bold with the camaraderie of the Freedom Fighters: "That may be true, Jen Jak. But, also, the Lord Farris is befriended by you and returns with your blessings."

And another, a stout woman carrying a butcher's cleaver, her bare forearms red and shining, said: "We know who has given us back our homes and our shops. No one stands over us but Jak the Drang, who is our lord. And we welcome the

173

Lord Farris because of that. Because he is set back in his place by Jak the Drang."

And the cry went up: "Jak the Drang, Emperor of Vallia. Hai, Jikai! Jak the Drang."

That, as I told the multitudes assembled on the next day, was the rehearsal for Vondium. They cheered. The broad kyro swarmed with people, packing in; the noise reverberated to the skies. Once the organizational details had been finalized here, a great host would march from Vomansoir and descend on Vondium. The timing was crucial. They must arrive when all the other bands congregated. If they were too late their help would be lost. If they were too early they might consume the countryside before we struck. Immense quantities of hoarded food were collected against that eventuality, and fresh weapons were secured from the arsenals, and the people cheered, and I sent the flier aloft heading for the Fredom Fighters ringing Vondium.

During all these periods of trouble an alert eye had been kept on the lookout for people who would serve in the future to create the better kind of Vallia these folk deserved. The positions of responsibility must be occupied by men and women with the welfare of the people at heart. Already a strong cadre of people who would take over once the invaders had been driven away existed. And, all the time, doubts assailed me. Was this a dictatorship of the worst kind? Well—no. Vallia would breathe easier once we had cleared the invaders away and could get back to living our own lives in freedom. So we all believed, and worked for, and, many of us, died for.

All these high ideals and abstract theories on the best forms of government were swept away when I landed at the rendezvous with Barty. He was there; but he was alone, and the bands were nowhere to be seen. His face looked pinched.

"Prince!" he said then he swallowed, and got out: "Jak! We must flee this accursed spot at once."

"Tell me."

The trees sighed in the night wind, a few stars pricked the cloud-covered sky, everything shrouded in the mystery of night. Barty shivered.

"The fighting bands have moved away. Hamalese came—a host. They are encamped less than an ulm from here. Let us go."

"Why is the spot accursed, Barty?"

He had waited for me. That had taken courage, seeing the

174

distress he was in. An elegant, refined, very proper young man. Barty Vessler, the Strom of Calimbrev.

"They set up an idol—a weird thing. They adhere to some religion or other—I do not understand it. But they are over in the next valley, a-worshipping and a-chanting—"

"I would see this."

"No! They have guards—they are a host—"

I marched off in the direction he indicated and he pattered along after. The night was dark, although not a night of Notor Zan. We reached the brow of the hill and so looked down onto the heads of Hamalese. In the center of the little valley, a dell in reality, an altar had been set up. An image shone above the basalt slab, an image illuminated in the light of many torches.

I saw.

"And they took a child from the village, and they are going—going to sacrifice it, I think. . . ."

I looked down on the assembled congregation and saw they chanted praises and genuflected to the blasphemous silver statue of a gigantic leem.

Lem, the Silver Leem, flourished most foully in Vallia. I watched and I shivered. This was not in the plans.

CHAPTER TWENTY-ONE

Vision at Voxyri

This I had not planned, had not foreseen. This was not abstract. This was here and now, red, bloody, fiery, utterly demanding everything a man can give, and more which comes from the spirit he does not know he possesses, and I was caught, trapped, held by the mirth of the gods in a vise that could be released in only one way. And that way could undo everything I had fought and struggled for for so long. . . .

"There's only one way to do this, Barty. Come on." I ran back for the flier. Barty, shaking, ran with me.

"What—?"

"It must be quick and sure and certain." I took the voller up savagely, smashed the controls over. If she failed me now, then this was the end of Dray Prescot. Through the night we

"The sacrificial knife lifted."

swooped, low over the wooded crest, skimming above the treetops. The torches burned brightly, illuminating that blasphemous statue. Lem the Silver Leem had no part in civilized men's scheme of life.

"Ready, Barty?"

"Aye, majister—ready!"

I took the voller down steeply aimed at the black basalt slab. The naked, pitiful, tiny form of a child lay there, crying. Priests moved in their cowls and hoods. The sacrificial knife lifted. Abruptly men were yelling. The flier hit the plinth and I was out, ripping the Krozair brand free. Two priests flew in four different directions. Blood drenched down onto the basalt slab, staining darker stains. Men were screaming. Guards charged toward me, their swords lifted. I slashed and swung and the longsword purred through the flesh and bone. The brand may not have been a true Krozair blade; but Ferenc the Edge had forged sweetly and true. Barty was out, a knife slashing the child's bonds. More guards tried to interface and the dripping brand cut them down as weeds are cut down.

A voice lifted among the multitude, for people were yelling and screaming, and moving dizzyingly this way and that.

"Dray Prescot!" screamed this voice, high and shocked. "I know that devil! It is Dray Prescot—"

"Aye!" I roared as I whirled the Krozair brand. "Aye! I am that devil Dray Prescot! And there is no place in all of Vallia for Leem Lovers—no! There is no place in all Hamal, in all Havilfar, in all of Paz for kleeshes like you!" And the stained brand bit deeply and chucked on, merciless, as Barty freed the child and leaped back into the voller.

"Dray! Ready!"

"I am with you!"

The longsword twitched this way and that and flying arrows caromed away. This was quite like old times. A last massive figure wearing the brown and silver of Lem attempted to stop me and the Krozair blade hit mercilessly and he screeched and fell away and I was in the voller and Barty was slamming the levers hard over and we lifted and soared away from that cess-pit of human depravity. Lem the Silver Leem! No, I shouted down, cursing them all, no, your foul creed shall never sully Vallia.

I was, as you will see, wrought up.

Only speed and audacity had done the trick, of course. Many a Krozair brother, many a Clansman, many a Djang, would have done the same. By Zair! Was there anything else to do?

We flew back to the camp and were able to press the child into the arms of his mother. That, by Opaz, was worth it all.

Then we set about the final preparations for the day of judgment.

The point must be insisted on; this was only the end of the beginning. Many songs were made of the events of the next days. One of the gates of Vondium is called the Gate of Voxyri, and two canals merge here, crossed by a bridge, called the Bridge of Voxyri. Outside the walls, which were tumble-down, extends a wide common land and this is called the Drinnik of Voxyri.

As our forces gathered, fierce, hard, determined men, they brought stories of how the Hamalese were everywhere pulling back to the capital. We could see the long columns winding along the roads and along the canals clumsily using commandeered narrow boats. Something vast was afoot.

These columns were attacked with vicious fury, using the guerillero tactics that struck from ambush and melted away. The provinces around the capital were emptying of Hamalese and their mercenary allies. We watched the capital walls and suburbs and surrounded the city at a distance, and we took prisoners.

These told us enough so that, when we pieced it all together, we understood the magnitude of the event. This was a moment of world history.

The Empress Thyllis in Hamal was recalling her army, was sending for many of the volunteers of her iron legions to return to Hamal. The full details were not known; but a revolution had broken out and there had been reverses in the campaigns in the Dawn Lands around the Shrouded Sea. Men were needed. Taking a calculating look at the situation in hated Vallia, Thyllis must have decided to relinquish those provinces in which organized and determined resistance was costing her too much. Phu-Si-Yantong, known as the Hyr Notor, had successfully arranged that those areas still securely under his thumb should remain so. The capital would be held, for its value was obvious and immense. So I looked at Barty and he made a face.

"It is great and glorious news; but it makes the taking of Vondium a thousand times more difficult, by Vox!"

"Maybe. They are short of fliers and must use them to keep open their lines of communication. The Flutsmen are already leaving, as we know, for there are scant pickings for

178

them now. We must redouble our efforts on the columns straggling in. But the plans go ahead."

"It is mortal difficult to infiltrate people into the city now—the mercenaries sew the place up like a spinster's—"

"Given a lead the citizens will rise."

Within Vondium some of our people spread the word. When our Freedom Fighters attacked then Vondium would rise. But I wanted to defeat the Hamalese and their allies and be seen to defeat them—not me, not Dray Prescot, not even Jak the Drang, I hasten to add. But the fighting people of Vallia—they were the ones who must defeat the Hamalese and be seen to defeat them.

Also, it was reported that the Prince Majister, Dray Prescot, had been seen in the vicinity. There had been Vallian witnesses to the events at the shrine of Lem the Silver Leem. It seems to me that in the events of my life I have been recounting there had been precious little of that old skirling helter-skelter hurtling into blood-red action—and yet, the truth is that in these vast confrontations, in these campaigns, in these secret machinations for power, the old blood still does go thumping along the veins, there is still the same old fey passion of combat. The fascination of men and women scheming obsessively for power is undeniable. All I was trying to do was to make sure that power fell into the hands of people with the general good at heart—and that is a trick beset with many pitfalls, by Vox.

My men spoke words that warmed me, and made me want to smile, words that were droll in their context, but words spoken from the heart, with passion.

"Dray Prescot? Aye. . . . Where has this Dray Prescot been in the days of trouble? It is Jak the Drang we follow and fight for. It is Jak the Drang who is rightfully Emperor of Vallia—and will be!" So spoke my men, stoutly.

Couriers spurred into camp with reports of a host advancing from the north and at the same time reports reached us from the city that the last group of infiltrators to go into hiding to await the signal to rise had been taken by mercenaries. We could wait no longer. The city would rise, we would strike from the outside, and the co-ordination would bring us the victory.

Then Nath Nazabhan rode into camp, disguised as a Resistance Fighter. At that, the truth acted as a disguise. I greeted him in my tent very warmly, already half-guessing what he had done.

179

"Aye majister—Jak the Drang. We owe you. I have brought a phalanx. We marched. We await your orders—"

Telling him how welcome he was did not soften my words.

"You have been warned many times that sword and shield men may not be directly attacked by the phalanx, except in exceptional circumstances—"

"We have many Hakkodins and archers—"

"Thank Vox for that. But this is city fighting, street fighting, dirty work. The brumbytes—"

"I shall bring the phalanx up, majister, and await your orders." He spoke with a persistent stubbornness I found at once infuriating and confoundedly familiar, for I recognized how much of my teachings had rubbed off on him. I nodded.

"Then await the signals. Volodu the Lungs will blow them."

"Quidang!"

So the phalanx of Nath Nazabhan explained the host from the north. We would have to take the city quickly, then. . . .

As he left he said, not off-handedly, but casually: "We have new flags for the Jodhris, now." A fine, dedicated fighting man, Nath Nazabhan, who knew why he fought." But the great tresh of Vallia flies over all."

The morning of the chosen day dawned fair and bright. The sky shone with a deep lustrous blueness. The Suns of Scorpio cast down their opaline brilliance in a sheening glory, the ruby and emerald mingling and streaming and illuminating everyone and everything as though revealing the inmost spirit and animation of human and object alike.

So I wrapped the old scarlet breechclout about me and drew up the broad lestenhide belt with its dulled silver buckle. An armory of weapons was girded on. Over my shoulder went the great Krozair longsword that had never been forged in the Eye of the World. And, also, because Delia had placed them in the voller I took a great Lohvian longbow and a quiver of shafts all fletched with the rose-colored feathers of the zim korf of Valka.

And so, on the day of Opaz the Deliverer, the signal was sounded.

Vondium rose.

The plan called for small independent groups to attack at selected points around the walls, aiming for particular gates and bridges. These were diversionary attacks, of course, and because there were not too many of them to reveal that fact to the Hamalese we trusted they would draw the swods off. Although the walls were in generally crumbled condition no

180

one seriously anticipated ill-equipped guerillas to be able to storm over in the face of professional opposition. We wanted the swods clear of the main thrust; my commanders were confident we could do it.

The main attack, aimed to get as many fighters as possible into the city in one overwhelming tumultuous mass, would go in over the Voxyri Bridge. The wide expanse of common ground, Voxyri Drinnik, had to be crossed first. The plan called for the civic rising and the diversionary attacks to co-incide, and then for the mass to charge into the city across the Drinnik, over the Bridge and through the Gate of Voxyri.

We had chosen the Voxyri complex because the bridge spanned a double canal making it the widest leading into Vondium, and the gate handled the heaviest traffic, and was the widest. These facts occurred in their calculations to the Hamalese high command.

No one ever proved a single thing. It was possible that among our own ranks *Punica fides* existed. The Bridge would have been taken without difficulty against a normal watch.

The Resistance Fighters in the immense mobs waiting for the signal to attack across Voxyri Drinnik were guerillas, Freedom Fighters. They were not line infantry, not even Peltasts or Hypaspists. They had been disciplined on the line of march and in camp and in respect of the proper behavior of fighting men; but they were quite out of hand now, when battle sounded. They would not stand their time in concealment.

Thin spires of smoke rose from the city and we could hear the first clangor from the walls and streets.

"Not long now," said Barty. He sat his zorca erect and his smooth face bore an exalted, shining look that afflicted me sorely. All about us the Freedom Fighters hunkered in cover. We heard trumpets from the city. These undisciplined mobs who fought for what they loved would not wait our signal.

They rose into the open. Screaming their hatred for the defilers of their country they ran out. Half-crazed, brandishing weapons, roaring, they burst all thoughts of discipline.

In a wild shrieking bunch they tore for the Bridge.

The combination of factors collided disastrously. Perhaps there was no treachery. Perhaps the swods merely acted as experienced soldiers. Perhaps in these latter days Catastrophe Theory can indicate on its models the unfolding progression of events, the upward line, the incurve, the downward trend that, curving through a million dimensions, abruptly explodes

181

into catastrophe. Whatever the inner truths may be—here and now, on Voxyri's Drinnik, we stared disaster in the face.

This screaming onslaught confirmed our intentions long before the Hamalese had been drawn away by feint attacks. The Bridge and Gate of Voxyri were the widest and quickest way into the city and therefore the best. They were and it was. Except—except that right here and now we saw cogent reasons why they and it were the worst possible ways we could have chosen.

From the Gate moved out long columns of soldiers, swods of Hamal in perfect line and dressing, trotting on with ranked shields, with crossbowmen flanking, with standards unfurled, trotting on to deploy into their long lines of armed and and armored men. They were ready. They had not suddenly been called up from barracks or billets, summoned with drumming urgency from their beds. They were ranked and ready—waiting.

And, from the narrower Gate of Rosslyn along the way giving access over the canal trotted squadron after squadron of cavalry.

For whatever reason, the Hamalian army had not been decoyed. Now they deployed, faced front, and advanced.

The roaring ranging mass of people hurtling down on them had no form or order. Archers and spearmen, swordsmen and axemen, all mixed up together in a boiling torrent, they spumed along like the primeval breakers of the sea itself. The long ordered lines of shields would meet them unyieldingly and the swords of the swods, blood-drenched, would be unmerciful.

As the iron legions of Hamal moved into view there was perceptible in the mass of crazed onrushing people the barest check. The noise suffused more reason. The regiments of Hamal marched out, deploying, ranking shields. And my people, gathering themselves as men do about to burst into burning buildings, gave a loud vociferous shout, a high shrilling moan of rapture, and flung themselves headlong on.

No rapture, no headlong charge, was going to carry partially armored and casually armed and shieldless mobs over or through that iron wall.

Useless to sound the recall. All there was left to do was to kick in heels and go pelting down after those crazed people of mine and burst through and so lead them, hoping that the inevitable stumbling falls of the zorcas might break a way through the shield wall.

I turned to bellow at my choice band, I lifted out my legs

to kick in, and I heard and saw the wonder, the marvel—as, indeed, I had surmised I might, hoping, and condemning my hope as evil.

The brazen trumpets shrilled high demanding notes into the heated air, all together, trilling blood-thumpingly on—sounding the "Advance." I saw—ah! I remember it—I remember it. . . . I saw the long serried lines of vosk-skull helmets, bronze-fitted, glittering, the crimson plumes nodding defiantly above. I saw the level wall of shields, crimson and yellow, gleaming. I saw the thickly-clumped forest of pikes, all slanting as one, rank on rank, I heard the heavy resonant blam-blam-berram of the deep-toned drums, and the trampling onrush of bronze-studded war-boots. Rank on rank, Relianch and Jodhri advancing, the files of the Phalanx pressed on.

A pungent smell of the red flowers of the letha tree wafted to my nostrils—hallucination, memory, evocation of another time and place where this advancing machine of glory, devotion, war and destruction had been born.

I trembled.

I, Dray Prescot, in the evil grip of grandeur, trembled. For Jak the Drang had warned and warned, and the brumbytes had laughed and not cared to listen. And I knew what I knew. My tumultuous mobs of undisciplined Freedom Fighters would be savaged and destroyed by the iron of Hamal. The temptation shook me, terrible visions of what would occur tormented me. The Phalanx advanced, perfect in order, moving as a single gigantic organism.

Could I? Dare I? What right had any man to demand the sacrifice of blood and life from another? Even with the fate of a country, an empire and all its people, at stake?

I knew what Nath Nazabhan would say. I knew what the answering roar from the brumbytes and the Hakkodins would be. And yet—the consequences of selfishness were incalculable.

So, shaking, filled with indecision, hating the fates that had brought me to this, I sat my zorca. What right . . . ?

Because a man is called emperor and sits in the seat of power over multitudes of men and women—does that give him the right? I did not think so. I had been called to be emperor by those crazed mobs who would so soon be destroyed and by those ranked and orderly pikemen who awaited my signal. They had placed the power in my hands, and not because I am blessed or cursed with the yrium. I cupped their fates in my hands. Worthy or not worthy, it was all down to

183

me, and to me, simple sailorman though I am, the fate of empire had been entrusted.

This vision of empire at Voxyri, this fleeting hallucination of power and glory as the Phalanx halted as one, glittering, splintered with sun-glory, waiting my signal—my signal!—overwhelmed me. I saw the flags proudly lofting above the Jodhris. Nath had told me the Jodhris had been given new treshes. Scarlet, those flags, scarlet slashed with the broad yellow cross. So he knew. Nazab Nalgre his father must have confided in him.

Over the brilliant and formidable mass of Phalanx awaiting my orders waved Old Superb, the battle flag of Dray Prescot.

So could I take the granite decision and into my own hands and heart allow the creeping death that such a decision might bring? And in the suns-sprinkled scene I saw a private chamber within some anonymous hotel or high-class tavern, the walls lush with rosy drapes, the samphron oil lamps shining, the wide white-sheeted bed, I saw the room clear as the trumpets pealed and the zorcas tossed their heads and the iron legions of Hamal advanced to meet that headlong, rapturous, pathetic charge of the Freedom Fighters.

And, in that room I saw a woman, standing, half-turned, the samphron-oil lamp's gleam limning her form, supple and sweetly curved, secretly shadowed. The rosy light glimmered on her flesh. I saw her head lift in that old familiar dear way and the heavy fall of her brown hair, rich with those outrageous auburn tints. Standing waiting in that room that was not our own, Delia smiled, and filled all my mind and heart, and I drank her in and slaked my desolation with her goodness. That welcoming smile, that special, secret, intimate smile between ourselves alone enfolded me and I could not feel the zorca between my knees or the helmet pressing my brow, and the dust and stink of armed and armored men shrank and faded away. I looked upon my Delia as I was wont to do in those precious moments of our deepest privacy. And a man moved toward her, taking her into his arms, leading her to the waiting bed. And I saw his face.

Palpitating with love for Delia and ready to cast all the mad desires for empire and power and dominion to the four winds and revel only in her, I saw his face, and saw he wore that tousle-haired, knowing, surely-smiling, handsome face of Quergey the Murgey. I sat the zorca like stone and the suns fell. Pain cleft me. I saw the bitter fighting as my Vallians reached those iron-hard shields and the thraxters struck, in and out, in and out, and scattered their red droplets upon the sundered bodies of my people.

The bodies clung together. The shield wall advanced. The pointed swords thrust in and out, in and out, and the tumbled bodies fell into the dust of the Drinnik. Naked flesh pierced by steel swords bled into the dirt. Together they forced themselves on and together they died.

No anguish touched me for the dead. Not then. The agony within me bit and burned as acid bites, corroding through everything, corrupting, defiling, destroying. My whole body flamed a single blaze of torment.

This obscene insanity was not real. The blood and death all about me was not wanted; but its evil was real. Better, perhaps, the ghostly hallucination than the dreadful reality. Surely better, certainly surely, that neither should be real! A spark I did not know I possessed flared and I saw and I understood. This was the work of Phu-Si-Yantong. He had thrown his powers upon me, using his kharrna to infect my mind with this horror. And the horror almost destroyed me. A Wizard of Loh is a bitter and implacable enemy to any man; but ordinary mortals are bitter and implacable, they do not wield the sorcerous and supernatural powers of a Wizard of Loh.

Yantong had determined to crush my will to fight. He infected my mind with diseased pictures. That room, that woman panting with passion for Quergey the Murgey, they were not real, they were hallucinations of the worst kind. But they had almost unmanned me. The crucial time approached as the ram of a swifter slices toward its victim's side. The noise shattered skywards. The stink of raw blood infected the air. Delia—my Delia—would have no truck with a vanity-feeding, suave, seeming-sincere seducer like Quergey the Murgey, no matter how badly I had treated her in leaving her abandoned for so long, for she knew I would come back to her, always.

Phu-Si-Yantong's vile trick had failed.

For my Delia knew me as I knew her, and our knowledge encompassed all of pain as well as love. For better or worse, for all the spaces between, in vaol-paol, we were the unity that transcends oneness, we were Dray and Delia.

Shouting like a crazy man—no, shouting as the crazy man I truly was in that anguished moment—I forced the zorca around and sent him haring across Voxyri's Drinnik. Straight at the figure at the right flank of the Phalanx I galloped. For there was a Phalanx there, two full Kerchuris. Straight at Kyr

185

Nath Nazabhan I rode, yelling, roaring, screaming at the top of my lungs.

"Jodhris!" I shrieked, whirling my sword above my head. "Jikaida! Jodhris!"

Nath responded instantly and the trumpets pealed. The even-numbered Jodhris from the right moved on; the odd numbers stood fast. The Phalanx formed a checkerboard. Square and trim in their alignments, the Relianches within the Jodhris halted and the glittering mass poised, in Jikaida, ready.

Volodu came crashing up behind me but to one side, for at my back rode Korero the Shield.

"Blow Archers to the Intervals, Volodu!"

He blew, the notes ringing out over the screaming racket erupting from the mobs of Freedom Fighters running across the Drinnik to follow their comrades as the bolts fell among them. I had to shut my ears to that frightful sound. The noise spumed on. The stinks drenched us with sweat. The brilliance of the suns splintering from bronze and iron dizzied the senses. The zorca moved under me, bounding on.

"Blow for the Cavalry!"

Now Nath was up with me, beaming, entranced, sitting his mount with the consummate ease of the true zorcaman, his armor a shining splendor.

"Well met, Nath. Your cavalry?"

"Coming up on the flank—there is a canal to cross—"

"You will blow the Charge?"

At once grave, he nodded, aware of the importance of the moment.

"As Varkwa the Open-Handed is my witness, majister, this is a moment that will be remembered in all Vallia." The barred visor half-shadowed his face. He drew a breath. "I will blow the Charge."

Nath called on Varkwa the Open-Handed, the spirit of generosity in Vallia, uniting all Vallians. I knew I had seriously hurt Delia by my enforced absences from her and that the oily minions of Quergey the Murgey would seek to take advantage of her unhappiness and defenselessness and sense of rejection. But I thought she knew me, knew me, plain Dray Prescot, well enough to comprehend that the necessary spaces between married couples were for us illuminated by the mutual light of love.

Life flows on like an ever-running stream and all things are mutable and must change, even to the rocks within that eternal flow no matter how hard their natures, and are sculpted into new and ever-changing never-repeating forms—so it is said. But there are things that never change. We poor mortals must learn to live in harmony with nature and adapt our ways as we progress through life bending with the current, always learning afresh—so it is said. But there are things we learn and know to be true and hold dearly.

The sorcerous trick flung at me by Yantong had failed. But it had jolted me in ways I would understand later. Delia and I should not bear the burden of secrets; between us they would be obscene, as obscene as the advantages taken by Quergey the Murgey in appearing understanding and sympathetic to a distressed wife and offering a fresh focus for affection, feeding vanity and the sense of crippled identity. His offers of help and a ready ear were self-centered. By their dark betrayals they destroyed where they purported to heal.

Phu-Si-Yantong had known only too well how to get at me, to cause me the deepest of anguished suffering, to steal from Delia and me, to betray and rob us, to tear me into pieces.

One day, I knew, Yantong and I would meet. On that day I would not forget his use of the despicable Quergey the Murgey against Delia and me.

So, with the name of Varkwa to guide us in generosity, Nath gave his orders. Volodu cast me a reproachful look as the trumpets of the Phalanx sounded; but the moment belonged to Nath and the brumbytes he had brought all the live long way from Therminsax.

The Charge blew. The brumbytes thrust their fierce plumed helmets forward, slanting in the sunshine, the shields locked, crimson and yellow. The pikes came down. The Phalanx advanced. As a checkerboarded mass of bronze and crimson the Phalanx picked up speed, moved with a beauty and power of unison, crashed across the Drinnik of Voxyri—Charged!

Watchful of the flank Jodhris, I saw they would be too far extended as the Drinnik narrowed before the Bridge. Volodu blew "Eleventh and Twelfth Jodhris stand fast," followed moments later by: "Under command Relianches, right, follow on." That would annoy the Eleventh and Twelfth. But what a tribute to their training and discipline! They halted, waited and then, tossing pikes, moved to the right and so followed on in the intervals.

The scene sprawled on that wide expanse of common ground presented an awesome spectacle. The background hemmed in the action. The walls and towers of a great city lofted, badly burned and scarred and now being rebuilt on a grander and vaster scale. Against those lowering walls the extended lines of Hamalese soldiers, smart and brilliant with weapons gleaming, confident in their ability to destroy the ragged hosts who ran upon their deaths, fought with the sureness of confidence. The mobs ran on, shrieking, waving their weapons, racing down to slam into that iron line of shields and those cruel swords. And, beyond all, flowing swiftly on, fired with ardor and passion, the solid masses of the pikemen pressed on with heavy tread and their archers in the intervals showered the foe with darting shafts.

"What a sight!" screamed Barty.

"It is a battle," I shouted back.

But it was not like any battle we had fought before.

The arrows criss-crossed. The Hamalese wheeled up their varters in the intervals between regiments, and the iron bolts loosed. Larghos Cwopin, a good man with a knife and a ready laugh, abruptly vomited from his saddle, the varter bolt piercing him through and through, iron and red with blood. The zorcas galloped on. The arrows fell. Men screamed and fought and died.

Korero the Shield performed prodigies, his four arms and tail hand manipulating his shields with that rhythmic grace of perfect mental and bodily co-ordination, a marvel.

Many feats of heroism passed unremarked. The red mask of horror floated before our eyes. The iron of Hamal remained unbreached. I could feel the armor upon my body, the helmet pressing my head, the grip of the zorca between my knees, I could feel all and know I was alive and yet feel nothing for death hovered near.

The noise roared on and now the brumbytes broke into a deep-voiced song, almost a paean, a heavy beating song that blended with the solid nerve-tingling blam-blam-berram of their drums. The flags flew. The name of the song does not matter—rather, as the armies clashed at last, the name means so much I cannot repeat it. It has been said that the best position for light troops to stand before the advancing phalanx is two hundred feet out. The guerillas of Vallia were much farther out than that; and so their fight, brief though it was, lasted far longer than I cared for. Then the Hakkodin were up with them and then—and then the savage bristle of pikes crunched into the shields of Hamal.

Even as the guerillas and the Hakkodins passed back in the intervals, the Hakkodins urging the guerillas on, and the archers faded to take up new positions in rear, drills gone through a thousand times, so the second line of Jodhris in the checkerboard smashed awesomely into the swods.

The Hamalian cavalry was caught as it debouched onto the Drinnik and was whiffed away as The Iron Riders had been whiffed away. The Phalanx moved forward, moved on and into and through the lines of Hamalian soldiers. They should not have done, of course. They should not have been able to do that magnificent thing. But the irregulars, the Freedom Fighters, the guerillas, had opened the way, had given the phalanx that little time it needed, and the phalanx swept on.

The thought hit me as I sent our little band hurtling on to enter the city as the Phalanx formed Reliance by Reliance to press on over Voxyri's Bridge and through the Voxyri Gate, the marvelous and yet vexatious thought, that there would be no holding the brumbytes now. They would believe themselves perfectly capable of going up as a phalanx against sword and shield men and of winning every time. And I knew that was not on.

Through the Gate and into the city I bellowed for Volodu to sound the "Brumbytes, stand fast." And then: "Archers, Hakkodin—General Chase."

General Chase. Yes, I know. But my old sea-faring days had dictated that, and now, how it fitted!

The city seethed and bubbled with conflict and the noise surf-roared into the heavens. This moment was the moment we had looked forward to, when ragged half-armed people swept crazily upon the army of Hamal and, far more particularly upon the masichieri. Getting these fighters into the city had been the trick and it would never have been done without the timely assistance of the Phalanx. So I believe. I know miracles occur; I can only say that a miracle had occurred there, on Voxyri Drinnik when the brumbytes of the phalanx toppled the sword and shield swods of Hamal.

The conflict rattled and roared and thundered on, surging this way and that. Many a poor devil toppled into a canal. The fight gradually assumed an order, a shape, and centered on the palace. Somehow I was out there in the front, loosing those deadly rose-feathered shafts, whipping out the longsword when the counter-attacks came in, urging on the men, urging them all on, guerilla and Hakkodin alike, cherishing them, giving them by example effective ways of fighting this kind of messy affair.

Every now and then a man or a woman would give a sudden, startled look. I would bellow out in the old intemperate, good-humored way: "On! On for Vallia!"

189

By the time the kyro before the palace had been reached we all knew that the city was ours. The remnants of the invaders clustered in the palace which reared, lapped in scaffolding, ringed by lumber and stone and all the bush paraphernalia of rebuilding. Phu-Si-Yantong had, indeed, sought to beautify his conquest.

The various leaders of the different bands and groups came together and, where necessary, I made the necessary pappattu. We stood, a group of ferocious men in the grip of the victory fever, and stared balefully upon the palace. The wink of weapons and the glitter of helmet and the flutter of plume and flag told us the place was still garrisoned.

"We will not attack," I said. "We do not have to lose any more good men. They will come out, all in due time."

There were arguments, of course. But I would not be swayed.

Many of my men were furious, and Nath Nazabhan and Dorgo the Clis and others of like ilk chief among them.

"How can we proclaim Jak the Drang Emperor of Vallia if we are not in the palace? That would not be right or decent!"

"Perhaps I do not wish to be emperor—"

"But you have the right!"

"The right of the sword."

"The right of leading us all, the right of holding men's hearts, the right of justice—Vallia cries out for an emperor to hold men together in amity—and you are the man!"

Even I, however reluctantly, could see the sense in that last sentiment. Vallia needed to be healed.

With a twinkling and altogether wonderful suddenness, flags of truce equivalent to white flags appeared along the battlements. Trumpets blew the parley. A deputation advanced from the palace across the kyro to where our group of commanders waited. Our people yelled, until our trumpets blew the still. In silence save for a little breeze that whispered with the flags, the men of Hamal, invaders in Vallia, advanced to surrender to the Vallians.

The scene struck brilliance and color, illuminated, stark, vibrating, it seemed to me, with the historical importance of the moment.

And here I must confess that although memory is not faulty, much of the ensuing event, many of the happenings that followed, echo back to me now vaguely, ill-defined, charged with an emotion and a wonder altogether marvelous—and embarrassing, too to an old sea-salt like me, a simple fighting man.

The commanders formed a semicircle and I found myself standing a little front and center. In that group of loyal men were many to whom you have been introduced; the roll call is profoundly moving. Behind them clustered, seething and yet silent and intent, the victorious forces of Vallia who had retaken their capital city.

The Hamalese made a brave show in their armor and uniforms, but they carried no weapons, and they looked strained and exhausted.

At their head marched a man I knew.

He had been in attendance on Queen Thyllis when that woman had dragged me through the streets of Ruathytu in her triumphal procession when she made herself Empress of Hamal. I had been lapped in chains and dragged at the tail of a calsany. This man, Vad Inrien ham Thofoler, had been a dwa-Chuktar then, a man bucking for power and position. Clearly he had reached both, for now he was a general, a Kapt, in command of the Hamalese forces in this sector of Vallia. He marched up, his heavy face with the bitter lines about the nose and lips held in that rigid look of disdain for what was going on. He halted before me.

The silence held, thin, acute, with only the little breeze to ruffle flags and standards and scurry leaves over the stones of the kyro. He slapped up his arm in salute.

"Hai, Dray Prescot, Prince Majister of Vallia. We cry quarter. We would negotiate—"

The pressing crowd at the back of the group of my commanders sucked in a single gigantic gulp of breath. A few small cries broke out, then more and more, a sudden tempest of yells and shouts.

"Dray Prescot! Dray Prescot! This is Jak the Drang! Our own Jak the Drang, Emperor of Vallia!"

And then—it had to happen, sooner or later—among the yelling Nath Nazabhan and the others brought order. They yelled in their turn, words that were picked up and repeated back through the hosts and along the avenues and boulevards, until the very sky over Vondium rang.

"This man whom you know as Jak the Drang is Dray Prescot, Emperor of Vallia."

The yells—the shouts—the astounded bellows of disbelief.

At last I signalled to Volodu the Lungs, whose mouth hung open foolishly, and he blew the still. Korero wore a tiny sly smile, and that confirmed me in my suspicions that he knew,

191

"I am Dray Prescot." I roared it out. "And I am Jak the Drang. And we Vallians have gained a great triumph this day of Opaz the Deliverer."

The incredulous uproar would have broken out again. I saw Korero move forward and he took out a certain scarlet bundle. I wondered with dizzied startlement just how much Delia had told him. He hauled out a pike and he tied on that old scarlet flag, to hoist it up. I heard the people yelling again: "Hai Jikai! Hai Jikai, Dray Prescot, Jak the Drang! Hai, Jikai!"

So I looked up, expecting to see Old Superb, that flag with the yellow cross on the scarlet field. And I saw—I saw a flag I had once seen in my mind's eye, seasons and seasons ago as we flew home from the Battle of the Dragon's Bones.

The yellow saltire of Vallia on the red ground flew there; but superimposed upon it gleamed my old yellow cross. The tresh formed a union of colors, a new flag, the new flag of Vallia.

A dark vision crossed my mind. We had Hamal to deal with, we had the vile religion of Lem the Silver Leem to transform into something of worth or suppress utterly, we had problems overseas and at home, and, looming monstrously over all, we had the shanks from over the curve of the world to resist or be finally beaten down. For only a small and precious space could we rest, rejoicing in what we had accomplished, for so much more remained to be done.

In a joyful procession amid a tumultuous host we moved into the palace of Vondium. The regalia was brought out. Where the false emperor Seakon had gone no one knew or cared. The precious objects, the ceremonial adjuncts, the crown, the throne, Drak's Sword—of which I shall have more to say—were brought out so that all might see. They sat me on the throne and the crown settled on my head and I took the necessary things, hand by hand, and the priests chanted and the trumpets blew and the people yelled.

Through it all a hollowness possessed me, for the rest of Vallia we had not so far liberated remained.

But the moment was sacred and meaningful.

For the fact was indisputable. I was the Emperor of Vallia, chosen by the people, emperor by their will, and seated on the throne because they willed it.

How long I remained there was something I, and I alone, I fancied, would decide.

Men and women passed before me, swearing allegiance. In turn they were promised support, that Vallia would be freed, that life and liberty would be theirs, and hapiness too, if they could contrive that profoundly difficult achievement.

I looked up. Of course. The Gdoinye and the white dove of the Savanti floated up there against the blue. They had not forgotten me. I would have more trouble from them in the future.

As I looked a voller fleeted in over the kyro and swooped for the palace. I saw her flags. Valkan flags, and the flags of Delphond and the Blue Mountains, Old Superb—all flew from her masts. But, over all, that new flag of Vallia floated, free, defiant, yellow and scarlet in the blaze of the suns, heralding a new epoch in the history of Kregen.

Surfeited on emotions both transcendental and foreboding and, just for this wonderful moment, blurring into a haze of thankfulness, I walked forward to greet Delia.

The whole of Vondium rang with the exultations.

"Hai Jikai, Delia, Empress of Vallia Hai Jikai, Dray Prescot, Emperor of Vallia!"

By Zair, I said to myself as Delia and I walked toward each other and the air vibrated with the noise and excitement. I must remember I am a Krozair of Zy and, too, I must not forget the Kroveres of Iztar. The Corruption of Empire must never foul this moment. The Sovereign State must serve every single person, each to each. If ever the corruption of power touched me, if ever megalomania assaulted my sanity, I would remember the good men who had died looking forward to this moment.

The truth was I had not wanted to be Emperor of Vallia; but if I had been chosen for that onerous task by the conjoined will of the people, then—for a space until I talked my son Drak into taking over—I'd be as competent and just and professional an emperor as I knew how, by Zim-Zair!

The uplifted swords glittered blindingly in the streaming mingled lights of Antares, the Suns of Scorpio. "Jikai! Hai Jikai!" roared the multitudes.

It was a moment to treasure, a moment to remember. . . .

"So you are the Emperor of Vallia in your own right, Dray," said Delia. She smiled and the suns glimmered pale in comparison. "Now what will you do?"

"Oh," I said. "Oh, I haven't even started yet."

A GLOSSARY TO THE VALLIAN CYCLE
OF THE SAGA OF DRAY PRESCOT

References to the four books of the cycle are given as:
SES: Secret Scorpio
SVS: Savage Scorpio
CPS: Captive Scorpio
GOS: Golden Scorpio

NB: Previous glossaries covering entries not included here will be found in Volume 5: Price of Scorpio; Volume 7: Arena of Antares; Volume 11: Armada of Antares; Volume 14: Krozair of Kregen.

A

Ahrinye: Star Lord of acrid tongue in apparent opposition to other Everoinye.

Arlton: Island to the north of Veliadrin. Name means pestle.

Aleygyn: Title of chief of stikitches.

"Anete ham Terhenning":   A tragic song of Hamal.

Ararsnet, Roybin ti Autonne: Secret agent working for Prescot. SES

Arial, Fair of: A fair held for the people of the Czarin Sea on the island of Drayzm after the pirates cleared away.

Arkadon: Pleasant market town in Delphond.

atra: Amulet, lucky charm.

audo: Military term for section of eight to ten men.

Autonne: Town on the west coast of Veliadrin.

Avandil, Rafik: A numin assigned by Phu-Si-Yantong to observe Prescot. Eventually unmasked as Makfaril.

B

Ba-Domek: Island on which is situated the city of Aphrasöe.

Bakan: High kovnate of Vallia situated to the south of the Mountains of the North.

The Ball and Chain: An unsavory hostelry a stone's throw from the Gate of Skulls in Drak's City in Vondium.

Battle of Sabbator: Final battle in which the Phalanx of the North East of Vallia overthrew The Iron Riders.

Battle of Therminsax: The fight in which the army of Therminsax with the Phalanx as the core gained its first success against The Iron Riders.

Battle of Voxyri: Climactic battle in which the Freedom Fighters and the Phalanx of Vallia defeated the army of Hamal and its mercenary allies across the Drinnik and over the Bridge and through the Gate of Voxyri.

"Bear Up Your Arms": A rollicking song of which this is the euphemistic title.

Beng Dikkane: Patron saint of all the ale drinkers of Paz.

Beng Drangil: Patron saint of Ovvend.

benhoff: Shaggy, powerful, six-legged riding animal of North Segesthes, with lean hind-sixths and a roll of fat across the chest. Used by the radvakkas.

Bet-Aqsa: Island west of Havilfar in the Ocean of Doubt.

"Black Is the River and Black Was Her Hair": A tragical ditty of Hamal which Prescot describes as farcical.

"Black Wings over Sabbator": A great song made in remembrance of The Battle of Sabbator.

Blade of Kurin, by the: A swordsman's oath.

Blarnoi, San: Either a real person or a consortium of misty figures of the dim past to whom many aphorisms and sayings current on Kregen are attributed.

blatter: Slang word for quick and successful assault and battery, a headlong attack.

Brassud: Brace up.

Bratch!: Move! Jump! Not as vicious as the infamous Grak! but still a powerful word of command implying move it or you know what will happen.

Bratchlin: The File Closer at the rear of each file of the phalanx.

Bregal: A small town of Ystilbur of the Dawn Lands of Havilfar.

brumby: A powerful eight-legged and armored battering ram of whirlwind destruction armed with a long straight horn in the center of his forehead, the brumby is thought to be either extinct or legendary.

brumbyte: Name for the pikeman in the files of the phalanx.

Bryvondrin: Imperial province of Vallia north of the capital.

C

Calimbrev: Island stromnate southwest of Veliadrin.

Cansinsax: Town of Aduimbrev where The Iron Riders defeated an army of Hamalese. GOS

195

Charboi, Dr: In the pay of Ashti Melekhi poisoned the Emperor of Vallia. SVS

chyyan: A large, heavy-winged bird, all rusty black save for scarlet eyes and claws and beak, with four wings like its distant cousin the zhyan.

Cleitar the Smith: Blacksmith who lost his family in the radvakka and Hamalian troubles and from then on carried Prescot's banner of Vallia.

Czarin Sea: Studded with islands off east coast of Vallia.

D

"The Daisies of Delphond": A charming song celebrating the ladies as well as the daisies of the Garden of Vallia.

Danmork: Leader of the fourth and tenth files in the Relianch of the phalanx.

Deb-sa Chiu: Wizard of Loh at court of the Emperor of Vallia. CPS

Delia: Mother Goddess generally associated with Delphond.

Deliasmot: Town of Delphond where a canal trunk system terminates.

deren: Palace.

Djondalar of the Twisted Staff: Spirit or deity of Kregen.

Dorgo the Clis: Tall, dark-complexioned man with facial scar who followed Prescot in fight against radvakkas. GOS

Drakanium: Clean, neat, sparkling city of Delphond.

Drak's City: The Old City of Vondium.

Drak's Sword: Part of the regalia of the Emperor of Vallia.

Drayzm: Small island of the Czarin Sea once called Nikzm and named for Dray Prescot.

drikinger: Bandit.

E

Eganbrev: Province to the west of Aduimbrev up to Great River.

Emerade, River: Runs from the Kwan Hills and joins the Great River where stands Thengelsax.

Enevon Ob-Eye: Prescot's chief stylor during the radvakka and Hamalian troubles. GOS

"Eregoin's Promise": A drinking song of Paz.

Ernelltar the Bedevilled: Runs of bad luck are attributed to this spirit or deity in North Segesthes.

F

Falanriel: Chief City of Falinur.

"The Fall of the Suns":   A menacing song, Prescot dubs this
   lay, for its cadences and images invite mournfulness. It
   tells of the Last Days when the twin suns fall from the sky
   and drench the world of Kregen in fire and blood, in water
   and death.

Falnagur: The castle fortress dominating the city of Falanriel.

Father Tolki: The All Mighty, chief deity of the religion of
   Vallia which ousted that of the Mother Goddess and was
   in turn superseded by the purer religion of Opaz.

Faxul: Leader of a file in the phalanx.

Fegter: Member of the Fegter Party of Vallia against the
   Emperor and anybody else who stood in the way.

Fist-tail or Hand-tail: Slang term for Pachak or Kildoi.

flamil: A sand-scarf of Ba-Domek.

Fletcher's Tower: Once called the Jade Tower of the fortress of the Falnagur renamed by Seg Segutorio. SES

Florania: Deity of a minor religion of Vallia patronized by
   millers and bakers. The Chief Priest of Therminsax out of
   good intentions attempted treachery against Prescot. GOS

G

Gate of Skulls: A gate giving ingress to Drak's City in Vondium.

Gelkwa: A trylonate of Vallia between the Kwan Hills and
   the Great River. Part of Hawkwa country.

Gengulas: Legendary monsters with the power of Medusae.

Gods sharpen both edges of a blade, the: A saying of Kregen which appears to imply that one evil may destroy another and in turn be destroyed.

Golden Feathers Aegis, by the: A Flutsman's oath.

"Golden Fur":   A song shared by numims and Fristles.

Great Chyyan: The black four-winged bird symbol of the
   evil and synthetic religion fostered by Phu-Si-Yantong and
   destroyed in Vallia by Prescot and the SOK and Naghan
   Vanki. Adherents called chyyanists. SES

Guiskwain, San: The Witherer, na Stackwamore. A famed
   necromancer of the North East of Vallia who lived more
   than two and a half thousand seasons ago. His corpse was
   revived to inspire the Hawkwa revolt. CPS

H

Hakkodin: The axe and halberd men flanking the files of the Phalanx.

Hawkwa: Term for the people of North East Vallia.

Himet the Mak: Rafik Avandil, lion-man, tool of Phu-Si-Yantong in preaching the artificial religion of chyyanism. SES.

hirvel: A stubby, four-legged riding animal, not unlike a nightmare version of a llama with tall round neck, cup-shaped ears and shaggy body and twitching snout with a performance similar to a good quality waler.

Hjemur-Gebir: a minor religion fallen into desuetude with a grotesque toad-thing as the idol of worship.

Hockwafernes: Temple and township of Gelkwa where San Guiskwain was resurrected. CPS

Hyr Notor: Alias used by Phu-Si-Yantong in dealing with the Empress Thyllis of Hamal.

Hyrvond: Imperial province immediately to the north of Vondium.

I

Ib Reiver: Soul Stealer—used in oaths.

Imlien, Trylon Ered of Thengelsax: A racter with whom Prescot had a smart run in over his daughter. SES

J

Jakhan, Jak: Name used by Prescot during adventures in Hawkwa country. CPS

Jak the Drang: Name used by Prescot to rouse Vallians against The Iron Riders and Hamalese. GOS

Jhalak, by: A stikitche oath.

Jhansi, Layco, Kov of Vennar: The Emperor of Vallia's Chief Pallan. When his plots against the emperor were frustrated by Prescot and friends, took to the field in the time of the Troubles in Vallia when Hamal and the rad-vakkas invaded.

jid: Bane.

Jikai Vuvushis: Battle Maidens.

Jikalla: A Kregish game.

Jodhri: A formation of the phalanx containing six Relianches totalling 864 brumbytes and 144 Hakkodin.

Jodhrivax: Commander of Jodhri.

Junka: A deity of the North East of Vallia.

Justicar: The imperial governor of province.

K

Kadar the Hammer: Alias used by Prescot in Vallia. SES

Kamist Quay: Wharves along the Great River in Vondium.

Kapt: General.

kax: Corselet, breast and back, cuirass.

Kerchuri: Formation of the phalanx containing six Jodhris of 5184 brumbytes and 864 Hakkodin.

Kerchurivax: Commander of Kerchuri.

kharrna: Manifestation of power exercised at distance by a Wizard of Loh.

Khibil: Member of race of diffs with fox faces, alert, strong, limber, excellent mercenaries used to outdoor life.

khiganer: Heavy brown tunic, double-breasted, the wide flap caught up over the left side with a row of bronze buttons from belt to shoulder and from point of shoulder to collar which is stiff, hard and high.

Kildoi: Member of race of diffs of Balintol with four arms and handed tail, very strong and courageous with apim-like features and a variety of hair-colorings.

"King Harulf's Red Zorca": Drinking song of Paz.

"King Naghan, His Fall and Rise": Song of Kregen with undercurrents of merriment and discipline and admonishment.

kitchew: Target for assassination on contract by stikitches.

Kwan Hills: Range of mountains in Hawkwa Country famed for their plenitude of game, good hunting country.

klattar: Parrying stick.

Korero the Shield: A Kildoi rescued by Prescot from torture at the hands of the radvakkas and a good comrade who carries a pair of great shields in combat at Prescot's back.

krahnik: Small form of draught animal of good pulling power.

Kroveres of Iztar: Members of Order of Brotherhood formed by Prescot on model of Krzy to ameliorate conditions in all Paz.

KRVI: Abbreviation for Kroveres of Iztar.

kutcherer: Knife somewhat like a butcher knife with a sharp pronged spike protruding from the heavy back.

Kyro of Jaidur Omnipotent: Brilliant plaza or square in Vondium.

Kyro of Lost Souls: Long plaza just within the Gate of Skulls of Drak's City in Vondium.

Kyro of Spendthrifts: One of the squares of Vondium famed for the expensive shops and stalls along the arcades.

L

Laik-Faxul: Quarter-file leader in Relianch.

laybrites: Precious gem of deep yellow color.

Laygon the Strigicaw: Stikitche who to his misfortune took a contract from Ashti Melekhi to assassinate Dray Prescot. CPS

letha: Tough, springy, elastic white wood.

Letha Brook: Runs through Therminsax.

Lio am Donarb: A minor religion of Vallia.

Liverspot Bark: Ingredient of the poison solkien concentrate.

Llanitch!: Halt!

Lornrod Caucus: Vallian political faction of whom it is said their only wish is to destroy everything and pull down what has been painfully built over the centuries.

Lushfymi, Queen of Lome: Popularly known as Queen Lush. A dark-haired violet-eyed woman of great poise and beauty sent by Phu-Si-Yantong to entrap the Emperor of Vallia. Her allegiance changed and she worked with Prescot to save the emperor.

M

"Maidens of Vallia, The": A lyrical ballad celebrating the virtuous women of Vallia.

Makfaril: Beloved of the Black, the Chief Priest of the Great Chyyan, the evil and artificial creed of chyyanism developed by Phu-Si-Yantong to destroy Vallia. Rafik Avandil, numim. SES

masichieri: Low-class mercenaries, not bandits but almost that, notorious for their rapacity and greed.

Maybers: A race of trading and sea-faring diffs from Donengil.

Mazilla: The high ornate collar much bejeweled and decorated worn by the nobility of Vallia, the simpler dignified high collar of the koters of Vallia. The nikmazilla is the smaller ornate collar worn with evening clothes.

mazingle: Swod's term for discipline.

Melekhi, Ashti, Vadnicha of Venga: A thin brittle and bright woman, hard-edged like a diamond, mannish, brilliant, with a flame about her that consumed all who were unfortunate enough not to know how to handle her. Came to an untimely end in her machinations with Layco Jhansi. SVS

Mellor'An: Local god of North East Vallia concerned with agriculture, husbandry and fertility.

Memph: A tree which yields a part of the deadly poison solkien.

MichelDen: Capital city of the kovnate of Forli in southeast Vallia.

Mustard Gate: A strong battlemented Tower-gate in an angle of the northwest walls of Vondium.

N

Naghan ti Lodkwara: Hawkwa member of the choice band who followed Prescot in the time of Troubles in Vallia. GOS

Nalgre, Nazab na Therminsax: The emperor's Justicar governing Thermin who loyally obeyed Prescot acting as Jak the Drang. GOS

Nath the Gnat: Alias adopted by Prescot in the struggle against the chyyanists. SES

Nath the Iarvin: A hard man, ruffler, Bladesman, bought body and soul by Ashti Melekhi, who came to an unexpected end on a Krozair longsword. SVS

Nav-Sorfall: Vallian province lush and rich with ponsho pastures to the east of Vomansoir. Naghan Vanki was made vad.

Nazab: Governor of imperial province ranking with kov.

Nazabhan, Nath, na Therminsax: Son of Nazab Nalgre, rose to command phalanx created by Prescot. GOS

Nik-Faxul: Half-file leader in Relianch.

Nikwald: Fortress town in the kovnate of Sakwara of Vallia.

Numi-Hyrjiv the Golden Splendor: Great spirit or deity of numims and fristles.

O

Olordin's Well: Insignificant hamlet where Prescot rendezvoused with Barty Vessler in south central Vallia. GOS

Opaz Enthroned: Day of festival dedicated to Opaz. The day on which the army of Therminsax sallied against the radvakkas. GOS

Opaz the Deliverer: Day of festival dedicated to Opaz on which Vondium rose against the Hamalese and the Freedom Fighters and the Phalanx struck in the Battle of Voxyri. GOS

Order of Little Mothers: One of the sororities of Vallia dedicated to good works.

P

"Pachak with the Four Arms, The": A song highly scurrilous of a fine people with an oblique reference to the Kildoi.

pakai: String of silver or gold rings taken from defeated paktuns by paktun victories and worn as badges of prowess.

Paltork: Commander of half Relianch.

Panadian the Ibreiver, the Vicissitudes of: Cycle of plays by the long-dead playwright Nalgre ti Liancesmot from which couplets, aphorisms and character analyses are often quoted.

Peral Gate: Imposing secondary gateway to the imperial deren of Vondium.

Phalanx: Created in Vallia by Prescot to oppose the Iron Riders. A phalanx consists of two Kerchuris totalling 10368 pikes and 1738 Hakkodin. In the field any close-order body of brumbytes called the Phalanx.

Poperlin the Wise: Mythical sage apostrophized by the workers of Vallia.

Prison of the Angels: A gaunt granite prison of Vondium.

Pyvorr, Tarek Dredd: The first martyr of the Kroveres of Iztar. SVS

R

radvakka's: The Iron Riders of North Segesthes.

Rakkle-jik-lora: A violent headlong training game played by the Clansmen of the Great Plains of Segesthes.

Relianch: Formation of the phalanx consisting of 144 brumbytes and 24 Hakkodin.

Relianchun: Commander of a Relianch.

Renberg, Marta, Kovneva of Aduimbrev: High-tempered, ambitious lady who assisted schemes of Phu-Si-Yantong. GOS

Rojashin the Kaktu: A Rapa paktun whose greed and overweening idea of his own importance drove him on to destruction and whose gear and pakai were used by Prescot in Hawkwa country. CPS

ronil: Precious jewel of red color.

Rosala and the Eye of Imladrion: An ancient legend of Kregen in its intentions paralleling the story of Pandora.

rosha: Orange-like fruit.

Ros the Claw: Name given to Princess Dayra of Vallia by virtue of the sharp steel gloved set of talons worn on her left hand with which she is very quick and cruel.

Rumil the Point: Tavern swaggerer who insulted Prescot

and dealt with by Rafik Avandil, lion-man, in The Savage
Woflo. SES.

S

Sabbator, River: In North East Vallia separates the trylonate of Zaphoret to the north from Urn Stackwamore, running into the sea opposite the island of Vellin.

Sakwara: High Kovnate of Vallia north of Aduimbrev.

Samphron Cut: A canal of Vondium.

Sapphire Reception Room: One of the ornate but less formal chambers of the deren of Vondium.

The Savage Woflo: Famous tavern of Vondium much patronized by the guardsmen and paktuns of the capital.

sax: Fort.

The Sea Barynth Hooked: Pot-house on the Kamist Quay of
Vondium catering to skippers of Vallian ships.

Shadow: Magnificent black zorca stallion freed from cruel
Kataki owners and ridden by Prescot in Ba-Domek. SVS

Shadow Forests of Calimbrev: Beautiful and rich forests in
the west of the island coveted by the Strom of Vilandeul.

Shalash the Shining: Fish deity or spirit called on by fisher-
folk of Vallia.

shandishalah: Merchandise of booths in the fish souks.

Shastum!: Silence!

Shkanes: Yet another appellation for the Shanks, the Shants,
the Shtarkins, Leem-Lovers, reivers from over the curve of
the world who ravage the sea coasts of Paz.

Shudor Maklechuan: A Chulik paktun known as Shudor the
Mak who was hired by Prescot with his band to fight for
Therminsax. GOS

signomant: An artifact created by a Wizard of Loh, often in
the form of a heavy brass disc covered with hieroglyphs,
by which he is able to observe events at a distance without
forcing a projection of himself to the required place.

Silversmiths Wharf: Canal side area where silver is traded in
Vondium.

Sisters of Patience: A sorority of Vallia.

Sisters of Samphron: A semi-secret sorority of Vallia.

solkien concentrate: A deadly poisonous compound that
secretly wastes the flesh, dilutes the blood and destroys subtly.

SOR: Abbreviation for the Sisters of the Rose.

Souk of Chem: Bazaar of the ivory traders in Vondium.

The Speckled Gyp: A tavern of Vondium smashed up by
Dayra and her cronies.

Stackwamores, The: Provinces of North East Vallia, the heartlands of Hawkwa Country, north, south, east and west Stackwamore.

stiver: Silver coin on Vallia.

"The Stylvie on the Slippery Slope": A risque song of Kregen.

T

tapo: Word of abuse with unpleasant connotations.

tarek: A rank of the minor nobility within the gifting of a kov.

Targon the Tapster: A Therminsaxer who became one of the choice band of followers of Prescot in the time of Troubles. GOS

Tarkwa-fash: A town of the North East near the Kwan Hills.

tazll: Applied to an unemployed mercenary.

Temple of Delia: An ancient ruined temple in Delphond dedicated to the Mother Goddess Delia where Prescot had a run-in with the masichieri of the Black Feathers. SES

Terfaxul: Leader of a file in the Relianch one rank higher than a Faxul.

Thengelsax: Town situated on Great River at point where River Emerade joins. One of the old line of fortresses against the North East of Vallia.

Therduim Cut: Canal connecting Therminsax and Thengelsax.

Thermin: Imperial province of Central Vallia.

Thiurdsmot: A sizable town of Aduimbrev.

Tholofer, Vad Inrien ham: A Hamalese Kapt who surrendered Vondium to Prescot and the Freedom Forces of Vallia. GOS

tikshim: Form of address used by superior to inferiors, equating with "My Man." The superiors consider it polite, the inferior are infuriated by its use.

Tolindrin: Place in Balintol with diplomatic connections with Vallia.

Tower of Incense: Contains the sorcerous chamber inhabited by the current Wizard of Loh in the deren of Vondium.

Trechinolc: A cactus, constituent of the poison solkien.

Trerhagen, Nath: The Aleygyn, Hyr Stikitche, Pallan of the Stikitche Khand of Vondium.

tresh: Flag or banner.

tsleetha-tsleethi: Softly-softly.

Tunnel of Delight: Leads out to the Kyro of Jaidur Omnipotent in Vondium.
Twitchnose: A chestnut zorca ridden by Prescot in Vondium.

U

Udo, Trylon of Gelkwa: Led rebellion of North East Vallia.
CPS
ukra: Flutsman's weapon, a polearm from seven to fifteen
feet in length with narrow blade and curved axe for aerial
work.
Ulbereth the Dark Reiver: Poem fashioned from the legends
of olden time on Kregen. The episode of the Black
Feathers tells of Ulbereth's disguise to enable him to ravish
a fair young virgin with golden hair.
unggar: Beast of burden.
Urn Stackwamor: Vadvarate of Hawkwa country in N.E.
Vallia.
urvivel: Saddle animal.
Uthnior Chavonthjid: A leem-hunter and guide with a fine
reputation who guided Prescot and Barty Vessler in the
Kwan Hills. CPS
Uzhiro, San: Necromancer of the Hawkwas who roused
corpses from sleep to aid North East Vallian rebellion.
CPS

V

Valhorta: Vadvarate province of Vallia immediately to the
east of the imperial Vond provinces and Vondium.
Vanti: Guardian for the Savanti of the Sacred Pool of Bap-
tism on the River Zelph of far Aphrasöe.
Varkwa the Open-Handed: Spirit of generosity called upon
in Vallia.
Vel'alar: One of the Hills of Vondium. The villa of the
Stromnate of Valka is situated on this hill.
Veliadrin: Large island high kovnate to the east of Vallia
whose name was changed from Can-thirda in remem-
brance.
Velyan techniques: Mystic martial disciplines of the Martial
Monks of Djanduin.
vener: Collective name for the vens and venas of the Canals.
Vennar: Kovnate province of Vallia between the Black
Mountains and Falinur.
ver: Title of pledge of loyalty of Kroveres of Iztar similar to
the pur of the Krozairs.

Vessler, Barty, Strom of Calimbrev: Amiable, chivalrous, brave young man befriended by Prescot. Desperately in love with the Princess Dayra. CPS GOS

Vetal: Island Stromnate to the east of the Czarin Sea.

Vikatu: The Old Sweat, The Dodger, the archetypal old soldier of Paz on Kregen, paragon of the military vices, legendary figure of myth and romance loved and sworn on by the swods.

Vinnur's Garden: Rich area in loop of Great River between Falinur and Vindelka whose ownership is contested by both.

volmen: Volim, crewmen of fliers.

Volodu the Lungs: Prescot's trumpeter in the choice band who followed him in the time of Troubles in Vallia. GOS

Vond: Imperial province to the west of Vondium.

Vondium Khanders: Political party of Vallia who looked to the business community for combined strength.

voswod: Aerial soldier of the vollers.

Voxyri: Complex of Drinnik, Gate and Bridge over two canals providing the easiest entrance to Vondium.

vydra tea: An excellent brew of the famed Kregen tea.

W

Walls of Larghos Risslaca: Inner defensive wall of the imperial deren Vondium.

wallpitix: Furry, bright-eyed household scavengers living in nest in hidden places of villas and houses.

Wellon, Nankwi, High Kov of Sakwara: A prickly kov who took the lead in Hawkwa after the disappearance of Trylon Udo and who was confirmed in his position by Prescot. GOS

"When the Fluttrell Flirts His Wing": A song of Hamal detailing the misadventures of an inexperienced fluttrell flyer.

Whiptail: Slang term for a Kataki.

Y

Yasi, Ranjal, Stromich of Morcray: Twin brother of Rosil Yasi, Strom of Morcray, in the pay of Phu-Si-Yantong and bitter foe to Prescot.

yasticum: An expensive and rare delicacy spread on the superb Kregan bread.

Yellow-tuskers: Slang term for Chulik.

Ystilbur: An ancient nation of the Dawn Lands of Havilfar.

Z

Zankov: Use-name of Hawkwa determined to overthrow empire, origins secret but subject to many rumors; slender, brittle; the man who slew the Emperor of Vallia. The Princess Dayra's name is coupled with his in unsavory ways. Zankov, the Tenth Duke, is almost a meaningless name.

Zarado: A Krozair of Zy who through some peccadillo wandered from the inner sea and hired out as a Paktun to assist Prescot in the defense of Therminsax. GOS

zim-korf: Bird of Valko with rose-red feathers whose quality is equal or superior to the blue fletchings of the king korf of Erthyrdrin.

Zunder: Krzy with the same history as Zarado with whom he is always in arguments.

ALAN BURT AKERS—

the great novels of Dray Prescot